In *A Slight Change of Plans*, Denise M. Colby weaves a tender and hopeful story of second chances, resilience, and quiet courage. Jenny and Ren captured my heart from the very first page with their gentle strength and longing to belong. With a beautiful balance of romance, faith, and a touch of mystery, this story reminds us that sometimes life's detours lead us exactly where we're meant to be.

KIMBERLY KEAGAN, AUTHOR
OF *PERFECT* AND *HEART OF HOPE*

With a cast of characters sure to steal your heart (including a rooster who steals the show!), *When Plans Go Awry* beautifully touches that deep need within all of us to be loved and accepted. This deeply layered story also reveals a truth we often forget—that innate desire to trust when life has proven to be untrustworthy.

CHAUTONA HAVIG, *USA TODAY*
BESTSELLING AUTHOR

This charming debut (*When Plans Go Awry*) from Denise M. Colby, about a young woman finding her bearings as a rural teacher in 1860s California, kept me smiling through the pages. If you love sweet historical romances with *When Calls the Heart* vibes and tender threads of faith, this story is sure to put a smile on your face too.

BECCA KINZER, AUTHOR OF *DEAR HENRY, LOVE EDITH* AND *LOVE IN TANDEM*

Best-laid Plans ✦ Book Two

A Slight Change of Plans

DENISE M. COLBY

Published by Scrivenings Press LLC
15 Lucky Lane
Morrilton, Arkansas 72110
https://ScriveningsPress.com

Printed in the United States of America

Paperback ISBN 978-1-64917-470-3
eBook ISBN 978-1-64917-471-0

Editors: Ann Harrison and Linda Fulkerson

Cover by Linda Fulkerson, www.bookmarketinggraphics.com

All characters are fictional, and any resemblance to real people, either factual or historical, is purely coincidental.

To my sons, Connor, Kyle, and Zach, and my daughter, Aimee.
Never give up on your dreams, no matter how long it takes.

And for Ken. Thank you for supporting all of mine. I love you.
Here's to thirty.

*"For I know the plans I have for you," declares the Lord,
"plans to prosper you and not to harm you, plans to give you hope
and a future."*
—Jeremiah 29:11 (NIV)

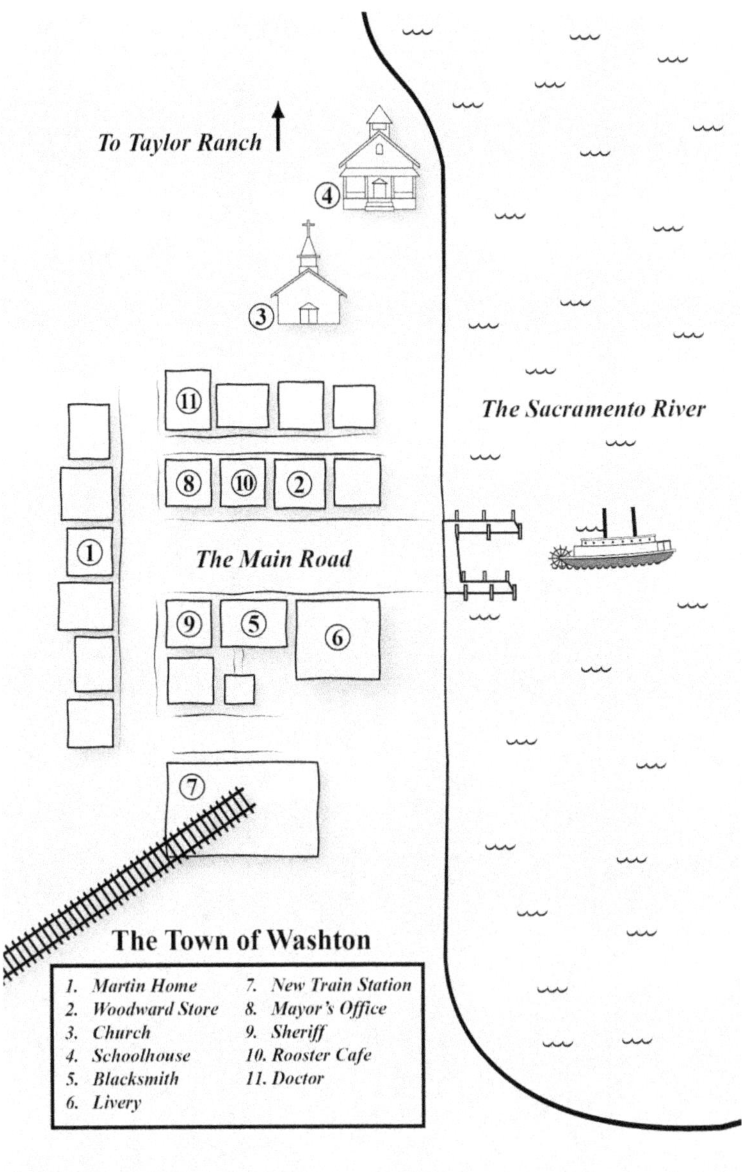

To Taylor Ranch
The Sacramento River
The Main Road
The Town of Washton
1. Martin Home
2. Woodward Store
3. Church
4. Schoolhouse
5. Blacksmith
6. Livery
7. New Train Station
8. Mayor's Office
9. Sheriff
10. Rooster Cafe
11. Doctor

One

This is the first journal I've ever owned. It's almost too fine for me to write in every day. Miss Beecher says to document our teaching journey as we head to California. I plan to save it for special occasions, the first of which, I have a roommate who is not a younger sibling. She goes by Livvy. She's quiet, yet very confident. Something I'm not.

—From the journal of Jenny Millard

Spring, 1870
Vallejo, California

"I'm sorry, Miss Millard, but there are no teaching positions available."

Jenny Millard closed her eyes for a brief moment at the school board director's words. "But ... I have a contract."

He nodded. "You *did* have a contract. With the first school in Copperville. But when they closed their doors and sent you here, it was canceled. We then secured a position for you at Mountain Ridge, but they, too, have closed their doors."

"Isn't there anything else?" Jenny strove to keep her voice steady.

The man winced. "I'm afraid not. Too many teachers have been sent here from area schools, and we don't have enough positions."

Jenny's gaze dropped to the floor as she pressed her lips together. Why would her life be different here in California? Within a short six months, she had failed two schools. Or those two schools had failed her. The wishes and dreams she had when she first arrived had fizzled out. Now, she was a teacher without a school, even though it felt more than that.

He cleared his throat. "You didn't do anything wrong, Miss Millard."

She glanced up. Had she asked her question out loud?

"None of this is your fault. The communities in the surrounding areas are struggling and can't afford a teacher right now." He glanced out the window.

Unfortunately, she understood all too well. Her own family lived in a rural area with few resources, which was why she had come west.

He reached into his pocket. "We don't have enough to cover your wages fully, but here's what I can provide." He slid over a few measly coins. "It's the best I can do. I'm sorry. I wish you well." He rose, indicating the discussion concerning her job was over.

And it was. Both the discussion *and* her teaching career.

What was she going to do?

The coins scraped across the desk as she scooped them into her hand. She followed the man to the door, picked up all her belongings, and stepped outside the one-room schoolhouse into the crisp morning air.

He bowed to her. "Thank you for your service."

She pasted on a smile and nodded to his retreating back. There was only one place she could go. Hopefully her one and only friend, Livvy, would help her. But she'd need to get to Washton first. The money jingled in her hand. She hoped it would be enough to purchase a one-way ticket.

She limped along the dirt road toward the train station, her suitcase bouncing off her leg with each step. After twenty minutes or so, she arrived at the heart of town. Her feet ached, and her shoes had worn so thin, the pebbles in the dirt poked through. She approached the boardwalk, lifted her foot and froze. A loose flap on the bottom of her left shoe almost caught on the wood. She gingerly lifted her leg high enough so she wouldn't stumble. What she wouldn't do for a chair and a cup of hot tea. But that had to wait.

Jenny shivered and wrapped her thin coat tighter to block the biting wind. She couldn't wait to get on the train and put the new past behind her. What should've been a fresh start had turned into a nightmare, much like the previous six years before she left home.

As she passed the mercantile, she overheard the excitement about the candy in the window display from a few young children.

"I've never seen so many colors. How many do you think there are?" asked the smallest girl.

The older boy next to her paused a moment. "I count six different ones, the color of the rainbow."

"How do you know the color of the rainbow?" she asked.

"I've seen one. You can trust I'm telling ya the truth, sis."

The young girl smiled at the boy and grabbed his hand. He didn't pull away, grinning back at his younger sister. What a stark contrast to her own lonely childhood. A bittersweet warmth spread through Jenny's chest.

None of her brothers had looked out for her like that.

Jenny continued walking, but her heart ached for the relationship she never had with her siblings. Maybe if she hadn't been the oldest, looking out for all of them, things might've been different.

A woman bumped Jenny's arm as she brushed past, causing Jenny to stumble. She caught herself, but not before a small grunt escaped her lips from the throbbing pain of her toes jammed farther into tight shoes. The lady didn't look back to see if Jenny was all right. Which made sense. She'd never had anyone look out for her or show they cared. Even just a little.

Oh, she was being quite the downer. Hard to be positive when the situation was not favorable. First, her family had asked her to leave because they couldn't afford for her to stay, then not one, but *two* towns where she'd taught closed their doors, leaving her with no work and no home.

The message was clear.

She didn't matter. She was disposable.

Tears threatened, and she swallowed the dark thoughts that clouded her mind. How could she support herself without a position? She was willing to put in hard work, but how could she do that without a job?

She sighed.

All the families in these towns faced a situation similar to the one she left behind. Two parents who worked long days to put food on the table for their family, with nothing left over because there were too many mouths to feed.

Is this how life was supposed to be?

Her stomach growled, reminding her she had yet to eat. Still, she needed to save the coins for the train ticket. The grumbling continued as she kept a steady pace along the boardwalk. It wouldn't be the first time she went without food.

She pulled the top of her bonnet down so it covered more of her face as she crossed the street and approached the train station. Even though no one should recognize her, she preferred to hide in plain sight. A habit ingrained at a young age.

Jenny handed over all the coins in her hand at the ticket booth, placing one last sliver of hope on her friend's willingness to take her in and help. There was no one else she could turn to.

Thankfully, this new rail line ran directly from Vallejo to Washton, which was where Livvy was situated. Jenny should arrive by mid-day. Passengers could arrive in Washton to board the ferry and cross the river to Sacramento to reach the main train station. Fortunately for Jenny, the route was frequent, making the journey more affordable.

The train whistle blew, notifying passengers it was last call to board.

Of course, Livvy was unaware of Jenny's struggles. She hadn't told anyone she had to move the first time, not wanting to be a burden. Which meant any letters from the teachers she had come west with would not have reached her.

Now, she wasn't sure what she would say once she arrived.

Clutching her ticket, she hurried to stand in line behind a young couple with a child. The little boy turned around and gazed up at her. She smiled back at him while her heart ached inside.

She couldn't leave fast enough.

Once boarded, Jenny headed to the back row to blend in, hoping no one would pay her any attention.

She must move on. Thinking about the past did nothing but bring her down. And it was important to cling to the little tiny dream she still held in her heart. For something more. For someplace to belong. To be loved without any strings attached.

If she thought too much, she felt as if no one wanted her—unless she was needed to watch the little ones. Or cook the food. Or wash the clothes.

There must be someone who wanted her for herself.

Maybe she would find that someone in Washton.

One could only hope.

* * *

"I HAVE to go out for a while." Ren Lyman's boss shouted over the clang of metal. "Do you mind watching the smithy?"

Ren paused mid-stroke. This was the moment. The chance for Ren to see if the people of Washton would accept him when Gideon Roberts wasn't around. What could he say? He couldn't very well say he wasn't ready. Besides, he was curious to know himself. No sense staying where one wasn't wanted.

Thankful to Gideon for opening his shop and home to Ren, he couldn't very well hide in the back forever. "Sure." He faced the man who treated him with nothing but kindness and held up his hand. "You don't think it will be a concern?"

Gideon shook his head. "I don't think it will be a problem as long as you don't make it a problem. Why do you think your scars would be an issue?"

Ren couldn't blame Gideon for making light of his deformity. Gideon wasn't the one who had to deal with the comments or the disdain others showed Ren because he had ugly, twisted skin all over his right hand and parts of his face. Scars which made it impossible to hold tools or write with his right hand. Ren adapted as a young child by switching to his left, but at school, left-handers were ridiculed and forced to conform. He couldn't, though, and thus, he was a freak. At least, that's what most people called him.

Still did in some towns. "It seems to have caused trouble in every town I came across on my journey here. You're the only person who never flinched or drew away from me when I reached out my hand. All my life, I have been teased and made to feel less a man because of this." He pointed to his face and hand.

Gideon tilted his head. "Do you feel you're less of a man?"

Ren's mouth fell open. No one had ever asked him that before. He responded without thinking. "No, not really."

"Why is that?" Gideon asked.

Ren searched his heart. "Because the Good Lord made me who I am, and I am nothing without him."

Gideon nodded. "Son, I don't think you have anything to worry about." He turned and walked away, "I'll be back in a couple of hours," he called over his shoulder.

Ren stood staring at the doorway, not quite sure what to make of his new boss.

An hour later, Ren pounded out the finishing touches on the wheel for Mr. Adams when the store bell chimed. He set aside his work and brushed ash off his leather apron. Leaving the mitts on, he passed through the doorway that linked the back of the smithy to the front. "Be with me, Lord. I like it here and don't want to have to move on again," he whispered.

A tall, lanky man stood at the counter. He wore a large brown hat and held his hands in his back pockets. He frowned when he saw Ren. "Where's Gideon?"

Ren reached deep to find the nicest voice he could muster. "I'm Ren. Been helping Gideon in the back for the past few weeks. How may I help you?"

The gentleman gave Ren a cursory once-over.

Ren felt as if he was cattle being inspected before a purchase.

The man acknowledged Ren with a tilt of his head. "Well, if

Gideon trusts you in his shop, then I do too. Name is Luke Taylor."

Ren blew out the breath he held and saluted the man with his gloved hand. "What can I do for you?"

The man pointed to the broken horse bit and horseshoes lying on the counter. "I need three new horse bits. And since I'm here, I should get some new shoes for one of my horses. These are run down."

"No problem. I can get to them as soon as I complete what I'm currently working on."

"My horses are at the livery while I run a few other errands in town. I'll check back in an hour or so."

Ren picked up the broken pieces and held them to his chest. Best way to avoid a handshake is to keep his hands full. "I can have it done by then. Nice to meet you, Luke."

Luke's hand gripped the rim of his hat. "Likewise."

A little disoriented from the positive interaction, Ren headed back to the forge. Voices from his childhood days haunted him, yet the kindness of Gideon, and now Luke, helped to lessen the sting of the memories. All of that could change once the man saw his hand. But for now, he would enjoy the moment of non-judgment and hope his next run-in would be with a stranger who was just as kind.

Gideon entered as Ren finished pounding out the metal on the anvil. "Any customers drop in?"

Ren put the finished metal into the water to quench it in place. Steam rose into his face, but he stayed near, twisting the tongs that held the metal. "Yes. A man named Luke."

"Oh, he's a good man, Luke Taylor. What was it he needed fixed this time?"

"Broken bits and some shoes."

Gideon put on his own apron. "He owns the large cattle ranch north outside of town. Inherited it from his parents. He's raising his two sisters. Recently got engaged to our schoolteacher. He's a good customer. And he'd be a good friend."

Ren shook his head. "I'm not here to make friends. I'm here to do a good job as a blacksmith and learn as much as I can from you."

He expected Gideon to praise him for focusing on his work, similar to how his father would've responded.

Instead, his boss placed a hand on Ren's shoulder. "Well, everyone needs to have at least one friend in their life." Gideon tied the string behind his back and picked up a sledge. "There's a lot of work for us before we break for lunch."

Ren nodded and went back to work. The two of them had established a compatible rhythm since the first day Ren started working for the man. Their techniques complimented each other, and his new boss was mindful not to talk Ren's ear off. In all of Ren's twenty-five years, he had never met anyone else who saw the world as he did. He wanted desperately to know if it was a sign from God to stay. His heart yearned to put down roots somewhere, and, so far, Washton seemed a good place to do that.

But was it the right place for him?

Time passed quickly, and the train whistled in the background, announcing the noon train would arrive soon. Ren had to go now before the railcars docked and the incoming crowd filled the streets. He set the pieces aside and walked to the nail on the wall, where he hung up his apron and gloves. "I'm going to take my walk now, if that's okay."

"Suit yourself," Gideon yelled over his own pounding.

Ren tapped his shirt pocket, making sure the piece of worn paper was still there. He exited out the front, then crossed the street and headed up the hill, entering the white building with the tall steeple on the roof. The sunlight beamed through the windows, highlighting the unsettled dust in the air as he approached the front pew. He sat and gently pulled out the piece of paper, being extra careful as he opened it for the umpteenth time.

His mother handed him this sheet filled with fifteen verses when he left home. She'd cried, hugged him goodbye, and told him these words would see him through wherever the Lord would take him. He carried the list with him all the time and had already read through it several times.

He picked up the small Bible sitting in the pew and turned the pages till he found the next verse on the list. As he reflected on the word of God, his thoughts kept returning to the idea of staying in Washton. He'd been protecting his heart for so long. Could he lower his guard and let people in?

His heart thumped double-time as if answering a resounding *yes*.

Two

Today, I'm traveling by train for the first time. It's very cramped and smelly, but the view is amazing. So many different landscapes within each state we travel through. I can't wait for my fresh start in California.

—From the journal of Jenny Millard

A hard jerk startled Jenny awake.

"Train station. Washton stop. End of the line," the conductor yelled.

Jenny shook the cobwebs from her head and stood, holding her bag close. She limped toward the exit, gingerly stepping down from the train. Not a single person greeted her, like the other passengers, so she hobbled around them to get out of their way. Her pinched feet throbbed, but she was used to the pain. She was more worried about the reception she would receive from Livvy, even though Livvy said she would always be there.

She glanced up at the sky as the midday sun shone on her face. School would still be in session, right? Should she approach after or during? What if her assumption she could stay with Livvy was all wrong?

With no other option, she had to try. She inspected her front and made sure her coat was properly buttoned. Her valise at her side, she headed away from the station with a smile pasted on her face. As she moved across the street, two ladies passed her with a friendly nod.

Jenny stood a little taller.

Stepping onto the wooden planks of the boardwalk, she passed along the side of the livery before stopping at the corner. Livvy had shared that the schoolhouse was beyond the church, so Jenny headed in that direction. She crossed the main street and continued on the boardwalk, eyes scanning the planks so she didn't trip.

Halfway, she set down her luggage to catch her breath and look around. According to her letters, Livvy's experience was different from her own. Her friend loved Washton, and the people here seemed to love her back.

What she wouldn't give to have had a town like this.

Water splashed against the shore from the nearby Sacramento River. The waterway was wide and vast, reminding her of the Bible story of the Red Sea. Why that reminded her of a Bible story, she had no idea. Maybe because of the newly painted building with the giant steeple sprouting out of the roof. As she studied the small structure, Jenny lifted her gaze to the cross at the top.

She had always wanted to attend church. But her family rarely had time for church or reading the Bible, like so many other families she knew. So, her youthful yearning to learn about God was replaced with a basic understanding. Jenny knew He was there. She just figured she was insignificant in His eyes.

Jenny couldn't stand there all day, so she picked up her luggage and gingerly stepped forward. Across the street, a gentleman exited the church doors slowly, placing something in his front shirt pocket. He strode across the middle of the street, and Jenny breathed a sigh of relief she would not encounter him on the boardwalk.

Her toe caught on something, and with her hands full, down she went. "Ow."

A few moments later she heard strong, solid footsteps approach. A gust of warmth engulfed her. "Are you hurt, miss?"

Jenny's gaze landed on soot-covered pants, then traveled farther up into the profile of a giant man with dark hair and dark eyes full of concern. He was the gentleman she saw exit the church doors. And he held her gently. She swallowed, not out of uneasiness, but because of the sensations she had never experienced before.

He leaned forward till his gaze met hers. "Are you sure you're not hurt?"

Her breath caught. Then she blinked and glanced down at his arms where they held her. Gentle and so full of care—for her. They were so inviting. Warmth flooded her on the inside as much as the outside.

Her gaze shot back to his, and the concern in his face lit a flame inside. What mesmerizing eyes. She could stare into them all day long. And they were close to hers. So close, in fact, she saw mottled skin under his right eye and cheek as if he had been burned a long time ago. She understood burns since she had done the laundry for her family of nine, along with her siblings. One of them received a burn one time that left a spot of discoloration, but nothing like this. What had hurt him?

He squinted, as if the sun was too bright. It broke her daydream.

"I don't think so, sir, but thank you." She tried to push herself up, but he hovered too close for her to move her arm.

As she struggled, he reached down, picked her up, and set her on her feet.

Heat rose to her cheeks as she quickly brushed out her skirts and set herself to rights.

He continued to stare at her without saying anything.

Her cheeks warmed. "Really, sir. I'm fine. I'm more embarrassed than anything."

He moved his hand behind his back, but continued to search her face. The way he focused on her was quite endearing. Jenny hadn't had many people fuss over her in all her twenty years. Not a family member, nor a friend, and especially not a handsome stranger.

She smiled shyly back at him, but he didn't respond in kind. Instead, he stepped back and made a sour grimace. "Well, if you don't need anything more, I'll be going now. Good day, miss." And he turned to walk away. After two steps, he glanced over his shoulder and then continued on.

Jenny didn't know what to think. But before she lost her nerve, she called out, "Sir, I'm looking for a friend. She is the schoolteacher here, Miss Livvy Carmichael. Do you think you could help me find her?"

* * *

Ren froze. His heart beating overtime. He turned around and saw the vulnerability on the face of this beautiful young lady and couldn't say no. And even though he did not know who this Miss Carmichael was, he would help this woman find her. Because he couldn't walk away.

She should be frightened of him. Most women were.

But instead, she'd asked for his help.

Half of him wanted to run and hide and never see her again, but the other half of him wanted to stay. To see how long before she was repelled by his ugly scars.

He should not be anywhere near here. The only reason was because he spent his lunch hours in communion with God at the church alone, which allowed him to avoid attending church on Sundays.

The wind blew, and she pulled her cloak tighter around her. The material must be thin, since it appeared to have seen better days. Not that he judged her—he just noticed things. That's how it was. He watched more than he participated.

Which was why it didn't escape his notice that her worn carpet bag looked like it carried everything she owned. And the dark circles under her eyes, causing the shadows around her thin face, told him she had eaten little lately. The way she felt in his arms confirmed that too.

His accelerated heartbeat urged him forward, so he took two steps toward her. "Yes, I can help. Let's check the schoolhouse first to see if your friend is there."

Relief flooded her face, and Ren found himself pulling his shoulders back, enjoying playing the hero for once. It wasn't something he had ever had the chance to do. Back home, the kids he grew up with mocked him or avoided him. And that didn't change as he aged. Which, so far, wasn't the case here. Although he didn't venture out much.

A blur of color came from around the corner.

Squawk.

The young miss glanced over her shoulder, screamed, and ran around Ren, hiding behind his back.

He waved his arms. "Shoo. Get out of here."

A rooster spread his wings and eyed him wildly. Then, he paced the ground, his beady little eyes focused on Ren.

He had never seen a bird act so peculiar. He stepped closer and glared at the mongrel.

The cranky bird stopped and stared back. Then he squawked, moved his head back and forth, and ran off in the direction he came.

Satisfied the threat was over, Ren picked up her suitcase.

She rushed toward him and tried to pull it out of his hands. "I can manage."

"You don't have to do everything on your own. It would be my honor to help. I'm Ren, by the way."

Curiosity sparkled in her eyes. "Wren like the bird? It's an unusual name."

"It's actually short for Clarence, but don't let anyone know." He whispered the last part and gave what he thought was a smile, but it felt more like a grimace. He had had little experience putting a pleasant look on his face, so it felt completely unnatural.

A beautiful smile bloomed from her lips as if the secret was a big deal. "My name is Miss Jenny Millard."

"Pleased to meet you, Miss Millard." He nodded, secured his position to her right side, and led her toward the schoolhouse. By the faint sounds of the children, they should find it soon.

The boardwalk ended, and they stepped onto the dirt road. Together, they followed it around the side of the church. He carried her belongings while she kept pace alongside him. His heart hadn't been this full in forever.

She'd looked so pretty standing on the pathway all by herself, with her straight dark hair clipped in back and her cute little hat perched on her head.

Cute? He frowned. He had never thought of cute things in

his entire life. He needed to focus on something else. Anything. But the only thing that came to mind was how to hammer metal on an anvil or to explain he was new in town and didn't know too many people. With no idea how to broach either topic and get a conversation started, he climbed the hill in silence.

She faltered, and he placed his arm under her elbow. Heat traveled up to his neck, but he didn't remove his arm. It was an honor to offer assistance.

The path straightened, and the children's voices grew louder. Good. They'd found the school quickly. Now to find the teacher so he could be on his way.

His chest tightened. Was it because he didn't want to say goodbye to Miss Millard? Or was it because the schoolyard brought about an influx of memories he'd rather not remember? Of course, this schoolhouse looked nothing like the one he'd attended. Gideon had mentioned the town had to rebuild it after the latest flood. It stood so tall and sturdy now, with a group of men working on the final touches. Ren couldn't imagine it damaged.

The children settled outside on the ground in a half-circle facing a woman who was most likely the sought-after Miss Carmichael. She sat on a tree stump. And that crazy bird paced back and forth right behind her.

Would the animal attack? Should Ren shout "Watch out" or something to warn her?

But as he focused on the scene, the teacher paid the rooster no mind. And the rooster clucked as he paced, stopping and looking at the students, as if he watched over them—or made sure they paid attention.

Had he been hit over the head with a six-pound rounding hammer? It could be the only answer to what Ren was seeing in front of him. And the only explanation for why he forgot all about his self-imposed isolation to help the black-haired beauty standing beside him. And for the mixed-up feelings on the inside, which he couldn't identify.

He might have to tell Gideon he was too sick to finish work today.

Three

Well, the new part of my life didn't plan out as I hoped. I no longer have a schoolhouse to teach in. I don't want to write about what happened, so I will just start over here.

—From the journal of Jenny Millard

Jenny heard the children before she saw them. By the time they entered the schoolyard, the children had quieted and were listening intently to their teacher's instructions. Jenny's heart leaped at seeing her friend.

What if Livvy wasn't happy to see her? Her stomach flipped, and her face flushed with heat at the thought of being rejected in front of this fine gentleman. She glanced his way as her mind raced with what thoughts he had of her.

But none of it mattered. She had no other options for a place to sleep for a night or two until she could figure out where she would go next. Livvy wouldn't say no to that, would she?

Ren put his hand out as if to protect her from something as

they approached. Taking his lead, she stopped before they were too close to interrupt. Then her gaze landed on the same rooster that had accosted them earlier.

She fisted her hands before she could stop herself. Were the students in danger? It didn't seem like it, but she was ready to fight. Roosters were mean. They would defend their territory and peck at fingers if the person attached to the fingers wasn't quick enough. She learned that lesson along with another at the young age of seven, the first time she ever collected the eggs herself.

The other being, if all the eggs dropped, there would be no breakfast for the entire family. The look of disappointment from her mother was something Jenny never wanted to have directed at her again. Yet, Jenny discovered as the years went by, her ma would scowl often at Jenny. It was not a fun feeling. And why Jenny hated to let down anyone.

Admitting to Livvy she failed two schools would not be easy.

Fidgeting with her skirt, her stomach growled. She sneaked a peek at Ren.

He glanced her way, eyes glimmering.

Her stomach dipped and chose to growl again. She forced a smile, then searched the area, counting to ten.

It was then she saw the schoolhouse. Her lips parted. Neither of her one-room buildings had ever looked this shiny. They were built with broken pieces of wood, where gaps leaked both heat and cold. Her townspeople, too focused on surviving, had given it no mind.

Here, several men finished whitewashing the outside walls. And inside through the window openings more men installed brand-new glass. One man backed into another, and they shared a laugh at the interaction. She might even call it friendly.

Her muscles eased a bit. People were kind here. Welcoming. She wouldn't be jeered at for existing.

Jenny shifted her feet, ignoring the pain that shot up her leg, not knowing what to do next.

One of the girls tapped Livvy on the arm and pointed toward them.

Her senses on high alert, Jenny felt ready to faint. This was the mo—

"Jenny!" Livvy exclaimed. She set down her book and rushed toward Jenny, holding her skirts up a little higher than normal so she could walk faster. That was a good sign, wasn't it? "What a pleasant surprise. What are you doing here? How long are you here? What are you doing here? Oh, I said that already, didn't I? Let me hug you."

Jenny opened her mouth, but knew if she said anything, her eyes would leak out the unshed tears forming, and her voice would croak.

"I'm so grateful to see you. I have missed you tremendously."

"I've missed you too," Jenny replied, relieved her voice didn't wobble. She closed her eyes as Olivia squeezed her hard and held on for a few extra minutes. Her heart sang at having someone hug her. Had she ever had this much enthusiasm in a greeting before? A memory she would pocket to cherish for the rest of her days.

Livvy stepped back and faced the giant of a man standing next to her. "Hello." She reached out her hand. "I'm Miss Carmichael, the schoolteacher."

Ren stared at Livvy's hand. Multiple expressions crossed his face.

Jenny frowned. What was wrong? He was so talkative and helpful with her, but now he was completely closed off. From the corner of her eye, Jenny saw him make a fist and then partially open his hand. She hadn't noticed before, but his hand showed different pigment colors with raised bumps all over his thumb, like his face. Was he embarrassed? Unable to shake hands? Her heart thumped faster, and she gestured toward him. "This is Ren. He saw me being clumsy and trip, and then he came to my rescue."

He glanced at her, surprise all over his face.

Jenny smiled at Ren, and he turned and nodded to Livvy, then proceeded to place his scarred hand behind his back.

Livvy lowered her hand and glanced between the two of them, smiling the entire time. Something about her glowed. Did she look more at peace than before she came to Washton?

Her friend grinned at Jenny. "What are you doing here? Aren't you supposed to be teaching in your school?" Livvy asked.

Jenny faced Livvy and pinched her lips. She didn't want Ren to know this, but what else could she do? She closed her eyes. "Yes. But they closed the school and let me go. I only had enough money to get here. I hope you don't mind I came."

"Oh, nonsense. I'm glad you did. I've been staying back at the Martins', and you can come with me." She held up her hand. "Don't say a word. You can share the bedroom with me, and I know you eat like a bird anyway, so it won't be an issue to add another place setting to the table for supper tonight."

For the first time in the last twelve hours, Jenny breathed out a sigh of relief. She would have a roof over her head and food to eat. There would be no need to fret over her predicament tonight. She would worry about tomorrow, tomorrow.

Livvy looked over her shoulder. All the children were watching intently. And the rooster too. He had jumped on the tree stump where Livvy had sat. "Why don't you wait for me to finish up here. It should only be thirty more minutes. Then we can walk to the Martins' together."

Ren cleared his throat. "If it's all right with you, miss, I really should get back to the smithy. I could carry your luggage over to—

Livvy chimed in. "That would be wonderful. It's Mayor Martin's home. The white house at the end of Main Street. You can't miss it."

He nodded and glanced at Jenny. "That way, you don't need to worry about it."

Jenny bit her lip. She didn't want to have her belongings leave her sight, but there was no way she could carry it herself. So tired, she might topple over if the wind blew hard. But could she trust him?

His lips twitched. "I promise to take it straight there, and it will be waiting for you when you arrive."

Livvy tugged on her arm. "Come and sit down with me, and I'll introduce you to my students. With everything going on, I could use your help."

Jenny instantly stood taller. Did they need more than one teacher here? She stepped forward, then stopped and faced Ren. "Thank you. For everything. I couldn't have made it all this way without your help. You are a true knight of service."

Livvy gasped and covered her mouth. "Oh. Don't mind me. It's just that I've said those exact words before to someone. And, well ... knights are rare, and hard to find, and not part of the plan sometimes. I'll explain more later."

Jenny's brows furrowed. What was she talking about?

Livvy waved to the children. "I'm coming." She looked over her shoulder. "You ready, Jenny?"

Jenny glanced at Ren, wanting to say more, but his back was to her, and he headed down the hill. An ache formed in her chest. Would she ever see him again?

* * *

THE SUITCASE BUMPED against Ren's leg as he headed back the way he came.

He should've said goodbye but couldn't get the words out. For that was what it had to be. *Goodbye.* He cringed as he replayed the interaction with the teacher. He was unprepared for a woman to reach out a hand to shake like a man. Reacted too slowly.

And then Miss Millard noticed his deformity.

He squeezed his hand closed and let the residual pain from the tightness in the skin numb the other emotions flowing through him.

Her hesitation over him handling her belongings punched him in the gut. There was no chance of continuing a friendship now. Although her words at the end confused him.

A true knight of service.

Why would she say that if she was horrified by his hand? He nodded his head as a thought clicked in his thick-headed brain. Maybe she saw him only as a servant. And did the only polite thing she could. Don't acknowledge the ugly. Focus on the task at hand.

And she needed his help.

His shoulders relaxed slightly. It was better than an outright rejection. Something he could accept. He would stay as far away from her as possible. Hide in the smithy. Help out in the background.

His stomach roiled at the thought of having to move on—again. Years of rejection from others hadn't softened the blow. And the schoolhouse behind him brought to the forefront painful memories of the taunting from his past.

With his ability to hold a conversation tapped out, he glanced at the luggage and cringed. Why had he offered to

24

help? He should've just left. But he had wanted to make sure the beautiful woman he had just met could get her belongings where she needed them. So, he offered.

Now, he was stuck.

He turned the corner on Main Street and continued on the boardwalk.

A sound came from behind, and Ren swung around.

That stupid rooster clucked closer while staring Ren down.

Screech.

"Shoo." Ren shook his head, turned, and headed down the boardwalk. The fowl following him did not help his mood. Thankfully, most people were not out and about, and he didn't have to bear his teeth in a resemblance of a smile and scare anyone.

Screech.

Why was this bird following him?

Ren's long legs moved him first by an empty storefront, then the general store, a new café, and then the mayor's office. The white house mentioned by Miss Carmichael stood at the center of the cross-street. Stepping up onto the porch, he raised his hand to knock.

The door swung open, and a lady about the age of his ma, smiled at him. "Yes, may I help you?"

"Uh." He lifted the ragged brown suitcase with his left hand, keeping his right one hidden. "Miss Carmichael asked me to deliver this to your home. It's Miss Millard's. She's come to visit." Based on the revelation about her job disappearing, he didn't think it was just a visit, but it wasn't his place to say anything.

"Oh, wonderful." She clasped her hands to her chest. "Another daughter to look after." She opened the screen. "Won't you please come in and put it in the bedroom over there?" The cantankerous rooster squawked louder. The kind woman smiled at the bird. "Bert, I see you. Thanks for making sure he found us."

Bert chirped and flapped his wings, and ran back down the street. If Ren didn't know better, he'd think the rooster could understand everything the mayor's wife said. Ren shook his head to clear it. He really needed to stay in the forge and pound metal all day.

His gaze moved from the bird to the opened door with the woman and the motherly expression on her face, welcoming him into her home. Unease swept through him, but he ducked his head and followed her gesture to the room she mentioned. Setting down the load in his hands, he settled his palms behind his back and headed straight to the front door to exit.

The kind woman stepped in front of him. "Would you care for a cup of lemonade or tea? Where are my manners? I'm Chrissy Martin." And she held out her hand. "My husband is Mayor Arthur Martin."

And for the second time today, he stalled. He couldn't be rude to the mayor's wife.

He pulled his left hand from behind and glanced down. "I'm sorry, my hands are all dirty. I don't mean to be rude. My name is Ren. I work at the Smithy." He glanced at her sheepishly.

"Oh, you're the person helping Gideon out? I've heard all about you, and I'm so thankful you showed up when you did. We need someone young and strong with all the railway work being done."

"It's nice to meet you ma'am. I really need to be getting back."

"Chrissy. Please." She reached for his arm.

He stilled. "What?"

She patted his arm and then let go. "Call me Chrissy. We will have you over for dinner soon."

There was no way he would subject them to his scars over a meal. But he could deal with saying no another time. "Thank you for the offer. I really must go." He focused on the door, counting his steps to ease his anxiousness. One, two, three, four. Opening the door, he nearly ran down the porch steps and into the warm sunshine to get away from the persistent kindness of Mrs. Martin.

"Thanks for stopping by," she called out.

He halted, and a swirl of dust skated across the tips of his boots. Looking over his shoulder, he waved with his left hand. Soon, he'd be back working hot iron in hot flames. Anything was better than the stifling conversation in the mayor's house, even the forge.

But, it was nice to know Miss Millard would be met with kindness. She looked as if she needed some.

That's why he'd offered his help. Because she was someone in need.

He stepped onto the boardwalk, heading back on the other side of the street, keeping his head down and walking as briskly as he could without drawing attention to himself. He didn't want any more encounters. He'd had enough today. Although, he didn't regret helping Miss Millard. Something about her drew him to her. Maybe it was a nudge from God, but he sensed something more, like when his heart thumped double-time when he held her in his arms. He shook his head. He sure didn't need complications if he planned to stay in Washton.

Cutting through the alley between the smithy and the livery, he entered from the back. His body relaxed as he set foot into the darkened room. Clanking sounds echoed off the walls as he grabbed his apron off the hook and slid it over his neck. This is where he felt the most comfortable. This is where he could hide and not worry about upsetting anyone. The shop was dark, poorly lit, and warm. Home.

"There you are." The pounding stopped. "Thought you might've left and wasn't coming back."

Ren grunted. He had thought about it. But where would he go?

"I can see you're not interested in talking, but Luke Taylor is in front wanting to go over the design of the gate you said you would make for him. Hopefully, he can understand your mumbling."

Ren placed his gloves on his hands and headed toward the front.

"Before I forget, did you enjoy your break?"

Ren grunted again. And then found his manners as he paused at the door. "Yes. I helped someone who needed assistance, so it took me longer to get back. I'll stay later tonight to make up for the lost time."

There was a long pause.

"You don't have to do that. With both of us working for the next few hours, we can finish today's work, no problem."

Four

I'm with my friend Livvy. She didn't send me away. Instead, she welcomed me. I've never been hugged, touched, and pampered like this before. Am I dreaming?

—From the journal of Jenny Millard

Jenny and Livvy arrived at the Martins' home shortly before the supper hour. On their walk from the school, Jenny listened as her friend explained all the repairs the town had made since the flood. When Livvy walked into the house as if she were a member of the family, Jenny stood on the porch, wondering if she would be welcomed as well as Livvy said she would.

"Chrissy! Chrissy where are you? I want you to meet my very dear friend, Jenny."

Jenny took a step inside.

A woman appeared wearing a smile and wiping her hands on her apron. "Oh, this is your Jenny!"

Jenny froze. "You know about me?"

"Oh, my, yes. Olivia has mentioned you several times, especially after receiving your letters. Please, come in. I assume it was your luggage dropped off by that handsome stranger earlier?"

Well, that answered her two questions. Livvy remembered her and still considered her a friend, *and* her bag with all her belongings arrived safely.

"My name is Chrissy Martin. You can call me Chrissy. Olivia is in the one extra room we have, but I'm sure she wouldn't mind sharing it with you."

Livvy laughed. "Not at all. I already told her we could share."

Chrissy smiled. "How long do you plan to stay?"

Jenny glanced around the front room, avoiding the answer. Furniture was sparse, and the inside smelled freshly painted. "Did you just move in?"

"It feels that way, doesn't it?" Chrissy looked wistful. "Unfortunately, the flood in January damaged our home, and we had to rebuild. Much of the town had to. It's sad to lose our things, but I count our blessings. We're alive and still have food to eat and a town to run."

"Run?" Jenny asked.

"Why, yes. My husband. He's the mayor. Been working so hard these past four months making sure everyone's had the help they need."

"He takes on the role of father here very seriously," Livvy added.

If only her town had been as concerned about her having a place to stay. "I'm sorry about the damage. I feel bad. Maybe I shouldn't have come."

Livvy touched her arm. "How could you say such a thing."

Chrissy shook her head. "Nonsense. This is what living is about. Things happen. Sometimes life is bountiful, and sometimes it's not. We need to have a hopeful attitude through all of it."

Jenny didn't know if having a joyful attitude about all that happened to her would help, but she nodded anyway.

Chrissy placed some bread and butter on the table and went back to the stove to grab the kettle. "Don't be shy. We have plenty. You look like you're hungry."

Jenny gave a sheepish smile. "How could you tell."

"You're eyeing it quite like a coyote eyes a rabbit." The older woman laughed.

Livvy joined in.

Jenny liked Chrissy. She was a straight shooter and had a great outlook on life. Her friendliness and the kindness in her eyes allowed Jenny to relax. At least she would eat and have a place to sleep tonight.

After they partook in some tea and refreshments, Chrissy sat back in her chair. "There's no limit, but I am curious as to how long you plan to stay?"

The concern and empathy on Livvy's face were enough to make Jenny cry. All sense of holding things back till they could talk privately broke down. "They closed the second school they sent me to." She burst into tears.

When Jenny's blubbering stopped, she found herself in both Livvy and Chrissy's arms. They patted her on the back. "I'm sorry." She pulled away.

"Don't be." Livvy squeezed her hand. "I'm sorry I haven't written in a while."

Jenny wiped the tears from her cheeks. "It wouldn't have gotten to me anyway." She shook her head. "I just don't know what I'm going to do."

Chrissy and Livvy shared a look. With a tiny nod, Livvy turned to face Jenny, then grabbed her hands. "Stay here with me."

Hope bloomed inside Jenny's heart. "Are you sure?"

"Absolutely." She laughed. "You have no idea. I think you're an answer to prayers."

She'd never been an answer to anyone's prayers. "What? I don't understand."

Chrissy laughed all the way back to the kitchen.

"Oh, you will soon enough. Let's get you settled in my ... no, *our* room, and then we can talk more at supper." Livvy grabbed her hand and led her to the bedroom.

The next hour was a whirlwind. Jenny's things were unpacked in no time—one, because she didn't have many belongings, and two, having multiple females unpack was much more efficient. Embarrassed to have Livvy see her well-worn clothes, she tried to tuck them away quickly. But Livvy stayed her hand, told her it would be okay, and then proceeded to hand her a pair of newer, worn shoes. She almost wept.

Jenny also found out that sharing her burdens with Livvy caused her less stress, not more. She still couldn't believe Livvy wanted her there, and that was a balm to her heart. She felt safe. Something she hadn't felt in a long time.

They came back out to the front room, and Jenny met the infamous Mr. Martin. He gave her a little hug upon introduction, and they laughed. They both felt as if they knew each other because of Livvy's letters. Her cheeks turned pink at the idea of the Martins reading them, but they didn't act like they minded in the least.

When they sat down to supper, Livvy rubbed her hands together. "So." She paused. "There has been a lot that has happened since we wrote each other last."

Jenny's stomach dropped. Was there some horrible news to be told?

"First of all, you can still call me Livvy. That will always be my name to you, but I go by Olivia here. Or Miss Carmichael."

"Olivia?"

Livvy scrunched her nose. "My true name is Olivia, but at the school in Cincinnati, I went by Livvy. "I'll explain more later."

Jenny frowned. Were there things she didn't know about her friend? Jenny wasn't sure what to think. It had been September of last year since they saw one another, and even then, they had only known each other for a month before. They had met when they trained for teaching, then rode out on the train cross country for ten days. Livvy came here to Washton, and Jenny ... well, Jenny went to a different place. One she thought would become her new home.

Chrissy smirked. "You never mentioned you went by Livvy. Isn't that what Luke calls you now?"

Livvy turned beet red.

Chrissy waved a hand at Livvy. "Don't be embarrassed. I think it's romantic."

Jenny tilted her head. "Who's Luke?"

"I wrote to you about him in a more recent letter. Did you never receive it?"

Jenny shook her head. "When I changed schools, I was so embarrassed, I didn't write to tell you my new address."

"Jenny, you have nothing to apologize for. I'm thankful you are here. And now I can tell you in person." Livvy smiled.

Chrissy grinned. "Luke is the *one* who will change Olivia's name from Carmichael to Taylor someday soon." Chrissy winked at Jenny.

Livvy glared at the sweet older woman. How could she get away with such a look?

An innocentness crossed Chrissy's face. "What? It's true."

Livvy huffed. "Let me tell her."

Chrissy rolled her eyes.

"Um ...see, I met someone and ..."

Jenny clapped her hands together and burst out, "You're getting married?"

Livvy's cheeks turned pink. "Not exactly."

"She will be—just as soon as she finds a replacement to take over teaching for her. There I said it." Chrissy looked at Jenny pointedly. "And you, my fine young lady are just the teacher to take over."

Jenny sat there, stunned.

"Whoa, hold on, Chrissy," stated Mr. Martin. "We have a school board that must approve these things."

"But don't you see? It's perfect. Luke and Olivia can be married, and the students won't miss one day of school." She winked at Jenny. "I've been praying, you know. And God has heard and answered those prayers."

Jenny didn't know if that was the reason. Surely, God wouldn't have put her through the past few months of struggle, closing two schools and having every family turn her away, all to bring her to Washton. Why, what type of God did that?

Livvy grabbed Jenny's hand. "Say you'll come by my classroom tomorrow. Maybe around midday? You can watch or help, it's up to you. Then we can talk about it further. No rush."

Jenny nodded, barely able to hold in her excitement. She was welcomed here. And she might be able to stay.

* * *

THE SOUNDS of the morning woke Jenny, and she found herself alone in a stranger's house. She pulled back the covers and moved out her legs so she could stand. The brisk air felt refreshing against her skin, while the sunlight pouring in the window warmed her. She must've slept late. Exhaustion, no doubt.

The Martins' house was very homey, and though not overly spacious, there was room enough for both Livvy and Jenny to move around. Jenny and Livvy had stayed up until late last night talking, Jenny filling her in on all that had happened since the last time she had written.

Livvy asked if they could pray together, and Jenny didn't have the heart to tell her that it wouldn't work. That she had tried praying. God had treated her like everyone else had. Invisible. Not there. Unnoticed. But she didn't want Livvy to know how she felt. She had done so much for Jenny already. Letting her pray was the least she could do.

Yet now, she felt refreshed. Renewed. A small bloom opened inside her heart. Much like freshly blooming flowers after taking a winter's nap. Spring was about fresh starts, and she was in the position to start over—again. She didn't know what her new beginning would be. But she wanted to find out.

Checking the timepiece on the dresser, she cringed. What would she do with the few hours before Livvy said to come to the schoolhouse? Doubts crept in, but she dismissed the negative thoughts and prepared herself for the day ahead. She entered the main room of the Martins' home just as Chrissy placed a plate of food on the table.

"Good morning, Jenny. How are you feeling this morning?"

Jenny wanted to look around and ask, *Are you asking me?*, but she didn't know if Chrissy would appreciate the sarcasm. She instead answered her with a polite, "Great." And really, she was good. She had gone to bed with a full belly, a soft bed, and excitement for her friend's upcoming marriage. Yet, she was still a little hesitant about what the future held for her here. What was expected of her? She was entering brand new territory, starting over again.

Chrissy studied her a moment, then motioned for her to sit at the table.

"Oh, no, I couldn't possibly have you wait on me. I should be the one to help around here."

Chrissy pulled out a chair. "Jenny, there will be plenty of time for you to work, but for right now, I'd like you to sit down so we can talk."

Here it was. Jenny knew what would come next. That she was another mouth to feed, and there wasn't enough room. Too expensive to let her stay. These were all things she had heard before. Numerous times. She knew when the door was closing, so to speak. Better say something now before it became awkward.

"No need. I will gather my things and move on today. I appreciate you allowing me to spend a night here. And for feeding me." Tears formed in her eyes. She was so weepy. It made her feel weak. Something she vowed to never feel again once she left home.

Chrissy gazed at her with a different expression than others normally showed.

Not contempt. Could it be compassion? But Jenny hadn't had much compassion shown to her, so maybe she didn't know what it was supposed to look like.

"My dear child. Where will you go? How will you feed yourself?" Chrissy clutched her hands at her chest. She showed true concern.

Jenny opened her mouth, but she didn't have answers and didn't have the energy to hide the truth.

Chrissy stepped closer. "Olivia filled me in on your predicament, Jenny. It is obvious you are not comfortable sharing with me all that is going on with you. But I do want you to know you have a place to stay as long as you need it. We are not going to kick you out to figure it out on your own. And Washton needs you."

Tears streamed down Jenny's cheeks. At this point, she lost the control to hide her fears, her pain, her loneliness.

Chrissy approached her, wrapped her arms around her, and squeezed. "Whatever you are going through, Jenny, you are not alone. I want to be your friend. And Olivia is your friend. And God loves you, even though it doesn't always feel like it. Together, God, you, me, and Olivia, will figure this out. You'll see. Now eat your breakfast before it gets much colder. Okay, missy?"

Jenny chuckled and swiped at the moisture on her cheeks. When her eyes could focus again, she glanced into Chrissy's warm expression and smiled. "Thank you. You don't know how much your words mean to me." Famished, she sat at the place set for her, picked up the fork, and ate her breakfast. She hadn't seen so much food in one sitting in a long time. Something she could get used to, if she didn't watch out.

After breakfast and cleaning up, Chrissy encouraged Jenny to help her with a task. "I could use your help in preparing some food for families who are still affected by the flood damage."

Warmth coursed through Jenny at being asked to help. Together, they prepared to cook enough food to fill several baskets. Thankfully, Jenny knew her way around a kitchen. Since the age of ten, she was cooking and cleaning for her family of nine, and by the time she was fourteen, she completely ran the household. Her job was the kitchen work as well as leading her siblings with the daily chore of laundry, including hauling water from the well several times a day. She was happy not to be doing that anymore, but thankful she could serve this sweet woman, who had shown her nothing but kindness.

After a few hours, they had five sets of meals, all placed in baskets.

"Help me take these out to the wagon." Chrissy pulled off her apron, grabbed three, and headed through the front door.

Jenny picked up the last two baskets, headed outside, and placed them in the wagon bed next to the others. She brushed her arm across her brow.

"I can see you're worn out." Chrissy chuckled. "Thank you for all your help. There's no way I would've gotten this done in time. While Mr. Martin and I deliver these, why don't you rest. We'll be back shortly."

She stood in the doorway, watching Chrissy cross the street to her husband's office. Jenny's shoulders sagged a bit. The exertion of the morning depleted her, and she had no idea why. She used to work in her family's kitchen all day as well as standard laundry loads, including batches for her mother's laundry business. She should have the energy for more than what they did this morning.

Uncomfortable to just sit in someone else's home, she went back to the kitchen to see what she could clean up. There wasn't much left, as Chrissy had done most of it while they loaded up the baskets. How nice it was to work in tandem with someone. *Teamwork* is what Chrissy called it.

Jenny had never been a part of a team before. She liked the idea.

There was something to be said about teamwork. Livvy and the schoolhouse appeared in her mind, and an idea surfaced. She hurried to compose herself for the next part of the day. One where she would learn all she could to become a teacher again.

Five

I'm looking forward to learning more about the Washton one-room schoolhouse and its students.

—From the journal of Jenny Millard

After leaving a note for Chrissy, Jenny hurried out the door, crossed the street and stepped onto the boardwalk in front of the mayor's office. Several townsfolk went about their business. Next door to the mercantile, the window held a for-hire sign. She slowed down to read it.

The new Rooster Cafe was looking for hired help to wait tables. Since she knew her way around a kitchen, maybe she could stay and work here if the teaching didn't pan out. "Don't get ahead of yourself," she murmured. Though a backup plan would be prudent, given her past experiences. Next to the new cafe, several people went in and out of the Woodward's Store. Through the window, Jenny saw two chairs and a chessboard in the corner.

Loud pounding emanated from the smithy across the street. The blacksmith's hammer continued in a set rhythm, and she wondered if the hammering was Ren and what he was making. Back home, she had always loved to see what the local blacksmith created. He didn't mind children watching from the open door and would form his extra metal scraps into fun shapes for them to play with. She smiled at the memory before she was brought back to the present, her heart pounding along in the same beat.

A sharp pang crossed her chest. Even if she did go home, life would never be the same. She didn't think her ma and pa would be able to see her for anything but a helping hand who could bring in more money to help feed and clothe everyone.

Someone bumped into her from behind. She found herself blocking people's way. "Sorry." She hurried along, trying to make herself appear smaller and out of the way. This was not the impression she wanted to leave with the townsfolk, especially if Mr. Martin was able to get the board to approve her as a schoolteacher.

A hissing sound came from the smithy, and she looked that way. Her pulse hummed as she searched in vain for a glimpse of the man who treated her kindly. Instead, she found a man leaning against the livery building next door. Horses neighed, but he just stood there and studied her. She looked away and focused on her steps as she approached the dirt hill, hoping to not trip like she had the first time. The sensation of being watched followed her until she came upon the church building.

At that moment, the door opened, and Ren stepped out, holding a piece of paper. He glanced up and froze.

"Hello." She waved, then approached him. "Thank you for carrying my bag yesterday."

He nodded. "Glad to help." He shifted his feet, keeping his hands behind his back.

An awkward silence descended between them.

For some reason Jenny didn't want the conversation to end. "Um. You're a blacksmith?"

His eyes lit up. "I am. How did you—" he searched her face "—know?"

She didn't want to call out that he had soot all over him, so what did she say? "You carry yourself like a blacksmith."

He smiled. "And how does a blacksmith carry himself?"

Her face heated, and she glanced at the ground.

"I'm sorry, I didn't mean to embarrass you." His voice cracked. "I'm not very good at this."

She looked up and his dark eyes held hers. Her heart flipped. "Not good at what? And you didn't embarrass me. I'm just unsure of myself."

He chuckled. "Well, then we can be unsure together. I don't have a lot of experience talking to pretty ladies."

Her eyes widened. He thought she was pretty?

"I said too much. See. Not very good." He turned his body to show his left side, his gaze never leaving her face.

It felt like a caress, and her cheeks heated. She needed something to talk about. "I think you're doing just fine."

A hint of pink appeared on his cheeks.

She needed to change the subject. "What's the paper you're holding?"

He hurried to stuff it into his pocket. "Nothing really. Just a few Bible verses I carry around with me."

"Oh." She looked away.

He cleared his throat, and her eyes found his again.

"Are you heading to the schoolhouse?"

"I am."

"Would you like an escort again?"

Her lips lifted into a smile. "I would love that. But I'm sure you have more important things to be doing."

"Uh. I don't mind." He turned and offered his left arm, placing himself between the dirt road and her.

She slowly reached out and tucked her hand into the crook of his elbow. Her arm felt as if a bolt of lightning was surging through it.

They each took a step at the same time with different feet, which had them pulling on each other's arms in the opposite direction.

Jenny laughed. She hadn't had this much fun in, well, never.

"I'm so sorry. My fault." Ren tilted his head her way. "Again, something I'm not really used to. Escorting someone."

"Really? Because I've never had an escort before."

"That can't be." He grinned her way.

She grinned back.

"Let's try this again." He took a step that matched hers. And he stayed by her side the rest of the way.

When the schoolhouse appeared into view, Jenny found no one outside. She caught movement from inside the building through the open door.

Ren stopped and dropped his arm. "I think they're inside. I must get back to the smithy. Looks like you'll be okay to handle things from here?"

Jenny nodded and dipped into a little curtsy. "I appreciate your assistance. Again."

His gaze searched hers, and his lips twitched in some semblance of a smile. He abruptly turned and headed back the way they came. For a large man, he moved fast.

She walked up the steps of the one-room schoolhouse and went inside.

Livvy's voice rang throughout the building. "Students, I

have a treat for you today. This is my good friend Miss Millard. She will be helping during class time."

Several heads swiveled toward her.

Butterflies trounced on her stomach as if they were as heavy as iron. It was time to put the skills she learned to use. She had a lot of catching up to do if the opportunity to become the next schoolteacher of Washton came to fruition.

* * *

THWACK.

Ren pounded on the thin piece of metal, flattening it so he could bend it into the shape he intended. The clang from the hammer hitting the iron, along with the gases spewing from the fire, were like a conversation for Ren. He could listen and interact with it all day.

Each strike was a release, a way to wallop out frustrations in his system—the past, the future, or anything in between. Such as how the image of a certain black-haired woman plagued him, disrupting his work and peace.

Thwack.

He'd pummel it out if it was the last thing he did.

Thwack.

Though hitting metal looked easy, it was a form of exercise for Ren, using strength and control to do the job well.

Thwack.

But he also liked to box.

At his dad's shop, his father had a pole with a bag of flour wrapped up in leftover burlap sacks they would pound into. His dad had seen the irritation in his son after the accident and let Ren hit at it whenever he needed. Boxing helped him deal with the emotions churning inside. And made him stronger. When he was ten, he was able to lift two times the weight of most boys. The bullies still tortured Ren, but it would've been much worse.

Thwack. Thwack. Thwack.

What was it about Miss Millard? He hadn't shared that many words within a twenty-four-hour period since he was a boy.

Thwack.

Then, the encounter with the mayor's wife. Ren didn't want to admit it, but she terrified him. She would push right through all the barriers he had built through the years. And then, who would he be?

Thwack.

Work alone would not be enough to settle his thoughts today. Glancing around the room, he saw a few sandbags he could use for the interim. "Gideon, would you mind if I used some of those bags over there to set up a punching bag?"

Gideon frowned. "You aren't thinking of going into fighting, are you? To my way of thinking, fighting does not solve anything."

Ren laughed. Between his size and the suggestion of a punching bag, he could see how that would send alarm through his new mentor. "No, I had a punching bag growing up, and I used it to build my arm strength and for exercise. I haven't done it in a while, and I feel some weakness in my arm."

Disbelief showed on Gideon's face. "Suit yourself. As long as you do the work necessary before you go punching, I'm okay with it."

"Thank you, sir, I appreciate it." Ren turned back to his work.

Thwack.

"I said not to call me sir. My name is Gideon." His words didn't have any condemnation in them. Just a reminder to Ren that Gideon was becoming more than a boss or mentor. To a greater extent, a friend. Treating Ren as such since the first day Ren showed up at the shop asking for a job.

Yet, Gideon didn't just offer Ren work, he offered him a place to stay. Widowed for several years, Gideon's house sat behind the smithy, a little cottage that looked like it hadn't been thoroughly cleaned in years. And it most likely hadn't.

Ren knew he'd found something truly special here.

Where other blacksmiths he met while traveling west found the way Ren worked odd and criticized him with harsh words, Gideon was different. He welcomed Ren and treated Ren as an equal right away, as if Ren added value to Gideon's shop.

And they worked much in the same way, their techniques complimenting each other. Gideon easily assessed others. Kept opinions to himself. Was mindful not to talk Ren's ear off, and ran his shop honestly, which showed with his patrons.

Most blacksmith shops were where the men gathered in town. News, gossip, and sharing of ideas passed amongst them, and Washton was no different.

Ren placed a new piece of metal in the pit, then stirred the coals.

Same could be said of Ren's father's shop.

Sparks crackled and floated upward.

Ren wiped his brow. Growing up with a father as a blacksmith, staying with Gideon gave him a little taste of home.

He moved the hot metal over to the anvil.

Thwack.

Home. There was another topic he had to pound out frequently. His family loved him, there was no doubt. But when others found out Ren had worked on their projects, they didn't think he was capable, and business disappeared. He couldn't do that to his father or his younger brothers, who were also in training.

So he left.

Thwack.

How were things going with his brother in the shop now? Did the Joneses keep needing their gate fixed every week? Did the shoes stay on Old Man Red's horse for longer than a week?

Ren really should write and let his family know where he was. His mom was probably worrying if he was eating enough, and his father would want to know if he was alive.

Thwack. Thwack. Thwack.

He stopped and looked at the flattened iron. Molded and controlled. That was how he planned to live his life. Thanks to God and the verses his mom encouraged him to memorize as a boy, God had molded him. Helped him find ways to keep his emotions in check. The anger from the past, the loneliness from the lack of friendships—all the things that clawed inside of him at times—kept in control.

Studying the metal, he found a small spot that needed more hammering.

Thwack. Thwack. Thwack.

Gideon placed his hand on Ren's shoulder and squeezed. "I think the metal has been pounded enough."

The hammer Ren held stopped mid-swing.

Gideon squeezed his shoulder again. For an older guy he still had a very strong grip. "Everything will be fine, son. I'll help you set up that bag tonight."

Ren nodded.

In this, Gideon reminded Ren of his father.

He briefly closed his eyes, and bowed his head. *Thank you, God, for finding this refuge for me, away from the stares, the glares, and hostility I have endured. May I not squander the peace you've provided. Amen.*

Gideon broke the silence. "Sunday would be a good day for you to meet more of the townsfolk. You keep hiding yourself away here in the back."

Ren now wanted to remove the word friend from his description of Gideon. "I'm not hiding. I'm perfectly happy where I am. Right here in the forge."

"You can't stay here forever."

"I wish I could. Makes life much simpler." His sarcastic tone was not lost on his boss.

"Nonsense," Gideon said with a bit more gusto than usual. "And you got out yesterday *and* today—and nothing happened."

A *lot* had happened, but Ren wasn't going to discuss the feelings twisting inside of him or about his encounter with Miss Millard. "I don't think I'm ready for that, or more that the town is ready for me."

"At this rate, you'll never will be ready. You're a grown man, so I won't push you, but I want you to come with me."

How could he get out of this and not offend the one person who offered his home, his work, and his friendship?

He closed his eyes again. Was this more molding God had planned for him? It sure didn't feel like he was in control. But maybe that was how it was supposed to be. *God, please help me here. I spend time with You on my own. But I'm being asked for more. Is this what I'm supposed to do now? I'll go where You lead. Just let it be crystal clear.*

*I'm not looking forward to being acquainted with the terrifying
rooster named Bert, who everyone in Washton
seems to love.*

—From the journal of Jenny Millard

The next day, Jenny rose when Livvy did. As Jenny dressed, she hummed along the way.

"That song, what is it?" asked Livvy.

"What?"

"The song you were humming?"

Jenny shrugged. "I have no idea, I just hum."

"I know you hum, silly. Remember, I was your roommate for over a month. You have a beautiful voice. But what specific song was it?"

"I don't know, something I made up. There're no words to it, I created my own melody."

Livvy studied her. "Well, if it's not a known song, you should write words for it."

No one would like to listen to music she wrote. "I'll think about it."

Livvy considered her a bit, then went back to her morning routine.

They entered the kitchen when a loud screech cried out.

Screech.

"There's Bert, right on time." A huge smile crossed Livvy's lips.

"What was that?"

"That's our timekeeper. Bert."

She must've had a crazy look on her face because Livvy laughed. "Yes, that's what I thought the first time I heard him. But he's actually quite helpful." She patted Jenny on the shoulder. "Just go with it, it's easier that way."

Jenny frowned. "Okay."

After breakfast they walked out onto the porch, and the same giant red, orange, and black rooster she saw the day she arrived stood in the street.

She stepped back as Livvy stepped forward.

Screech.

"Good morning, Bert. I'd like you to meet my friend, Jenny."

He flapped out his wing.

Screech.

Jenny didn't move. "You know this rooster was at the schoolhouse with you?"

"Yes. He's well known here and walks me back and forth to the schoolhouse." Livvy smirked, then cupped her hand around her mouth to hide her words. "Say hi."

"What? No." Jenny shook her head. "I don't have a great affinity for roosters."

Livvy's gaze searched hers. "What happened?"

"Long story." Jenny winced. She didn't want to remember.

"Well, Bert is different. It took me a while to warm up to him. Hopefully, you won't need as much time as I did."

Jenny studied the massive bird. This was silly. She didn't talk to roosters. And neither would Livvy, or so she thought. But both her friend and Bert looked at her expectantly.

"Um. Uh. Hi?" For sure, her cheeks were bright red. Her head felt on fire too.

Bert ducked his head, turned, and walked away.

"We're to follow his lead." Livvy waved her arm in the direction he went.

And like that, Jenny walked with her friend while following a chicken.

This Bert fellow strutted at a clipped pace, making it easy for them to keep up. Onto the boardwalk. Past the storefronts. Jenny never felt so ridiculous. Although, standing outside her closed schoolroom, not knowing what to do next, came in a close second.

"Wait." Jenny stood immobile in front of the cafe. "Is this the rooster that this Rooster Cafe is named after?"

Livvy smiled and tilted her head at the sign hanging overhead. "The one and only."

"Oh, my." Jenny shook her head.

Screech.

Bert stood at the corner, honking at them.

"Exactly." Livvy linked arms with Jenny and spurned them on.

The walk went fast, and soon they passed the church and headed into the large yard of the schoolhouse. A few men knelt on the roof, hammering, while others hammered the railing.

It all reminded her of the day she arrived—and of Ren.

Livvy glanced at Jenny. "The flood pretty much made it uninhabitable till we cleaned it up. Now it's all going to be fresh and new again. I was so thankful to be inside yesterday, although it brought back a few unpleasant reminders."

"You were inside the schoolhouse when the river crested?"

Livvy's gaze was far away. "Yes."

"Wow, Livvy. How scary."

"It was. But God protected me."

Jenny figured God was too busy protecting everyone else that He didn't have time for her. It wasn't like she went to church or anything. She didn't really know God or how the whole church thing worked. She always had a pile of laundry to work on on Sundays for her family.

Bert perched himself on the chopped-down tree stump Livvy used and crowed loudly.

"He's telling the children it's time to come to school." Livvy smiled.

"And they hear him?"

"Well, some do. But other roosters on neighboring ranches pick up his call and carry it on. So, in a way, yes, they do."

Jenny studied Bert. "It's neat, but also a little scary that he's so smart."

"Oh, you have no idea. He's very helpful. Takes a little getting used to, but you will." Livvy sounded so sure that Jenny was sticking around. She didn't want to get her hopes up too much. Circumstances changed like the wind for Jenny.

Jenny stood still. "I'll stay here for now and keep my distance as much as possible."

Livvy laughed as she walked over to Bert and shooed him off the stump.

Bert strutted to a block of trees, squawking at the students entering the schoolyard.

Livvy waved her over, and Jenny settled on the grass next to the stump.

The following few hours passed while Jenny observed from

the sidelines, then joined in with the younger students when Livvy asked. Livvy interacted with her students constantly and conducted lessons like they had been taught during their teacher training. All the students showed great respect and wanted to learn. Jenny's ribs squeezed tightly. How she wished her own teaching experience could've been like this.

After the students were released, a man who had been working on the schoolhouse roof approached them. He had a disgruntled look on his face. Jenny turned to face him, but Livvy grabbed her arm. "Let me handle Mr. Chapman."

The man frowned. "Hello, Miss Carmichael." He glanced at Jenny. "Hello."

Jenny nodded.

Olivia pulled her shoulders back. "Mr. Chapman, this is my colleague, Jenny Millard."

Was Livvy embarrassed to call her a friend?

She faced the unpleasant man. "Pleased to meet you, Mr. Chapman."

He crossed his arms and nodded at Jenny. "I see what you are up to, Miss Carmichael."

Livvy matched his stance. "And what am I up to, Mr. Chapman?"

"You're training your replacement."

Jenny gasped.

"So, I'm correct."

"Mr. Chapman, it just so happens that Jenny did come from the same school I did. In her town." She paused and glanced between them.

Jenny held her breath.

"They didn't have need of her services."

"So, she failed."

"Mr. Chapman!" Livvy exclaimed.

"Well, I'm just stating the facts as I see them." His

narrowed eyes focused on Jenny. "I had hoped to be the next schoolteacher." He placed his hands on his hips. "But I'm learning God might have other plans for me."

"I hardly … "

"Save your breath." He turned and spoke over his shoulder. "Let's see what the mayor has to say about this."

Jenny stood stock still.

Olivia tried to hide her smirk. "Don't mind him. He's just a jealous man who has nothing better to do but to ruffle feathers."

Screech.

A blur flew by as Bert pounced near Mr. Chapman's feet, pecking his heels.

The disgruntled man yelped and ran up on the schoolhouse porch.

Jenny and Livvy burst out laughing.

"I feel bad." Jenny covered her mouth to hide her smile.

"Don't. He does nothing but stir up trouble. Although he's been the most involved person during all the repairs since the flood and has had a better attitude toward everyone, including me."

"Is it because he thought he'd get your job?"

"Possibly. But we don't need to worry about it. Arthur Martin understands everything perfectly."

"But what if the rest of the town doesn't."

"Didn't I tell you? They want a woman teacher. Specifically requested one, which is why I'm here. He's not from here but from Sacramento and comes over on the steamer daily. He has been trying to squirm his way into the position of teacher since the beginning. Although I've heard he has inquired about renting the old Cooper place. I've tried not to pay him any attention more than I must. Again, you have nothing to worry about."

Jenny wasn't too sure. It seemed that no matter what task she took on, it always turned into something else entirely. Was she a horrible teacher? Did she not have anything to offer her students? Was she lacking in some way?

Would she be able to prove to herself and everyone else she deserved to stay in Washton?

* * *

REN SHOWED Luke the completed parts when he came by in the morning. Luke had just dropped his sisters off at the schoolhouse. At the mention of the one-room schoolhouse, Ren thought of Miss Millard and how he escorted her yesterday. His heartbeat accelerated as Luke studied the finished product.

"I'm impressed with the speed and quality of your work. I have some additional ideas I want to run by you. Would you be willing to come out to the ranch to see what I'm needing?"

Ren nodded. "I'm glad you're happy with them. Let me know when. I have a horse I board at the livery who would love a long ride."

"How about next week, then?" Luke reached out to shake his hand.

Ren had his body turned so that the left side of his face showed. Would now be the time to see how Luke would react? He slipped off his right glove and extended his hand, facing forward to make the connection.

Luke's grip was solid and firm. His shrewd gaze locked onto Ren's. Never dipped away. "Much obliged. See you next week." He released Ren's hand and gripped his hat brim, smiled, then turned and walked out the door.

Ren stood there dazed.

Gideon clapped him on the shoulder. "Told you it wouldn't be any big deal."

"You did. But I didn't believe you." Nervous energy flowed through him. Luke was a large ranch owner, and if he didn't have an issue with Ren's scars, then maybe no one else would. "Let's get to work on those broken chains that just came in." He put his glove back on and strode into the darkened forge.

Gideon followed, his chuckle echoing off the walls.

Ren picked up the broken metal and sunk it into the hot coals. He pushed air into the fire with the bellows, creating more heat. Sparks flew as he waited for the metal to turn color. The darkness in the forge allowed blacksmiths to see when the metal changed colors. In order to bend the iron, it had to be bright orange and red, just before melting.

The fire had always called to Ren. When he was too young to know better, he had reached out and touched the hot poker and froze with the searing pain. He was only four years old.

He was so grateful he healed enough to use his injured hand in some capacity. Most people, including his father and the doctors, thought he would never be able to use his right hand. But Ren had proved them wrong. Even though it hurt, he pushed to stretch his hand and do the daily exercises needed to keep it flexible. He had learned how to grip things differently and at odd angles so he could still work in his dad's shop.

Unaccepted at school by the other children, Ren wasn't invited to play in any of the outdoor games, so after a few years, he stayed home and worked, becoming good at what he did. He loved creating things with the sledge and unrefined metal and finishing the day with something solid to show for it. Sometimes, it didn't always turn out because the heat wasn't hot enough or the metal he used wasn't able to bend in the direction it should. But most of the time, the pieces turned out well, like the parts he made for Luke.

Thwack.

Why did these memories plague him these past few days?

Thwack.

Last night, the boxing bag was set up in no time with Gideon's help, and Ren was able to spend an hour in exercise, which helped tire his body. Unfortunately, it didn't alleviate his trailing thoughts about Miss Millard.

Thwack.

Thunk.

Gideon's hammer found a rhythm with Ren's.

Did Miss Millard like it here in Washton? Was she walking around by herself? Was there something else he could do for her?

Thwack.

Thunk.

Able to ignore his divergent thoughts while fabricating metal all day, now those thoughts intruded with a loud clang. He needed some air. "I'd like to stretch my legs and go for a walk."

Gideon chuckled. "I used to need to do that myself when I was your age, Ren. Go ahead and go. I'll finish up in here."

"Are you sure?" asked Ren. "I can help finish up first."

"Yes, I'm sure." Gideon grinned. "Besides, maybe you'll run into someone who needs assistance."

Ren's eyes widened.

The joys of living in a small town. Even the men shared gossip.

He decided not to respond and instead banked the fire, then cleaned up his station. A part of him hoped Gideon was right. He wouldn't be opposed to offering assistance to the same pretty lady with the dark, soulful eyes.

He put away his apron and reluctantly set down his gloves, then patted his pocket for the slip of paper he kept there. He left out the back, walking around to the front between the livery and the smithy.

The sun was shining bright, although sunset approached.

He patted his pocket again. Even if he didn't see Miss Millard, he really needed some quiet time with God for some more molding and shaping. Anything to set his mind back to rights.

Seven

I hope I made a good first impression.

—From the journal of Jenny Millard

As Jenny and Livvy passed the church on their way back to the Martins' home, Jenny's heart fluttered. She darted her eyes this way and that, hoping to see Ren, but all she saw was Bert, trailing behind him.

She was being silly. Why would Ren be around here now?

Screech.

Her eyes widened, and she turned back around. Would she ever get used to the rooster shadowing her and Livvy wherever they went?

Not seeing Ren, she focused on the dirt path to avoid tripping in the same spot as the day they met. She didn't know when their paths would cross, and it would be difficult for her to seek him out. Well, maybe not so difficult as—

"Well, hello again." Livvy's voice cut through Jenny's thoughts.

Jenny glanced up and froze.

"Uh, good afternoon." His gruff voice stirred up a hornet's nest in her stomach.

His eyes searched hers, and all thoughts fled.

Livvy nudged her and broke loose Jenny's jaw.

Jenny swallowed, and her lips lifted into a small smile. "How are you today?"

His eyes shone. "Well, thank you. It's nice to see you again." He fidgeted with his shirt pocket. "Uh. I must be going. Gideon is expecting me."

Livvy stepped closer to Ren, pulling Jenny with her. "That's right, you work at the blacksmith's shop. Luke was excited about picking up something from there today."

Bert clucked behind them, but didn't squawk or peck at Ren's feet like he did at Mr. Chapman's.

Ren eyed the bird. "He did come by this morning. He seemed pleased with the work." He didn't say more. Just stood there gazing into Jenny's eyes.

Jenny couldn't look away.

Livvy cleared her throat. "How long have you been in Washton?"

He blinked, then shifted his gaze to Livvy. "I've been here a few weeks. Staying with Gideon. And he's probably looking for me. I should go. Nice to see you, again, Miss Millard. Miss Car ... uh."

"Carmichael. Nice to see you again too. Have a nice day." Livvy grinned as he walked away, then leaned into Jenny, smiled, and pulled her arm in Jenny's tighter. "I think he's sweet on you. He seems even shier than you are, if you can believe it."

She couldn't. And he wasn't. Was he? Jenny could feel her heart beating throughout her entire body. "He's just being polite. Everyone here is so nice."

They stepped onto the boardwalk and continued past the storefronts.

"I would agree everyone is nice. Except for a few people, that is. Let's visit Mr. Martin at his office on the way home and tell him about Mr. Chapman." Livvy led Jenny inside the last building on Main Street that had a sign marking it as the Mayor's Office.

"Good afternoon, Olivia." The woman behind the desk nodded solemnly to Livvy and then to Jenny.

"Hi Mary Ellen. This is my friend, Jenny."

"Nice to meet you." She looked at Jenny expectantly.

Jenny nodded. She roamed around the front room and stopped in front of a daguerreotype of the schoolhouse hanging on the wall. Students stood on the porch, with Livvy in the middle.

"We took that during our Founders Day celebration. Since I'm the first teacher and the town's first time using the schoolhouse, they wanted to have a photograph. It was impossible to get everyone to stand still for so long. You can't see all of the children's faces because of the blur. Still, Arthur insists it hangs here." Livvy shrugged.

Jenny chuckled. Livvy sure had a different experience. The town embraced her in a way Jenny's town never did. And Livvy never struggled with being paid or the children not showing up. She made it all look so easy.

"The people in Washton really like you. They built you this beautiful schoolhouse."

Livvy shook her head. "They didn't build it for me. It was here before I got here."

"But you're the first teacher," Jenny said.

"I wasn't supposed to be."

"What do you mean?" Jenny faced Livvy.

"They originally started with another lady who was swept

off into marriage before she even taught for one day," Livvy stated.

"How romantic." Jenny sighed.

Livvy laughed. "I don't know if it was romantic. If you haven't noticed, there are fewer women here than men, so when someone new comes to town, there are men who strive to win her favor. I think in her case, she was so overwhelmed that she was whisked away before Mr. Martin could warn her. He knew better when I came to town. Everyone had to leave me alone."

Jenny gasped. "Really? How did they manage that?"

"Well, I had to sign a contract agreeing to all the rules for an entire school year. That would give them time to send for another teacher."

"But how are you engaged, then?" Jenny raised her eyebrows.

"It's sort of hard to fight against Mother Nature's plans. And God's." Livvy grinned.

"Have you regretted signing the agreement?"

"When I got here? Absolutely not. But now ..." She paused, then shrugged.

Livvy had never really opened up to Jenny before, so Jenny wanted to hear what she had to say. She hadn't really had a close friend growing up, and her mother didn't confide in her. She relished hearing thoughts and opinions from others. Sometimes, she wondered if the way she saw things was correct or not. Was the world how her brain saw it?

Livvy's gaze caught Jenny's. "I love teaching. And I swore I would be independent all my life. But God has a way of changing things. His plan sometimes is so different than our own ideas. Once I believed and trusted that, I could see he had so much more for me. And the people here wanted to see Luke and me together." She laughed. "So, they are okay with him courting me until my contract ends."

"But with me here, that could change, right?"

Olivia shook her head. "No, I couldn't do that to my students. It wouldn't look right. I want to follow the rules. I plan to live in this town a long time, I don't want there to be any talk."

Jenny remembered Livvy mentioning something about being gossiped about back home and knew that was a sensitive subject for her. "Whatever you think is best."

Livvy looked thoughtful. "Maybe we should pray about it. We can spend some time in prayer tonight before we go to bed."

Jenny nodded. She'd pray with Livvy, but wouldn't expect any answers.

"Sorry to keep you waiting, ladies." Mr. Martin approached them. "To what do I owe this honor?"

"I wanted to share the conversation we had with Mr. Chapman a moment ago." Livvy raised her eyebrows.

"Ah, I see. Come back to my office, and you can tell me all about it." He reached out his hand for them to precede him.

Jenny didn't know what to expect, but Mr. Martin's office held only a simple wooden desk in the middle with a high-back chair behind it and two wooden chairs with blue cloth on the seats on the other side. There was one window on the far wall, and one trunk that must hold important papers inside.

Livvy took a seat immediately and patted the chair next to her.

Sitting, Jenny held her hands in her lap and let her friend explain.

Mr. Martin looked at Jenny. "Don't let Mr. Chapman get to you. He has an authoritative air about him, but he's all bluster. And he knows it. Olivia is the official teacher. And her contract won't be completed for a few more months. After, we all know she and Luke will marry, and we will need to find another teacher. Since you are from the same school, we should be able to offer you the same contract for one year, if you are interested in staying. How about you help Olivia in the meantime, stay with us, and see what plans you decide to make?"

Jenny blinked. Her pulse increased and her hands perspired.

"I think you've rendered her speechless, Arthur," said Livvy.

Jenny smiled. This was exactly what she wanted. "I don't know what to say."

Mr. Martin held up his hands. "You don't have to say anything right now. Get yourself settled, and see how you like things in Washton."

"I will do that, sir."

"You don't need to *sir*, me. Arthur or Mr. Martin is fine."

Livvy stood, and Jenny followed. "Thank you, Mr. Martin."

He chuckled as he stood.

Livvy wrapped her arm around Jenny's. "We can find our way out. See you at supper."

Jenny glanced over her shoulder and smiled.

Mr. Martin waved back at them, a fatherly smile with a sparkle in his gaze. It was as if he saw Jenny. *Truly* saw her. More than her own father ever had. As if she might matter to him.

* * *

THE SUN HAD SET by the time Ren left the smithy with the metal stakes the rail depot needed. He passed the livery and headed for the platform across the street when he saw the livery worker, Goose, leaning on the backside of the livery, smoking a cigarette, watching people come and go at the depot.

When a couple of ladies passed him, a leer crossed his face. His gaze remained on them long after it should have. Ren had to admit most men took a look now and then, but there was something in Goose's demeanor that put Ren on alert.

Before Ren could garner his attention, Goose turned and followed the two ladies. Ren had much experience observing, so he followed to see what Goose would do. A good judge of assessing situations, he knew something was wrong with this one.

The ladies were so busy chatting, they had no idea they were being followed. Goose moved stealthily closer, until he reached out and grabbed one of them around the waist.

"Hey! Let me go," she screamed. Her feet kicked out, but she couldn't make contact. She swung her fists, hitting him in the arms, but it did nothing to deter him from carrying her off.

"Stop it, you big bully!" Her friend threw her reticule at him, but it didn't stop Goose. "Let her go!"

Ren ran over grabbed Goose's arms, freeing the lady. "What do you think you're doing." Ren hissed.

A look of surprise crossed Goose's face. He scowled. "Leave me alone. Mind your own business." No slurring, but the smell of whiskey was apparent. Ren knew that alcohol could alter a person's behavior.

As soon as the lady was free, she ran toward her friend, grabbed her arm, and together, they ran off down the path to the main part of town.

Desire to punch the man throbbed through Ren, but he knew violence wasn't the answer. He held Goose's arms behind his back as Goose squirmed. "I'll let you go if you promise to go home."

"I don't need to make any promises to you, Ren. You have

no idea what you just did. You'll pay for this." He shook free of Ren's hold and stormed away.

Ren knew deep down he was correct in interfering, but Goose's threat gave him pause. He didn't want to cause strife here. He didn't want to make enemies. And Goose had been in this town longer than Ren. He would be the one to leave if people took sides. He had learned during several stops along his journey that the newcomer was never in the right.

He scuffed back to pick up the package of stakes that had clattered to the ground before he jumped into the melee. Dusting off his clothes, he continued to the depot. Thankfully, the last train had left, and no one was around. He was sure the look on his face would terrify anyone who saw him.

Ren clenched his jaw. What kind of monster would attack a lady in public without any thought as to how it would affect her reputation? Had Goose done something like that before? Who else had he preyed on? So many questions whirled in Ren's head, his stomach took an unpleasant dip. He would need to watch Goose more closely. Surely, Goose wouldn't do anything now that he'd been caught.

Dropping off the package in the container used for holding needed supplies, he headed back to the smithy. He shook his head to clear the images of what had happened. He'd kept his cool, but his blood boiled.

It was way too late to pound any metal tonight. Too unsettled, he did the only thing he could do at this time of the evening—pray.

God. I pray for those ladies tonight and thank You that they were not hurt. I pray for Goose and ask he will not try something like that again. And I pray somehow it was all a misunderstanding. Thank You that I was able to help. I pray You can use me to protect people if that is what You need me to do, God. Amen."

Ren walked between the livery and smithy to the pathway

that led to Gideon's cottage. Though he prayed, he still worried Goose would try again. He hoped he could be there if it happened so he could stop him.

The following morning, Ren sat on a barrel in the back space of the shop with his Bible in his hands. His quarrel with Goose had created much turmoil in his heart. He had hardly slept and wanted God's wisdom and guidance to deal with it. He opened his Bible, and the pages fell open to James 1:12, and he read, '*Blessed is the man that endureth temptation: for when he is tried, he shall receive the crown of life, which the Lord hath promised to them that love him.*'

He read it again.

Sometimes verses spoke to his heart, as if God was speaking directly to him. His entire life had been one big trial. Well, that wasn't true. He had found a way to survive. But moving west and paving a way for himself had been a trial. Catching Goose and possibly making an enemy of him could be an even bigger trial. But through it all, Ren had tried to lean on God, listen to His guidance, and stay faithful to Him. This verse promised that there would be a reward in heaven for those who persevere.

The Bible never said following Jesus would be easy. In fact, Ren knew life could be much harder because things in the outside world could tempt and distract him to take his eyes off God. He was thankful he had been able to persevere. But the fight was not over yet. Sometimes, it was a daily battle to stay the course.

Ren looked across the backyard. With the fence open in the back, he could see the new train station being built. Movement caught his eye, and Ren saw that crazy rooster strutting down the street. Bert glanced Ren's way, his head bobbing up and down as if heading somewhere specific.

He shook his head at his own absent-mindedness. The

town was starting to wake, so Ren bowed his head to pray before he was distracted again.

Dear God. Please forgive me for when I do not follow You. Keep my heart focused on You, Lord. He paused and swallowed. *I pray for Goose to stop his bad ways and that there can be healing in our relationship. Let Your spirit guide me today, God. Amen.*

Ren kept his head bowed for several minutes. He loved being still and listening to God in the morning before starting his day.

He had just put on his apron when Goose ran into the forge. He pulled up quickly and glanced around. "Uh, hiya, Ren." Goose looked everywhere but at Ren directly. Would you mind watching the livery for an hour while I take care of some things?" His eyes were red, his hair mussed, and his voice cracked.

Ren didn't think God would answer his prayer so quickly, but he took the olive branch being offered. "Sure, Goose. Do you need me now?"

Goose focused on the ground. "If you can come over within the quarter hour, that would be ideal."

"Done." Ren didn't know what the reason was, but he was happy to trust God and find out.

Eight

Staying with Livvy and the Martins, I feel as if I've been wrapped up in a warm blanket.

—From the journal of Jenny Millard

Screech.

Jenny woke up to a loud noise. Since she was in such a deep slumber it was difficult for her to place what it was. Blinking the sleep from her eyes, she opened them and saw a faint light shining through the curtains.

"Sounds like Bert wants to get an early start this morning." Livvy stretched out her limbs and removed the covers so she could rise.

Jenny laughed. "Does he do this every day?"

Livvy shrugged. "Mostly."

"It's Saturday." Jenny yawned.

"I know." Livvy dragged out the last word slowly.

"Where does he go at night?"

"I've wondered that myself." Livvy splashed cold water on her face.

"You mean, you don't know?"

"No. But I've thought about following him."

Jenny clapped her hands together. "We should do that sometime."

Livvy laughed. "The only reason I haven't was because I wanted others to respect my privacy, I felt I needed to do the same to him."

Jenny contemplated her friend.

Livvy shrugged. "I know. Sounds silly."

"Yet understandable." Jenny nodded.

"A lot has happened. I really haven't had the time. Let's hurry and help Chrissy this morning. I can't wait for you to meet Luke and see the ranch."

Jenny squeezed her friend's hand as they left the room. Livvy had met the love of her life, even when she'd had no plans to ever marry. Although Jenny hadn't met Luke Taylor yet, she had met his adorable sisters, Rose and Caroline, who were Livvy's students.

After an enjoyable breakfast conversation with the Martins, Jenny and Livvy set out to retrieve a buggy. The air was crisp, but the sun shone, and the birds chirped in harmony. It was a perfect day to get outside.

Arm in arm, they walked down the boardwalk. Jenny had no idea what the day would hold, but it would be an adventure. One of many she had had in the last few days. Never had she done so much walking, exploring, and talking. She'd mostly stayed at home working her chores. And since they lived in the rural area in north Kentucky, there weren't many people around. The first time she faced a large crowd was when she attended the teacher training school in Cincinnati.

Livvy directed them across the street toward the livery. The large building sat on the corner lot next door to the smithy. Horses' neighing came from inside.

"Since when did you learn to drive horses? You had never ridden one before when we met?"

"The town taught me."

Jenny tried to hide her surprise. "The *town* taught you?"

"Well, actually, Luke did the teaching, but the entire town felt I was too green for life out here, so they taught me to drive a wagon, ride a horse, and shoot a rifle."

"You know how to shoot a rifle?"

Livvy laughed, "Yes, and it is so much fun. Have you ever shot one?"

Jenny recalled the time her father found her holding his gun, asking if he would teach her. She shook her head. "No, I haven't. My father felt that womenfolk stayed in the kitchen."

"Well, if you haven't noticed yet, in the West, women have to do some of the same things as the men in order to have food on the table or to manage these ranches. Did the families in your school have specific jobs, or did everyone pitch in?"

"I didn't really pay much attention. I was so worried about how good of a job I was doing and how the children were. Their well-being meant more to me than anything."

"And that's what makes you a great teacher."

Her shoulders sagged. "Then why did they close the school?"

"That was beyond your control. There's a Bible verse about that." Livvy paused. "Therefore, do not worry about tomorrow, for tomorrow will worry about itself."* She squeezed Jenny's arm. "Something like that."

---

* Matthew 6:25 (NIV, paraphrased)

Jenny knew the words were meant to help, but they didn't penetrate the shield around her heart.

They entered the livery, where a buggy with one horse sat ready and waiting.

Livvy walked up to the horse and patted her nose. "Hi, girl. You ready to go see your friends today?" She glanced at Jenny. "Go ahead and climb in."

Jenny glanced first at the horse, then Livvy, then the buggy. Fear niggled her mind. Was this a good idea?

"Do you need help getting in, Miss Millard?" asked a familiar gruff voice.

Jenny's heart lifted at the realization it was Ren. And then dropped as she remembered how he walked away from her. *Twice.* He must think she was frightened when she was more sad, lonely, and scared about her future. Which had nothing to do with him. She needed to show him.

"Yes, please." She turned to face him straight on and smiled. Even with the scars on his cheek, he was striking, with a strong jawline and dark eyes.

She must've caught him off guard if the surprised look meant anything. A hint of a smile lifted on one side of his handsome face. Then it dropped as he reached out with his left hand to help her step up. He kept his right hand close to his side.

Warmth flew from where their hands connected all the way up her arm. She held on, not wanting to let go. "Thank you." She squeezed his hand and gazed into his eyes a moment longer. He seemed nervous, and she wanted to show him that his scars didn't bother her. One nice gesture, one act of kindness, could mean so much to the person on the receiving end.

Maybe it was because she didn't have them happen to her very often.

He glanced away.

Not wanting to make him more uncomfortable, she seated herself and adjusted her skirt.

Livvy climbed up after her. "Thank you for fixing the wheel. Is there anything I should be careful about?"

Ren held the horse's head. "Everything should be in tip-top shape. I looked it all over. Next time, stay out of the ditch if you can." His lips twitched, and, much to Jenny's delight, a genuine smile bloomed on his face.

Jenny's pulse quickened.

He was a very handsome man. Tall with a large build that reflected his strength. The soot and hay on his clothes showed he took his work seriously, which made him that much more appealing.

Ren stepped back, and the buggy lurched forward.

Jenny gripped the seat tightly as Livvy guided them out the larger side door and onto the dirt road. In that moment, his words registered. They passed the church, then the schoolhouse. "You drove into a ditch?"

Livvy laughed. "It was one time, and there was a good reason. The Taylor ranch is on the outskirts of town. We'll be there in about twenty minutes." Livvy glanced at Jenny. "How am I doing?" Light glistened in her eyes.

Jenny released the seat and surveyed the area as they traveled. She smiled at her friend. "You're doing great."

The clomping of horses' hoofs and the swaying of the buggy created a rhythm Jenny relaxed into. Neither spoke.

They crossed under the ranch sign after twenty minutes.

A few minutes later, they rode up to the ranch house. Two girls stood on the porch waving, and a man strode toward them as Livvy pulled on the reins. He was tall, lean, and moved with confidence. His hat settled on his head as if it was made for him.

"Welcome." He approached Jenny first and helped her step down. "You're Olivia's friend from school? She's talked so much about you. The girls loved hearing the newspaper story you sent her. She read it in class, you know." He grinned at her.

Jenny looked at Livvy in amazement. "Really?"

Livvy nodded. "They loved it."

Warmth settled in the crevices of her heart.

"You're going to stay around here a while, we hope?" He winked.

She smiled. "It seems like it."

"Good. We are much obliged to you." He headed to Livvy's side. "Let me take that, darling." He bent and lightly kissed her hand.

Livvy blushed.

After hearing Livvy's story about her ex-fiance in Cincinnati, seeing her friend truly happy with Luke was a sight to behold.

What must it be like to have someone to depend on completely?

Sure her family needed her to help run the farm and take care of her siblings. But as soon as they needed to reduce the mouths to feed, they told her she couldn't stay. No one really needed her for who she was—only what she could do for them.

A sharp pang shot out from her chest.

She still didn't know if she had done the right thing. Although, standing there, watching Livvy and Luke together, a fragment of anticipation stirred in her heart.

Would she ever have someone take that much interest in her to want to spend the rest of their life together? What would that be like? A strong, scarred man appeared in her mind, but she shook it off. He was too timid in his approach to her. She needed someone who'd declare his love to her in a big way in order for her to believe it. And that wasn't going to happen.

* * *

REN HELD onto the wooden sliding door as the two ladies drove off in the buggy.

His hand still tingled from where Jenny had placed her hand in his. Being close to her had been unexpected—and probably unwise. Yet, her presence soothed him in a way he hadn't felt before. Her smile twisted his heart into an unfamiliar shape. The blacksmith in him was unsure if he approved of its new design.

He closed the door and returned to the desk, grateful for the distraction of a new customer. Ren busied himself boarding the gentleman's horse for the day. With the task complete, the unfamiliar sensations came back to the forefront of his mind. He looked at his unscarred hand. When was the last time someone willingly laid a hand on him? When had he ever offered a hand to be touched?

A long-buried memory surfaced. *He had reached out his hand at school, while standing in a circle with the other students. The one next to him screamed and cried, terrified she would catch what he had. After that, no one else would stand near him. Because of the burns and scars on his hand.*

A horse nickered, and he turned toward the stall. "All right, all right, Coal. I have your food right here. Don't worry. You won't starve." The black chestnut raised his head up and down. "You noticed her too?" Another nod. "What do you think I should do?"

His horse didn't have any insight. He just wanted his food.

Ren laughed as he filled the bag with hay. The livery and the smithy worked in tandem with each other. Ren usually made rounds, checking horseshoes and buggy wheels every couple of days. That agreement allowed Ren to board his own horse here. Spending time with the animals was easier than being around people, so he enjoyed the work.

He made his way around the entire barn, feeding all the horses, securing the same unhelpful answer to his dilemma from all of them. Maybe he would need to consult a human being after all, especially if he kept seeing Miss Millard about.

Back at the front, looking for something else to do, Ren stacked crates until Goose finally returned, along with a man who had a hard, dangerous look about him.

The man leaned against one of the stalls as if waiting for Ren to leave.

Goose fidgeted with something. When he turned around, his eyes wouldn't meet Ren's. Ren didn't know if he was hiding something or couldn't look at his scars.

Goose had been gone for a couple of hours. What was he up to? Why the livery owner, Stevie, let Goose be in charge while he was out of town, Ren didn't know. He might need to come over more frequently to make sure everything was on the up and up. "All the horses have been fed and watered. There's a new horse boarded in stall one. Is there anything else you need me for, Goose?"

Goose looked at him then, as if just realizing Ren was there. "Uh, thanks, Ren. Dusty and I can take it from here."

The other man jerked at the mention of his name, then pulled his hat down low and faced Ren. "Nice to meet you." His voice had an accent Ren couldn't place.

Ren didn't want to judge. Not yet, anyway. He was new in town too. "You as well. I'll be at the forge working, then. I'll come back to check on the horses tomorrow."

Goose and Dusty headed to the back of the barn and hadn't

acknowledged Ren's goodbye, so he strode out the front gate onto the main street and headed next door.

Voices came from the front of the shop, so Ren cut into the side alley and around to the back.

Ren wasn't ready to join in the discussions yet. Listening from afar suited him quite all right for now. Even though he was a grown man, voices from his childhood still rang loud in his ears.

"Your middle name is Eugene? That's a funny name."

"You aren't normal. Your hand is ugly looking. You can't play ball with us with only one good hand."

It hurt at first, never being included. The other kids stared at his deformed hand, thinking he was incapable of helping them win the games they played.

And even though he learned to use his left hand for everything, others viewed not using the right hand as the devil's handiwork. Or someone who practiced witchcraft. Ren had never heard of these things, but others had. And they let it be known to both Ren and his parents.

He looked at his scarred hand and opened and closed his fist.

His mom had done a good job that day, treating the wounds as best she could. No one knew the pain he was in for weeks after the accident. That pain still resonated in the tightness of the skin and the phantom heat that never went away.

At first it made him sad, but he soon learned to ignore it. Then he learned to channel it. All that pain, absorbed into determination, where he focused on being the next best blacksmith in the family.

When he showed up each day, his father taught him new ways to create and build things. Sometimes he even designed works on his own. In the beginning, his father's customers didn't know, but they liked what they bought from his father, and so his father let him continue working.

His mother insisted he go to school and meet other children and learn reading and writing.

But the other children didn't want to know him.

They never included him in the games they played before school or at lunch recess. So he practiced his reading inside. He found he could escape to another time and place when he read. Reading taught him patience and perseverance. One of the only books available was the Bible. He read about David and the Giant and Daniel and the lion's den. They all had a huge amount of faith. He saw them as the weaker characters who, with their faith in God, could do anything.

That was who Ren wanted to be. David.

"Ah, there you are." Gideon entered the back area of the shop. "Goose back again?"

Ren nodded.

The invitation to go to church with Gideon sat in Ren's chest. He would go. Have big faith in God's plans for him. To trust in all things.

"You joining me tomorrow at church?"

Ren lifted his head, and his gaze collided with Gideon's. His heart hammered.

Gideon grinned and rubbed his hands together. "You won't regret it."

Ren didn't know about that. But there was no turning back now.

Nine

—From the journal of Jenny Millard

Sitting on a blanket, eating the noon-day meal with all
the others, Jenny couldn't believe what she witnessed
on the Taylor ranch. Everyone had pitched in to put the
meal together. The foreman Jimmy, the housekeeper Evalyn,
the girls, and even Livvy and Luke. Such another lesson in
teamwork for Jenny. Everyone laughed and smiled while doing
their chores, and then the group took a break from their work
for the meal, even though there was still work to be done.

Never had her family taken an afternoon off to enjoy each
other's company. They had to continue working on the never-
ending chores in order to keep food on the table.

Yet, for all that work, it was never enough.

But here, family was cherished. It was obvious by how Luke interacted with his sisters. And even how he interacted with his workers. There was mutual respect.

Rose came over and tugged on her hand. "Come see our new horse."

Jenny followed over to the wooden fence by the barn.

A young mare approached the fence.

"This is Fanny. She's new here and looking for a friend." Rose leaned on one of the fence posts.

Jenny held out her hand. "Hello there, Fanny."

"Here." Caroline walked up and handed Jenny a carrot. "You can feed her this."

She placed the carrot in her turned-up palm and held it out. The mare sniffed and then nibbled, her large lips tickling Jenny's hand.

All three of them giggled.

A warmth spread from Jenny's heart through her body. She glanced over at the girls, then farther at Luke and Livvy and the others, feeling a sense of belonging. Something she'd never felt before.

"Thank you for introducing me to Fanny." Jenny had always wanted her own horse.

"Maybe you can come visit her again sometime." Caroline extended the invitation with no hesitation.

Jenny's heart squeezed. "I would like that very much."

"Are you going to be our new schoolteacher once Miss Carmichael becomes our mom?" Rose peered up at Jenny with beautiful, innocent eyes.

"Don't put her on the spot, Rose. She's still new here, and we don't know what's going to happen," Caroline stated.

"Thank you, Caroline, for answering that question so well," said Jenny.

They headed back to the others, who were picking up the remnants from their meal.

Jenny hurried over, worried her little bit of enjoyment had caused someone else extra work. "Let me help."

"We got it." Livvy and Luke both piled everything into the baskets. "There's nothing else that needs to be done."

"Are you sure?" Jenny asked.

Livvy nodded. "Once I get back, we'll load up in the buggy and head home, okay?"

Jenny stood there not sure what to do.

"I'll walk with you." Luke picked up the baskets and offered his elbow to Livvy.

"They lovvee to do chores together." Caroline came to stand by Jenny. "They don't see each other that much during the week, so this is the only time they have together."

"And they spend a lot of it kissing." Rose made kissing noises with her mouth.

Jenny laughed.

"It was nice to meet you." Jimmy grabbed the brim of his hat, swung up into the saddle, and rode off beyond the barn.

Evalyn hurried after Luke and Livvy. Possibly to chaperone or make sure they did their chores.

Jenny sighed. "Well, I guess I don't have anything to do."

"Can you tell us a story?" Rose asked.

Jenny studied the two girls. "I guess I could. Come, let's sit over here. I have a great story in mind."

"Yippee." The girls skipped over and sat close to Jenny.

Jenny dove into one of her favorite tales.

She finished as Livvy walked up. "Time to go. We have an afternoon tea to attend."

Jenny narrowed her eyes. "We do? You didn't mention anything about a tea."

"Oh, it must've slipped my mind." Livvy's face said more than that, but Jenny would not ask until they were alone.

Luke had the buggy ready and helped each of them step into the seat.

As soon as they crossed beneath the sign, Jenny turned. "What's this about a tea?"

"Chrissy will be there already. I didn't say anything because I truly didn't know if we'd make it back in time. But we will, and it will be good for the ladies to meet you right away. Now, don't fret about it. Tell me what you think about Luke?" Livvy smiled at the mention of Luke's name.

Jenny's smile matched Livvy's. "I'm so happy for you, Livvy. Luke is the perfect match for you."

Livvy's face turned pink. "Do you think so?"

"I do." Jenny nodded.

"I didn't. At first." Livvy shrugged. "Writing about him in my journal helped me figure it out."

Jenny's eyes widened. "You wrote about him in your journal?

"Who else was I going to talk to about my feelings?"

"The book Miss Beecher gave us in school? The one you wrote in during the entire train ride west?"

Livvy smiled. "Yes, that book. And don't tease me. I had much to capture. But things have changed since then.

"How's that?" Jenny loved that they were sharing things about each other. On the train ride west, Livvy didn't want to talk about much at all. Jenny had respected her privacy, but Livvy was more open now as well as happier. Is that what had caused her to change? Writing in her journal?

"I used to write a letter to my diary covering facts about the day and my opinion on what I saw. But since moving here and a series of events, a little I've shared already, now I write prayers to God. It's a great way to spend quiet time with Him." Livvy smiled.

Jenny didn't know what to say. Prayers to God? She didn't have any experience in saying prayers, much less writing them down. How did one write a prayer to God? She cast an eye out on the fields as they passed. Beautiful colors of yellow, white, and purple dotted the land. Birds flew all around.

Livvy pulled on the reins to turn the horse right. "Do you still have your book?"

"Y-yes." She turned back toward her friend.

"I can show you what I mean later."

"Okay." Every once in a while, Jenny wrote in her own journal, but she saved the pages for very special occasions. She'd never had something so fine and desired to make the pages last as long as possible. Did she want to write prayers in there?

"For now, we have each other to talk about things." Livvy reached and squeezed Jenny's arm.

Jenny's heart leaped with joy. She'd never had a friend to share her thoughts with before.

"But that doesn't mean you still shouldn't write in your journal. Like I said before, you can write prayers to God. And you'll be able to look back and see how God answers those prayers. Because even when we think He doesn't, He truly does."

Jenny was afraid to ask, but did so anyway. "What makes you say that?"

"It was weeks later, but I went back and saw all the answered prayers. They may not have been the way I wanted them to be, but He did answer them. The answers are hard to see. A subtle response here, then another one here." She pointed her finger in opposite directions. "I prayed for my students. I prayed for their situations. I think it's easier to see God working in someone else's life than in my own."

They both grew quiet as Livvy drove back into town.

Jenny wiped her hands down her skirt. So many things were changing, it was difficult to keep up. She swallowed. She wanted to stay. To be a part of Washton. But anytime she wished for something, the opposite happened. She didn't want to get her hopes up. To write down prayers if it was all going to be for naught. Jenny glanced at her friend. She wouldn't know if she didn't try. Maybe this time would be different.

* * *

As the hired gun, Dusty's job was to track down the person he was sent to find and take back what was rightfully his boss's in the first place. But this time, it was proving harder and much longer than he originally planned. No one expected the Carmichael heir to hightail it out of Cincinnati and go West.

He couldn't wait to get out of this forsaken place and back to civilization.

Her trail was a bit challenging to find at first. No one knew where she went. She hadn't told anyone except her servants. Usually, servants didn't know the comings and goings of their masters, but hers did. It took him way too long to figure out that they knew. And then, a while longer to get the answers out of them.

The effort paid off, even if he had to roughen up Jasper and Agnes a bit. He didn't hurt them exactly. Just scared them after he punched Jasper and gave him a black eye. Agnes finally bent at that point and shared one small bit, even though Jasper yelled at her not to. It was enough.

Even though all he got was the name of a school for women.

Breaking into the American Women's Educational Association to rifle through papers wasn't so hard. Just long. Took him a few weeks, but he finally found the papers that listed out where every single woman was sent. Another week or so to figure out how to travel hidden all the way to California.

This small town of Washton was another unexpected development. Because she left, his boss believed she took something of value with her. But so far, he hadn't seen anything that would say wealth attached. He thought she would stand out with her high and mighty ways and money. But that wasn't the case.

She was working. As a teacher, no less. And living with others. Searching her belongings or snatching her wouldn't be easy. The gal was never alone.

Rubbing elbows with the livery employee had proved helpful. Goose was a funny name, but once he explained about the large goose egg he had gotten as a child, it all made sense. The man was a bit odd, but it served Dusty well. He had a place to sleep and a place to watch people come and go. And it was so close to the train station—an easy escape out of town if he needed it.

Now, he might need it.

Goose had introduced him to another, using his name. He wasn't sure yet if this Ren fellow would be suspicious or not, but Dusty should lie low for the rest of the day before coming back tomorrow to think up a plan. He'd need to find a place to bed down for the night.

Besides, with the Carmichael chit out with her friend today, Dusty would be waiting around anyway. Goose had shown him around the outskirts of town today, so he had a good lay of the land already. "I need to leave town for a bit. Don't worry about bringing me food tonight."

Goose startled. "Oh, okay. Where ya going?"

Dusty gave a hard glare. "Probably better to keep that to myself. Understood?"

Goose nodded. "Forget I asked. Let me know when you're back, and we can hang out again."

Dusty would wait and see. It might be time to venture out on his own.

Squeezing out the back door, Dusty waited for his eyes to adjust. The sunset and clouds closed in overhead. He glanced back at the livery. He would miss the covered roof tonight, but there wasn't anything he could do about it. He strolled over to the depot, around the train tracks to the other platform, picking up his saddlebags hidden underneath.

Screech.

His head bumped on the wood above him.

Screech.

He stood and found himself being glared at by a rooster. "Shoo." He kicked out his foot.

The fowl flapped his wings and got away before he could make contact.

Screech. Squawk.

"Stop that racket." Just what he needed. Attention drawn his way. He fished into his pockets, finding some crumbs wrapped in a handkerchief. He picked out a piece and threw it to the ground.

The animal ignored the treat thrown his way.

Squawk.

What did he want?

Thankfully, no one was around, and the train wasn't due in for an hour. But how could he ditch the bird? He searched the area. He wanted to go south, following the train tracks. Would the rooster follow? He couldn't take the chance of someone seeing him leave that way. Instead, he strolled around the platform and up the step, sitting on the bench as if waiting for the train.

The rooster followed, squawking and clucking. His beady little eyes never moved from watching Dusty. After pacing for a few minutes, he screeched, flapped his wings, then ran off.

Dusty waited until the bird was no longer in sight. Then stood, threw his bag over his shoulder, and jumped off the platform, following the train tracks out of town. There was a stand of trees about a mile out where Dusty had stayed before. It was a walk on foot, but should keep him well away from any other spying eyes.

Ten

I think I like being part of a team. It's not so lonely.

—From the journal of Jenny Millard

Ren found himself restless. The smithy was closed for the rest of the weekend. Gideon was napping, and Ren sat on the porch step, trying to read his Bible. His mind was all over the place. First on Miss Millard, then on church tomorrow and the imagined gasps from people when they saw him there, to the mystery of this Dusty character Ren met earlier, and then back all around again. He hadn't been this stirred up since he'd decided to leave home.

His Bible was open to the next verse on his ma's list, and he read it again. *'Being confident of this very thing, that he which hath begun a good work in you will perform it until the day of Jesus Christ.'* As a blacksmith, Ren knew the time it took to mold and shape metal. The same could be said with God. He was still molding and shaping Ren. Ren knew firsthand that nothing ever stayed the same, but boy, was it hard to let things go sometimes. The worry, the what-ifs. He didn't have all the answers, but he wanted them. Without all the turmoil. Ren could either let go and trust God in all these changes or not. It was really that simple, even though it felt anything but.

Which was how he felt right now. Maybe a ride would help. He'd have to cross paths with Goose again, but he could possibly stir up a conversation with Dusty and learn more about him.

When Ren entered the livery, Goose was nowhere to be found. Ren stood there in the middle of the barn searching, till he saw a shadow of a form up in the loft, soft snores echoing in the rafters. "Goose. It's Ren. I'm taking Coal out for a run."

The only response was another snore and Coal neighing at the sound of Ren's voice.

Ren went to work saddling him, then pulled him out of the stall.

Goose stood and leaned over the railing. "Ren, thought I'd heard you." He rubbed his eyes. "It was quiet, I laid down for a spell."

More like laying down on the job. Ren tried to keep his mind away from unkind thoughts. "See you in an hour." He pulled himself into the saddle and moved the reins to lead Coal out of the barn, heading across the street toward the train station.

Squawk.

A colorful blur sped toward him right in the middle of the street.

Ren kneed his horse to stay in control. "Bert. What are you doing?" He hissed.

The bird raised one wing and circled around till his head was facing south. Flapped his wings.

Squawk.

Ren's eyes narrowed. Was Bert trying to tell him

something? Ren glanced around. No one was here at this hour, and the train wasn't due yet. What could he be up to?

Bert paced forward, looked over his shoulder, then took a few more steps south. Waiting. He flapped his wings again.

Coal moved his head up and down and took a step, as if the two animals had come to an agreement. Ren loosened the reins and let Coal lead. Follow might be the more accurate term. Because Bert was leading. Past the platform, past the water filling station, and out into the wilderness, south of town.

The tracks followed the river on the east, while the west had trees and wildflowers dotting the landscape. All prime for something to be lurking within if anyone went three yards away from the train tracks. Bert stayed within those three yards, following the route, stopping every few steps, checking to see if they were still behind him.

Ren glanced up. Rain clouds formed. He should head back. He did not want to be caught in whatever storm was brewing. Though following through with this escapade seemed important, so he would continue.

What would they find wherever it was they were going? Ren wished he had his gun. He owned one and knew how to shoot, but it wasn't something he carried with him. That would be dangerous near the hot fire in the smithy. And he hadn't had need while he worked. But now he wished he did. He could run into all sorts of things. Trouble came in several different varieties.

Bert stopped and raised his wings. As if pointing. He cut into the brush, and only the top of his head could be seen bopping up and down as he moved.

Ren guided Coal to follow. As they moved farther away from the tracks, a grove of trees came into view. Thicker and denser than the trees in other areas. Ren looked at Bert. "What type of trouble have you brought me to, Bert?"

Bert circled around Ren and pecked the ground. It was up to Ren to figure this out on his own. He jumped off of Coal and staked him to the nearest tree, under the shade. Ren wiped his brow. How he wished he had a hat. He didn't own one, but most others did in town. He'd have to ask someone.

Quietly Ren stepped forward, placing his body behind a tree as he went. He still didn't know what he was looking for, but Bert did. And Ren would find out soon enough. He was almost to the grove when a red cloth caught his attention. Ren darted back behind the tree. His chest on fire as he calmed his heartbeat. Someone was in there. But who?

An image of the stranger Ren met earlier floated in his brain. Could his hunch be correct that Dusty was up to no good? He squatted and crawled on his hands and knees, working hard not to make a sound.

Soon, a voice carried in the wind. "Why me? Why did I have to be the one?"

That weird accent. Ren would know it anywhere. It *was* him. The man Goose had called Dusty. Ren held his breath while crawling a little closer. How did Bert know? Ren glanced back to where he left Coal and Bert, but couldn't see a thing in the high weeds. He couldn't hear them either. How far had he crawled? Could he make it back without alerting Dusty he was in the vicinity?

"What am I going to do?" Ren could see the man running a hand through his hair. He was here for something. The question was—what?

Thunder roared off in the distance, and both men jumped. Dusty dove under a tented blanket, so Ren used the noise to backtrack. He found both animals munching on field grass.

They lifted their heads in unison and waited.

"Bert. I'm not sure if you can understand me, but you were right to bring me here. Something isn't right. We'll have to be on guard and wait till he makes a move. For now, though, let's get back to the barn before those clouds let a downpour on our heads.

Bert raised his wings, quietly clucking as he raised his head up and down. He turned and ran off.

By the time Ren was in the saddle, Bert wasn't anywhere to be seen. He headed back to town the same way they came, letting Coal stretch his legs. The wind helped clear Ren's head as he'd originally planned. One thing was crystal clear—someone was up to no good. He didn't want to raise alarms, but he would keep an eye out. And pay more attention to Bert.

Such an odd bird. Yet, Ren couldn't help but be impressed with how astute he was. Washton was lucky to have him. And the fact he watched over Miss Carmichael, and now Miss Millard, gave Ren a bit of comfort. Together, he hoped they could catch Dusty before someone got hurt.

* * *

"Do you think the ladies will welcome me?' Jenny asked. Livvy had explained that this group gathered one time a month for tea and to catch up on things. Sometimes there was a Bible study discussion. Today was to share on all the rebuilding since the flood.

"Of course, they will. They will love you. What's not to love?" Livvy answered.

Jenny had on only one of two dresses, and she was saving her best one for church tomorrow. This dress had been sewn back together many times, but it was not too faded and the lace that lined the hem still held its shape. She was nervous what the ladies would think of her. She learned the basics of taking tea at the American Women's Association, where she and Livvy were trained. She was grateful for the lessons, but she hadn't been able to use them much yet.

A knot twisted in her stomach.

She'd watched from afar a tea get-together in her community when she was younger. Neither she nor her ma had received an invitation. Jenny had hidden behind the bushes to catch a glimpse of the ladies talking, laughing, and eating tiny foods that made Jenny's mouth water and sip liquid so warm steam rose from the cup well after pouring it.

Growing up, she was lucky if her food was lukewarm or if it was enough to fill her belly. The meals she and her mom prepared were never as fancy as what she'd seen served that day. To be a part of a tea herself gave her goosebumps. If only her ma could see her now.

She frowned. She missed her ma, but she didn't miss the constant criticism or the constant work.

"I wouldn't think going to a tea would cause a frown like that. What's the matter?" Livvy asked. She took Jenny's arm in hers as they walked along one of the streets lined with small homes.

"Oh, don't mind me. My mind was in the past. Where it should stay. It really is a pretty day today." Jenny said.

Livvy squeezed her arm. "I know you've had a lot of firsts lately. Don't worry, I'll be right there with you."

Jenny leaned into her friend. "Thank you."

"Don't worry about it. You were there for me. In the beginning, when we first met. And you're here for me now. That's what friends do." Livvy's beautiful smile lit up her entire face.

Yes, that's what friends do. Jenny just hadn't had a friend before. She grinned back.

They approached a walkway full of colorful flowers with perfect stems for cutting lining each side. The door was open, and voices traveled from inside, bringing hope to Jenny's battered heart. As she walked in, she was surrounded by several women all at once.

Livvy introduced her to the hostess, Mrs. Timbly.

"Welcome to my home, Jenny. I'm so happy you could join us." The woman cupped her hands in hers. "Let's introduce you to everyone." She walked Jenny around the room and presented her to every single person.

She felt like royalty. All of them were kind and friendly.

When the ladies sat, Livvy made room for her on the covered loveseat. "Are you enjoying yourself?"

Jenny leaned into Livvy. "Yes, Everyone is so nice."

Livvy smiled. "They are." Her eyes held a gleam in them that Jenny couldn't interpret.

Before she could ask, Mrs. Timbly brought in two beautiful plates of those little sandwiches Jenny had eyed when she was a child. Now, she would have an opportunity to try one.

She wiggled her fingers as she reached over, selecting the top sandwich on the pile. The bread was soft and fresh. Rotating it around, she saw a slice of ham and butter. As she bit into the delicate parcel, she closed her eyes and savored the moist, fresh taste as it melted in her mouth. It was everything she imagined it would be. She quickly ate the rest of it, washing it down with a sip of very hot tea.

Not wanting to be rude, Jenny waited patiently for all the others to pick their refreshment before reaching for another one. This time, she knew what to expect as she took a small bite. Pure warmth traveled all the way to her toes. She was sure her face revealed how much she enjoyed the treat.

As she downed the second sandwich, she was asked a question. "Tell us Jenny, where did you travel from?" The lady perched on the seat across from Jenny leaned forward. Jenny thought her name was Mrs. Barbara Woodward.

The sandwich stuck in her throat. She swallowed. Which answer should she give? Where she was from originally, or where she had most recently come from?

Livvy came to her rescue. "Mrs. Woodward, Jenny is a teacher as well. Her school in Copperville recently closed, so she's come to visit me before her next assignment."

"How lovely. We have two teachers in our midst." Mrs. Woodward nodded and winked at both Jenny and Livvy. What a friendly demeanor she had. And it seemed as if she knew Livvy well. "I find it a very honorable position."

Jenny liked her immediately.

"If you have to work, then that is the position to have. But what will you do about getting married? Being a schoolteacher seems to diminish your chances of being a wife, does it not?" A woman named Mrs. Oliver asked.

"Did you know only a male schoolteacher can court while teaching?" Another woman added. Jenny couldn't remember her name.

"Why are the rules different? Why can't women court while still teaching? In fact, isn't that what you're doing, Olivia?" The lady made a face. "Oh, sorry, I may have let the cat out of the bag with that piece of information. It's not well known yet about you and Luke, is it?"

The ladies tittered.

Jenny caught Livvy and Chrissy sharing a look and then smiling back at the others.

"Is it true your pay is not as much as a male teacher?" This from the same woman who seemed to enjoy sharing a bit of gossip.

Jenny truly did not know the answer. She glanced at Livvy, whose lips were pinched together, but her eyes held a bit of mirth in them. Jenny covered her mouth with a napkin to conceal her smile. Small towns really did have no secrets.

"My Sterling says that he has to help the younger ones with their additions. What is it you do all day that the older students must help you teach?" asked a lady sitting in a corner.

Silence engulfed the room.

Jenny didn't think these ladies were meaning to attack Livvy, but they had no clue how a one-room schoolhouse operated. Juggling multiple grades with students at all sorts of levels of skill could only work with the older students helping the younger ones. Besides, those students learned more by showing a younger child what they knew. They had to communicate the knowledge, which reinforced what they had learned. It was an important technique.

"Well, my Sally says Miss Carmichael is the greatest teacher she's ever had!"

"She's the only teacher she's ever had, Evie." Chrissy smiled at the woman.

Everyone laughed.

"Doesn't matter. She loves going to school and learning her numbers and letters. Why, she says she's the best speller in the entire first grade, isn't that right Miss Carmichael?"

Livvy looked at the lady and nodded. "That's right, Mrs. Smith." She mumbled to Jenny. "And she's also the *only* one in first grade right now."

Jenny smiled. There were two sets of parents. One who never seemed to notice anything their children were doing, and those who noticed only their children but not what the others were doing.

Unsure how parents became either type, her own family came to mind. What made her ma and pa have all these children only to make them feel they weren't wanted or cost too much money? Or was it just her and not the others?

Her heart lurched, but she reined it in so that she could

focus on the conversation. It would be rude to not pay attention.

The conversation lulled. The ladies set down their tea cups and rose.

"Jenny," Mrs. Timbley asked.

Jenny looked over at her hostess. "Yes?"

"We're glad you have joined us today. Know you are welcome any time."

"Thank you, Mrs. Timbly. This has been more than lovely." Jenny stood with the others.

As Livvy and Jenny said their goodbyes and exited the house, Jenny glanced up to see dark clouds overhead.

Livvy's gaze followed Jenny's. "We might have some rain showers soon."

"The weather is so different from Cincinnatti." Jenny still couldn't believe she was in an entirely different state than where she grew up.

Livvy nodded. "I'm used to it now, so I don't give it a thought, but yes, it's amazing how different the weather can be in one part of this vast country versus another."

They both stood, observing the sky a moment longer, neither saying anything. It was nice to have someone who understood.

Chrissy joined them. "Studying the clouds?"

Jenny sheepishly glanced at Chrissy. "The weather is very different here."

"That's what I hear. We might have a storm blow in later. Let's head home." She took the first step forward, with Livvy and Jenny joining on either side.

Many things were different from back home. Some harder to adjust to than others. But she had a lot to be thankful for. She was healthy. She had a friend. And she currently had a roof over her head. In that moment, she didn't regret leaving home. It was a very freeing thought.

Eleven

Being social is exhausting. But I'm thankful to have people who actually want to talk with me.

—From the journal of Jenny Millard

Thunder rattled the small home as Jenny and Livvy settled in for the night. Bright lights flashed long after the rumble roared through. Soon, pinging hit the rooftops in quick succession, providing a symphony of sounds in their bedroom.

With each boom, Jenny found it harder to drift off to sleep. She sat up.

"Jenny?" Livvy sat up as well.

"It's so loud. I can't sleep."

"The storm?" Livvy asked.

Jenny stared straight ahead. "No, I think it's more than that. Everything is so different here. How connected you are to the residents. How helpful people are. Setting foot in church tomorrow. There's just so much change. It's all wonderful things, so I'm not upset, it's just all so different from anything I've ever known. It's overwhelming." She placed her nightgown over her legs and hugged her knees to her chest.

Livvy lit a candle, and the light cast moving shadows across the walls. "I guess that would be expected. I felt something similar when I came here as well."

"What did you do?"

"I changed my point of view. Although it didn't happen overnight." Livvy reached for her journal. Opening the book, she turned to the beginning. "Here I was observing. And fearful." She flipped through some pages. "Here I started opening my heart. Read this entry. You can see it's different."

Jenny took the book and read the words. *Help me, God. I'm not sure what I need to do. Have I been approaching this all wrong?* Glancing at her friend, Jenny reached out and squeezed her hand. "This sounds so personal. Are you sure you want me to read this?"

Livvy nodded, tears in her eyes. "I was staying with the Woodward's, and Emily wanted to know what I was writing. She put this into words so much better than I can, but she basically challenged me to start saying 'Dear God' when I wrote an entry and write it as a letter. Those letters are really prayers, because God wants us to talk with Him. When I started writing my entries this way, I didn't feel so alone. I had someone to share my utmost thoughts with and help me sort out my feelings. It helped." Livvy shrugged.

"I haven't ever gone to church. I don't know God," Jenny whispered.

"Doesn't mean you can't start writing a letter to Him tonight. You could ask Him to be with you tomorrow."

Jenny climbed out from under the covers and walked to the bureau. She opened her drawer and pulled out her journal. She only had a few entries, saving the pages for special moments. This was a special moment, right? Livvy had just shared her heart with her. And Jenny was going to try something new.

She sat on the bed and opened the book to the next blank page.

"Here." Livvy handed her a sharpened pencil.

"Thanks." Jenny held it in her hand. Closed her eyes. The last few days flashed in her mind. Meeting Ren, seeing Livvy, the Martins, seeing Ren again, the Taylor ranch, and the tea. Ren again. What if the flutters she had felt with him meant something, especially after watching Luke and Livvy together? She liked him. When he was near, her worries didn't seem so big. She felt safe. What if—her hands grew clammy. Could there be something there? But she couldn't be a teacher and be courted by him. She'd have to choose. She gripped the pencil tightly.

Livvy placed a hand on Jenny's shoulder. "Don't overthink it, Jenny. It doesn't have to be perfect or pretty. God doesn't care."

The raindrops softened and slowed to a slow dripping sound.

Jenny placed her pencil in place and wrote.

Dear God,

This is my first time writing You. I hadn't written before because I didn't know I could. Also, I really didn't think You cared. Livvy says You do. I just didn't think I mattered to You since You have so many other people to watch over. But maybe it's because I haven't written to You yet. So, here I am. Writing to You. I'm not sure I have the right to ask for anything. But if I do, I'd like some help finding a home. A place to belong.

That's all,

Jenny

She closed the book and sighed. Weird, how a weight lifted

off her shoulders. He hadn't answered anything, yet it felt … nice.

* * *

Dusty arose to an early morning engine whistle as the first train rode by his small camp. He cleaned himself up the best he could, in case he came across anyone and headed back into town. He didn't want to look memorable.

Of all nights to not sleep in the barn. The sudden rainstorm that swept in late in the afternoon yesterday was not great timing with him sleeping under the stars. When he'd finally gone to sleep, he was wet, cold, and miserable.

Still damp and cranky, he walked along the train tracks, figuring out what he needed to do next. He'd have to search her things. She was most likely hiding the stash somewhere. Or had a key to a bank box. The question was, where?

He skirted around the train station platform, avoiding the passengers coming and going. Once he reached the back of the livery, he followed it around to the front, where a large set of bushes and trees were gathered. He climbed into the large bush where he had hollowed out the middle. From this angle, he had full view of the house where she stayed and the road to the schoolhouse. He had learned her patterns over the last couple of weeks, following at a distance. So far, she went back and forth between the schoolhouse and the house where she stayed. Lately, there was another young lady with her. He had yet to find out her name.

Movement at the house had him watching closely. Four people exited and headed north. That meant everyone was away at the same time. Where were they going? How long would they be gone? He closed his eyes while his brain fought to figure out what day it was. Wait! Today was Sunday, which meant everyone would be at church.

An idea popped in his head, and he hightailed it out of the bush and entered the livery. He'd have to be cautious with how he went about this. He couldn't risk running into that crazy rooster and having him make a ruckus. And he hoped to sleep in the loft again if Goose could keep quiet about it. It was easier than hiking back out of town all the time, and definitely more comfortable.

* * *

Jenny's stomach churned as she walked alongside Olivia and the Martins toward the church for the Sunday morning service. "Now, tell me again what I should do?"

"Jenny." Olivia looked over at her. "Don't fret. It's not that formal. You won't do anything wrong, so don't worry."

Jenny forced a smile and nodded. She fortified her countenance on the outside, but inside, she was a mess. Well, that wasn't exactly true. She did feel different. Her talk with Livvy last night had given her a whole new outlook on things. But it didn't take away the nausea and faintness she also felt. She was sure she would make a blunder.

She put her hand up to cover the yawn that escaped her.

"I'm sorry, Jenny, for keeping you up so late last night."

"I didn't mind." She squeezed the arm threaded through hers. "You've given me much to think about."

"And there's more to share." Livvy squeezed back.

Chrissy walked on Jenny's other side. "I agree with Olivia. Sunday is the one day each week we all stop our work and gather. People are happy to be able to see their neighbors, along with the opportunity to worship the Lord together. You can follow along with Pastor William's instructions, and you'll fit right in."

As they turned the corner, a small group gathered at the entrance. She expected them all to stop, turn, and call her an imposter. She didn't know anything about God, so that's what she felt like. However, if there was anything she'd learned about herself during the past six months, it was that she had the courage to try new things. And she had the support from people she now called friends.

The clump of people at the door entered the building, except one. He turned and faced their party with a large smile in place. "Chrissy, Arthur, and Olivia. Welcome." He reached out his hand.

Chrissy put hers in his. "So good to see you this morning, Will. Beautiful day, isn't it?" She glanced back and nodded to Olivia, then she and Arthur went inside.

Livvy linked her arm in Jenny's elbow. "Pastor William, I'd like you to meet my dear friend, Miss Jenny Millard."

The pastor turned his entire focus solely on her and reached out his hand. "Welcome, Miss Millard. You picked a lovely day to join us."

She hesitated, then placed her fingers in his. "Thank you."

He must've sensed her unease. "You can call me Will or Pastor. Either is fine. I answer to both."

"Thank you, Pastor."

He squeezed her hand and then let go. Being on the receiving end of his intense gaze made her want to squirm. He was younger than she expected and quite handsome, although in a different way than Ren. Why she compared the two of them, she didn't know. Her stomach didn't buzz around like it did when she was around the blacksmith. She wasn't sure what that meant.

Livvy steered her forward, and Will faced the people standing behind them. "Good morning," he said.

She released her breath. He must focus on everyone the same, then.

Jenny and Livvy entered the small foyer of the white building and then passed through another set of doors into the main part of the structure. People were everywhere. Some she recognized, others she did not. Jenny really hadn't been around such a mass of folks growing up, although her family of nine was large all by itself. But this was something more. A few sat in their seats already, while others stood talking in small clusters throughout the aisles.

Livvy led Jenny around most of them until they found the Martins sitting in their seats. Jenny slid into the pew next to Chrissy and placed her hands in her lap, ready and waiting. Livvy sat next to her. Soon Livvy's beau, Luke, walked by and winked at Livvy, who blushed. He sat in the front row to the right with his sisters.

At the front of the church was a large cross and a podium the pastor must use for his sermons. It was raised higher. That must be so everyone could see better when sitting in the pews. To the side of the podium was an area with a wooden banister around it. Jenny wasn't sure what that was for.

Iron candelabras stood near the podium, one on each side. Candles lit, their glow gave the church a homey feeling Jenny had to admit was welcoming.

Others took their seats as Pastor Will strode to the front. A commotion in the back ended with the creaking of wood as someone sat behind her.

After a welcome greeting, Pastor Will spoke. "Will you please stand and turn your hymnbooks to page twenty-four?"

As everyone stood, the shuffling of clothing and paper

filled the room. A lady stood near the wooden banister, opened her mouth and started to sing.

Since she didn't know the songs, Jenny listened to the music and let it wash over her. She could hear everyone in the room, especially a man behind her. His bass voice was lovely, and he held his notes well. She began to hum, blending her soprano to his baritone.

The man stopped singing. She wanted to hear more, so she glanced over her shoulder to see what the matter was. Ren's widened eyes stared at her, and she quickly faced forward. Was that him singing with the beautiful voice? Softly, the man's bass joined back in. Sure enough, the voice she heard was him.

The swarm in her stomach dipped. As she heard him sing, a quiet peace engulfed her. Soon, the song was over, and everyone settled back into their seats.

As the service led to a close, Jenny observed several things. Attenders sang loud and off key, children fidgeted in their seats, and an older gentleman fell asleep when Pastor Will was talking.

Growing up, all she ever heard from her ma was, "Those high and mighty Christians think they're better than us. They'll ask for all your money on Sunday and leave you high and dry the rest of the week."

Her ma told her to never set foot in church. And Jenny had never wanted to cross her ma, who would pile on extra chores if she did.

This church wasn't anything like what she was taught.

In fact, she didn't feel like anyone took something from her. Instead she felt she was given something, filling her up. Was this normal? She couldn't wait to talk with Livvy about it. And she wondered if Ren felt the same.

Twelve

Tomorrow I will be attending church for the first time. I'm not sure what to expect.

—From the journal of Jenny Millard

The church looked small on the outside, but it was amazing to Ren how many people fit inside. The wooden pews were full of all the townspeople, and they sat shoulder to shoulder. As far as Ren could see, every inch of space had been taken. When he and Gideon entered before the service started, they found room to sit in the middle of a pew. A family near the edge of the pew scooted to the middle, so Ren and Gideon could sit on the end.

Right behind Miss Millard.

Even amongst all the chaos of settling in their seats, he spotted her right away.

Then the hymn began. Children sang a little off-key, and no one seemed to care. They all were worshiping God, singing praises, and raising their voices. As Ren looked at the hymnal Gideon held, he joined in, his deep voice adding to those around him.

He closed his eyes and sang from his heart, and then a soprano voice intermingled with his. The sound was so beautiful, he couldn't breathe.

He stopped singing. When he opened his eyes his gaze landed directly into Miss Millard's.

Her mouth dropped open, and she turned around.

A little frightened now to sing too loud, he opened his mouth and sang softer. Was she appalled or just as nervous as him? He had no idea how to interpret her reaction. And he wasn't about to ask.

Thankfully, Gideon didn't noticed the interaction. He had his head down, reading the hymnal word for word.

When worship was over, the parishioners around them welcomed him and went on their way. No one cringed or refused to speak to him. It all felt so normal. And made Ren glad he had come.

"Would you like to meet Pastor Will?" Gideon asked.

"Sure." Although he didn't know how to handle things if he was asked to shake hands. It had been easy to forget about his scars since living with Gideon and the recent interactions with Luke, the ladies, and Chrissy Martin.

He followed Gideon to the front, where Luke and Will were talking. Two younger girls stood nearby, visiting amongst themselves.

Luke gestured to Ren. "Ren, I'd like you to meet my best friend, Pastor Will."

Ren nodded, keeping his hands behind his back. There wasn't anything he could do about the scars on his face. He had come to grips with that not too long ago. "Hi, Pastor Will. It's nice to meet you, sir."

"Please call me Will, and it's nice to meet you, as well." He held out his hand. "I understand you are working with Gideon at the Blacksmith shop?"

Luke grinned. "Nothing gets by Will, as you will quickly learn."

Ren stared at the hand offered. He had wrapped his hand in cloth this morning so that no one would see the scars and would think it was a current injury. He extended his wrapped hand and saw Will look at it. He quickly switched hands and put out his left one. "It looks like you have an injury, why don't we shake with the other one?"

He swallowed to cover up the loss of words. "Thank you. I appreciate it. It's an old injury that flares up now and again." And he shook hands with his left hand.

Luke chimed in. "I'd like you to meet my sisters, Caroline and Rose. Girls, this is Mr. Lyman. He works at Gideon's shop."

"Hello." The older one curtseyed.

"Hi." The younger one copied her sister.

He bowed to them both.

They giggled.

As Ren stood upright, the schoolteacher, Miss Carmichael, came into view. He opened his mouth, but then he saw Jenny out of the corner of his eye. Knowing he had to say something, he forced his grimace smile into action. "Hello, ladies. Nice to see you again." Had he spoken those words?

"You met Olivia already?" Luke asked. He placed his hand at Miss Carmichael's back.

"We've passed each other on our walks to and from the schoolhouse. He helped Jenny find me the first day she was here." Miss Carmichael smiled at Luke and then smiled at Jenny. "Right, Jenny?"

Jenny's eyes met his. "Y-yes. He provided me assistance."

Gideon stood next to Ren, but didn't say a word.

Ren was sure Gideon would ask questions when they got back to the cottage.

"We discussed him coming to the ranch soon so he could take a look around." Luke glanced at Miss Carmichael.

Ren nodded. He'd never been invited out to someone's place before, although this could be business only—

Miss Carmichael clapped her hands. "And then have a grand meal together. We could make a day of it." She beamed at Jenny. "Wouldn't that be fun?"

Jenny bit her lip and glanced at each of them. Was she as uncomfortable as he was? Yet, the idea of spending more time with her put a lightness in his chest he couldn't ignore.

"Can we plan on next Saturday, then?" Ren asked.

Luke grinned. "Let's make it a date."

Jenny's eyes widened.

Ren's heart thundered in his chest.

Rose clapped her hands. "Another picnic?"

"Yes, won't that be fun?" Miss Carmichael clasped the girl's hands. She looked at Luke. "Would ten o'clock be all right?"

Luke nodded. "Works for us. Ren?" He looked at him expectantly.

He swallowed, glanced at Miss Millard, who studied her hands. Did she want him around? What choice did he have to say no? Besides, he *would* like to spend time with her. His gaze traveled to Gideon, who stood, smiling. Back to Luke. "Yes, that would be fine."

Luke clapped a single clap. "Great. Should be a swell time, then."

Mrs. Martin and a man Ren could only assume was her husband joined them. "I'm so glad everyone is here together. How about you all come back to the house right now for supper? That includes you two." She pointed to Gideon and Ren.

Ren looked at Gideon, who raised his eyebrows at Ren. Ren shrugged.

"We'd be honored to come," Gideon answered.

Everyone else agreed and headed out the door. Ren found himself walking outside with a large group of people, who considered themselves family or close friends.

Was he in some sort of dream? Could this mean he was accepted as one of them?

His spirits lifted. Between the church service and being invited to lunch, his heart had never felt so full.

If only Miss Millard showed some interest, his life might be complete.

JENNY'S SENSES were on high alert as they gathered together in the Martins' living room. Afraid of saying the wrong thing, she sat at the end of one couch, holding a plate of food, content to listen to the conversation around her. When Chrissy shooed Ren into the seat next to her, she almost choked on the bite in her mouth.

Their stilted conversation so far had been endearing, but awkward. How she wished she could converse with him like she did everyone else.

He cleared his throat. "Are you enjoying yourself?"

She nodded while she swallowed the bite of chicken.

"Sorry. Finish your food. Then we can talk some more. I'm starved." He bit into his own serving of cold fried chicken.

Thankful for the reprieve, she continued to eat.

Chrissy carried over more potato salad and added another helping to Jenny's plate. She really wanted to say no. She'd eaten so much food this past week, the cost to feed her always at the forefront of her mind. But when she would refuse,

Chrissy would put food on her plate anyway, and she would not let it go to waste. As the week progressed, the hunger pains subsided, and she felt better. Although the memory of those as a child remained with her. She didn't ever think she'd forget those feelings.

She appreciated the Martins' hospitality more than they knew. She felt safe. And cared for. Each person in the house right now truly cared about one another and enjoyed each other's company.

Together, she and Ren sat and ate. No words were exchanged while they finished their food.

He wiped his hands on a napkin. "This food reminds me of home."

"Where is home for you?"

He startled and then glanced her way. "I'm originally from Missouri. But I hope to make Washton my home." His eyes sparkled with something she couldn't identify. "What about you? Where are you from?"

"I originally lived in Kentucky. Went to Cincinnati to train to become a teacher."

"And now you are here."

"And now I am here. Life is vastly different in California, isn't it?"

He smiled. "Sure is. You have a lovely singing voice, by the way."

She looked at the plate in her lap. Held in a smile. He had a wonderful voice too.

"I'll take those plates if you are all finished," Chrissy said.

Jenny glanced up, and Chrissy winked at her. Her cheeks grew warm.

"Thank you, ma'am. The food was delicious." Ren handed her his plate and helped handle Jenny's. He really was a thoughtful man.

"I'm so glad you could join us, Ren. I told you we'd have you over for a meal. You didn't believe me, though," Chrissy said.

He laughed. "You are correct about that, Chrissy. I didn't want to spoil anyone's food with my scars."

Jenny frowned. "Why would people be bothered by your scars?"

Chrissy walked away, calling out to one of the girls to help her clean up the kitchen.

The blacksmith Gideon came over and placed a hand on Ren's shoulder. "I'm going to go take a nap. Please stay." He smiled at Jenny before he walked out the front door. Had he heard any of their conversation?

She turned back to Ren, wanting him to answer her question.

His lips were pressed together and he visibly swallowed. "I've never had anyone talk with me about them, other than to point them out, laugh at them, or comment how ugly they were."

"I don't think they are ugly. They are a part of you and your story. They are what makes you, *you*." It would be improper for her to tell him he was handsome, but she couldn't have him believing his scars made him ugly.

His neck reddened and his eyes sparkled. "Thank you for that—

"What are you two over here talking about?" Livvy interrupted.

Jenny groaned inwardly. She wanted to know what Ren was going to say. She was enjoying their conversation and had found that she could converse with him without tripping over her words. Her heart ached for him, and she wanted to help him see himself the way she saw him. But maybe they were getting in too deep. She had to remember she had plans. Plans that included signing a contract and teaching, once Livvy married Luke.

"We've been sharing about our homes and how different California is from where we came from." Jenny peered up at her friend.

Livvy nodded. "I concur in that assessment. It does take a little getting used to, doesn't it?"

Luke joined them.

"He wouldn't understand." Livvy laughed.

"What wouldn't I understand?" Luke put his arm around Livvy.

Livvy's gaze fell on Luke's and she smiled. "How different living out west is. How old were you when you moved here, Luke? I know you've told me. But I can't remember."

"I was a little boy. And our ranch was just a field when my pa laid down roots here."

Ren studied Luke. "So you've seen lots of change occur here over the years, then."

Luke swallowed. "Change is hard, but necessary." He glanced at Livvy. "Even in the hard things, there are blessings, though."

They smiled at each other, a hidden communication between them.

Luke cleared his throat. "So Ren, what is Ren short for?"

Ren grimaced. "Clarence. But I've always gone by Ren."

"I like it. It fits you," Jenny said.

Their eyes met for a brief moment, then Ren tilted his head. "Your first name is?"

"Jenny. Just Jenny. That's all it's ever been." She shrugged.

"I like Jenny," Livvy said. "And Ren, you can call me Livvy or Olivia. We are all friends now."

Ren opened his mouth, but before he could say anything,

Caroline and Rose ran over. "Luke, Chrissy sent us over to tell you Evelyn and Jimmy are outside readying the wagon."

"Guess that's our cue to go home." Luke held out his hands to his sister.

"Aww. Do we have to?" Rose crossed her arms.

Luke picked up Rose and tickled her. "We do. We all rode to church together, remember." He reached for Ren's hand with his free arm. "Great seeing you at church today, and I'm glad you came and joined us here."

Ren stood and shook Luke's hand. "Likewise."

Jenny loved that Ren was making new friends here as well. Luke and Livvy, and Ren and her, were around the same age. If they were a couple, they could become old married friends.

Her eyes widened.

What was she thinking? She couldn't let her mind go there. Even if it wanted to.

"I'll walk you out." Livvy looked at Jenny. "I'll be right back."

Ren sat back down. "Miss Millard. About what you said earlier. I wanted to make sure you know this and don't think of yourself as less than. There's nothing *just* about you. Jenny is a fine name, and I think it fits you well."

Jenny blinked back the moisture forming in her eyes.

"I know this may be forward of me, but would it be okay if I called you Jenny now, instead of Miss Millard? That's how I think of you. Jenny. And I think we've become friends now, or so I hope. Like what Livvy said. And I'd like it if you would call me Ren ... and I'm rambling." He chuckled. "Can I admit to being nervous? I'm not used to being in too many social settings."

All thoughts of her future plans escaped her at that moment as her heart soared. Wouldn't asking to use first names be a sign of interest? And he was nervous around her? A nobody who didn't have any work or a place to call her own.

He grinned at her.

She grinned back. "Yes, you may call me Jenny, Ren."

Thirteen

I enjoyed church very much. My heart hummed a beautiful melody for the rest of the day. Then we found out some disturbing news.

—From the journal of Jenny Millard

After supper, Jenny and Livvy went to their room to settle in for the night. Jenny opened her drawer and frowned. Had she left her belongings in such disarray?

Livvy shrieked.

Jenny ran to her side. "What's the matter?"

"My things seem to be all tossed around together in my drawer." Livvy held up an unfolded blouse.

"That's odd. Mine are too."

"They are?" Livvy placed her hand over her mouth. Her eyes darted back and forth.

Jenny frowned. "Was someone in our room? Why would they go through our things?"

Livvy hurried around the room, checking every single

thing. "Nothing seems to be taken." She sat on the bed. "No. It couldn't be."

Jenny sat next to her friend. "What is it?" What deep dark secret did Livvy have? Jenny couldn't think of any reason someone would search their things. Did someone from Jenny's last school think she took something? Or worse, think she had more than them and followed her? Her ma and pa wouldn't come after her, would they? They didn't even have money to travel west.

Livvy interrupted her racing thoughts. "My father. He ... he made some bad business dealings and lost everything. I lost everything. My home. My life as I knew it. All our furnishings were taken away. I never knew by whom. My parents died in a carriage accident a few weeks prior. And then everything collapsed, and I had to leave town."

"How horrible." If this is what Livvy had to deal with before Jenny met her, no wonder she'd been quiet and didn't share much.

"I really didn't know who to trust." She frowned. "But then I came here and found a wonderful place to live, and I've mostly moved on from my past. But, I can't help but feel this incident is related."

"Is anything missing?" Jenny felt this could be a good reason for someone to ransack their things. But what were they looking for?

"It doesn't seem like it. I don't have much. Just my teaching clothes, my riding habit, and my journal." She jumped up and ran over to the corner table. "Oh, no!"

"What?"

"It's missing!" She knelt and searched on the floor and under the bed. "I can't find it anywhere."

Jenny went to the drawer where she kept her journal. She had hidden it under her clothing which had been moved around. Had they taken her journal too? She pulled it out. Jenny had rarely used it, so she noticed right away how all the pages in the back had been thumbed through. "Whoever it was, found mine, too, but didn't take it."

They looked at each other.

"What are we going to do?" Jenny asked. Her skin crawled as she thought of someone in their room, touching her things, reading her innermost thoughts. How could she sleep tonight?

"First, we need to tell the Martins. It's their home, after all. And the sheriff, too, I guess. And Luke. Then, I don't know." Livvy gazed outside. "But whoever it was didn't find anything and might still be around."

Jenny shivered. "So, we aren't safe? What are they looking for?"

"I don't know." Livvy stared at the empty bedside table. Held back her shoulders. "But I'm not going to go back to being scared and fearful." She glanced at Jenny. "I'm sorry I dragged you into this."

Jenny reached for Livvy's hand. She was thankful to be there for her friend. What ill intentions toward Livvy could there be? What did they want? "Maybe this isn't you, but me? I wouldn't know why, but we don't really know anything—just that someone has been here, looking through our things."

Livvy put her other hand on top of Jenny's. "I'm glad you're here."

"Me too." Livvy's hands lifted, then her arms wrapped around her shoulders. Jenny circled her arms about her friend and squeezed. Hugs were few in her world. That's why she hugged the children often. When was the last time she had someone hug her? And she had someone to hug back? Livvy accepted and loved her just as she was. Her body warmed, and a peace filled her. She was grateful she bought the train ticket to Washton. She hadn't known what to expect. She had only hoped Livvy would be kind enough to let her stay.

Instead she had a friend. Actually two. Livvy and Ren, which meant she wasn't alone anymore.

* * *

DUSTY HAD GONE through the entire room and came up empty-handed. All the drawers were full of clothes, and under the bed and any other furniture, he found nothing. He had lifted the rug, hoping to find a loose floorboard or something, but still nothing.

When he'd opened the journal and saw so many entries, he decided to take it and read through the entire thing. Something in there should have a clue. Anything that might hint about what she did with hidden funds.

He sat in the loft of the livery thumbing through the book. The journal started once she joined the school. After she lost everything. Her first entries were simple, then she wrote about her parents' deaths. He studied those quite a lot, and from her perspective, it was an accident. She never mentioned anything about receiving money or hiding any.

He slammed the book closed and threw it on the hay pile, then tilted back his head on the wooden slats. Could it be there was nothing left?

She sure lived as if she had nothing.

"You up there, Dusty," Goose called out.

"Yep. Just resting." He opened his eyes and picked up the journal. He couldn't let Goose see he had this. As long as the livery worker stayed put, he'd sit here and keep reading.

He read, turning the pages slowly to not make any noise.

Once she arrived in Washton, the only things she wrote about were the places she went and what she did. Then her feelings entered the picture. And then she was talking with God.

What happened to her? If he didn't have such a thick skin, he would've closed the book. But he kept reading. His skin tingled as he read her words about leaning on and trusting this God fellow. What must that be like?

He shook his head. He had a job to do here and needed to get back to Cincinnati and check on his younger sister—the one person he was responsible for and cared about. If he didn't find any money, he couldn't keep her safe, fed, and protected.

What was he going to do? Would Miss Carmichael be worth anything back in Cincinnati? Could he kidnap her and take her back with him? Ten days was a long time to keep her tied up and gagged. People noticed those things. And she wouldn't go willingly. And he didn't have enough coin for two people to travel across the country anyway. He was supposed to use some of the funds he found to get himself back home.

He really didn't have many options left.

Ren rode the thoroughbred named Boaz through his paces after lunch the next day. Luke had boarded him at the livery and asked Ren to refit his horseshoes. Boaz meant strength, and this horse had it in spades. He had taken him far from town to stretch his legs and allowed him to run.

They galloped north along the main road before Ren turned him into a meadow and then a hay field. He wanted to test him in different terrain. The ride had been exactly what Ren needed as well. Focusing on the horse's needs was a good way for Ren to clear his own head.

He'd never been in a situation like he found himself yesterday, at the Martins' after church. Plenty of food, laughter, and sharing. And they included Ren as if he was one of them.

Luke even shook his hand. So did the mayor. Chrissy hugged him. And Miss Millard, Jenny as he now thought of her, permitted him to sit by her, again.

Bless Gideon, the interfering man that he was. He gave Ren a reason to visit with her longer because Gideon went to take a nap.

He and Jenny had eaten in silence, but he couldn't take his eyes off of her. He struggled to find something to talk about, yet she never made him feel small or dumb. Her beautiful black hair was neatly pulled back in an updo that highlighted her cheekbones and dainty chin.

His heart galloped along with the horse he was riding just thinking about her.

How could that be? What was it about Jenny that drew him to her? She was beautiful, but it was more than that. Her shyness? The fact they could sit in silence together? He'd never met someone who was similar to him in that way. She'd had a lot happen to her before she arrived. He knew that much. Her quiet resilience was apparent, and it attracted him to her even more.

A protectiveness grew in Ren over Jenny's well-being. He knew it wasn't his responsibility, but he wanted it to be. Not as a brother or friend, but more.

Boaz sped up, feeling the tension in Ren's body.

Deep down, he cared for her in a way he never had for someone. Admitting so was terrifying and freeing at the same time. Much like allowing this horse to run, with all the power behind his size and strength.

What was he supposed to do now?

With no plan sorted out, he turned the horse around and headed back to town, reining Boaz down to a slow trot. He had ridden over new ground, so he was unfamiliar with where he was.

Thankfully, these horseshoes had not come off. The horse responded well, and they both gained exercise. He wasn't paying attention when the horse cut through behind a field near town. The horse seemed to know where to go, and they entered a clearing with the schoolhouse coming into view.

The horse reared up.

"Whoa, boy." He pulled back on the reins.

Screech. Squawk. Screech.

What was going on?

Directly in front of him, Bert flapped and squawked at him, keeping the horse in check. Beyond his open wings, the two teachers faced him, eyes wide, with the children all huddled behind them.

They must've heard him coming, and he had scared them.

Squawk.

The fact that this small fowl had the courage to step in front of a moving horse filled Ren with respect. He didn't want to think of the consequences otherwise.

He swung the reins hard to the left and darted to the far side of the clearing behind the schoolhouse. Walked the energy off a bit. He waited for his heart to stop pounding, then swung down and strode back to apologize to Jenny and Miss Carmichael, horse in tow.

Screech.

The rooster stepped in front of the ladies.

Ren halted.

"I'm sorry for that scare a moment ago. I didn't fully know where I was until I came out of those trees. Are you all right?"

They both laughed nervously.

"We're all right, aren't we children?" said Miss Carmichael.

The children spread out and cautiously eyed him and the horse.

He nodded at the rooster. "That's one interesting bird."

"Isn't he? He's sort of famous around here." Miss Carmichael turned to Jenny. "Didn't I tell you he'd be our guard?"

The topic of their discussion paced between Ren and the ladies, swiveling his head back and forth, clucking small chirps along his path as if making sure the danger was over. Ren now knew that's what Bert was doing the first day he had met Jenny. A watchbird.

Jenny looked at her friend, then the rooster, and then at him. Her eyes softened. Wow, she was beautiful. Protectiveness surged within, and he shifted his weight back and forth. Anything to keep from reaching out. He wanted to take her in his arms and hold her close. Tell her he was sorry for scaring her.

But that would be incredibly forward.

He rubbed his hands through his hair, bowed to them, apologized again, then turned and got back on the horse. This was no way to endear him to her. How was he to gain her interest if she was scared of him?

"Excuse me, Ren?" Miss Carmichael called out.

He stopped and glanced over his shoulder. "Yes?"

"Is that your horse?" she asked.

"No, miss."

She nodded.

"Why do you ask?"

She tilted her head. "He looks like one of Luke's horses."

Ren was impressed. Not everyone could identify other's stock. "He is. I was testing out the new shoes I put on him."

"He's used to running through these trees. A little wild,

that one. No wonder he brought you this way. Is Luke at the smithy, then?

"No, not yet, but he's meeting me there in a few hours."

"Thank you." She turned to Jenny. "Are you all right with us stopping at the blacksmith's before we head home? We can bring the girls to him there." She glanced at the children, who now all sat on the grass, waiting.

"If you don't mind, I need to get the horse to the livery. Sorry again for startling you." He waved his hand. He needed a hat if he was going to be out and about greeting people like this. He liked how people gestured with one without saying words.

"Nothing to worry about, Ren." She turned to face her students, clapping her hands.

Jenny's gaze landed on his and held. Her lips shifted into a small smile.

His heartbeat tripled, and the horse side-stepped.

Screech.

Bert flapped at him.

Ren had to break eye contact even though he didn't want to.

The bird blocked his way, and he had to turn and go around the schoolhouse along the river's edge. So much for escaping out of town to flush out his emotions. He couldn't wait to see Jenny later when she came to the smithy with Livvy.

Fourteen

How different my life has become in such a short time frame.

—From the journal of Jenny Millard

Jenny's mind spun while she walked with Livvy, Caroline, and Rose to the blacksmith shop. All the excitement caused such an interruption to the lesson, it was impossible to start again. It wasn't every day a horse came running into the yard during class time.

Bert clucked behind them.

Jenny couldn't believe what she saw. A rooster as an escort and guard? However, after seeing him in action, she trusted the noisemaker. A far cry from when she was a girl and being attacked by one.

Her nerves were still on edge from when Ren had galloped into the field. The commotion he'd created outside matched the commotion he caused inside her heart.

He was handsome, kind, and commanded that large horse well. Genuinely concerned for their well-being, he dismounted and made sure everyone was okay. What's not to like about someone who did that? She sighed. But Jenny couldn't think about those things. If she wanted to take over Livvy's contract, she shouldn't be walking to the blacksmith's shop now, where he would be.

She didn't want her attraction to grow.

Maybe they could find Mr. Taylor quickly and be on their way.

As usual, Jenny didn't get what she hoped for. Mr. Taylor was there, as well as a slew of other men who sat on barrels and a rough wooden bench.

To her amazement, they stopped what they were doing, and all rose to their feet.

"Miss Carmichael, what a pleasant surprise." Several men murmured to Livvy. Some even approached her and kissed her hand. In front of Luke. Jenny thought they were too bold, but Livvy took it in stride, paying them the least amount of attention without being rude.

Then their attention fell on Jenny.

"Tell us, is this your friend? We saw you at church yesterday. Welcome to Washton." A blond-haired man with a black cowboy hat held out his hand. "I'm Wade Schreiber. And you are?"

"Spoken for." Luke Taylor stepped to Jenny's side.

Her heart stopped.

What was Luke doing?

Wade placed his hands on his hips. "You cannot claim every woman who comes to our town, Luke."

Luke laughed, glanced her way, and winked.

"I can if the same rules apply to Miss Millard."

The men groaned.

"Who made you in charge, Luke?" This was from the man next to Mr. Schreiber. He fingered his mustache, a slight grin of mischief in his eyes as they landed on Jenny. "Miss Millard, is it? My name is George Henly. I'm a friend of Luke. Pleasure to make your acquaintance. I can show you around town any time. All ya got to do is ask."

"George! She's a guest in Arthur Martin's house. A teacher from the same school as Miss Carmichael, with the same signed agreement. If anyone doesn't abide by that, they will have to answer to Arthur or me."

At the mention of the mayor, they all restrained from commenting.

Except one. "Let one of us escort her around. You already have Miss Carmichael." Both Wade and George swatted the man's arms with their hats. "What? You each had your say." But he stepped back and wasn't facing her anymore.

She swallowed the lump in her throat and turned to Luke and mouthed, "Thank you." There was a story here. She'd have to ask Livvy about it later. For now, she was thankful Luke stepped in. She didn't want extra attention. Well, maybe from one man and only one man.

Luke saw his sisters and opened his arms. "Caroline, Rose."

"Hi, Luke." Caroline and Rose ran over and circled their arms around their brother, effectively changing the topic.

The men all chose to sit down again and mumble to themselves. The enthusiasm they first showed toward her abated.

Livvy put her arm in hers and pulled her off to the side of the shop. "Don't be alarmed. Luke was setting boundaries. Necessary, even if it's a little embarrassing. Remember when I said the first teacher was swept away before setting foot in the schoolhouse? It's related to that."

Jenny watched Luke hug his sisters. He then spun to finish his conversation with the man behind the counter.

Jenny swung her gaze in that direction and froze. Ren had

been standing there the entire time? Her cheeks flushed with embarrassment until she noticed his expression.

Fury filled his eyes as he stared down Luke.

Did Ren hear Luke declare her off-limits too?

Afraid any movement would tip the scale in the wrong direction, Jenny held her breath.

She didn't know if she should feel relieved or sad.

* * *

REN STOOD at the counter between the forge and the customer waiting area, where he had watched Luke put his arm around Jenny and proclaim her spoken for. His blood boiled as hot as the melted iron he usually worked with.

Was Luke interested in Jenny? Wasn't he engaged to Miss Carmichael?

Luke stared back. And then his lips twitched. "Can you show me the tool you've been making for me in the back, Ren?"

Ren breathed deep through his nose, then pivoted and entered the darkened room, not caring whether Luke followed or not. Whatever it was Luke wanted to see, it better be quick. Ren needed to pound something, and he didn't think Gideon would appreciate it being his best customer.

"Ren," said Luke.

Ren warily turned around.

"I can tell you care for Jenny. Am I correct?"

Ren fisted his hands. What gave Luke the right to use her given name?

Luke raised his palms. "I'm just asking."

Ren narrowed his eyes.

"Is it a protection thing? Something that comes from here?" Luke placed his hand on his heart.

Ren pursed his lips. What was Luke getting at?

"Good." Luke nodded.

Ren did not like how that scene had unfolded. All those men gazing at Jenny adoringly. None of them had scars. She could easily be interested in one of them without giving Ren a second thought ...

"She'll need someone in town looking after her. Most everyone knows Olivia and I are engaged. But when Olivia first arrived, they surrounded her, harassed her at the schoolhouse, and challenged Arthur's rules. Jenny is new here, so their attention could easily go in the same direction. I live too far out of town. She does live at Arthur's home, but she needs someone else to watch over her when Arthur isn't around. Someone I can trust."

Did this mean Luke was giving him his blessing to be near her, after he just told all those men in the front to stay away?

"Until Arthur figures out who the next schoolteacher will be, I don't think Jenny will be available for courting. If she teaches, she will have to sign a contract that clearly states courting is not allowed."

"Doesn't Miss Carmichael have a current contract?" Ren asked.

Luke chuckled. "Olivia had made things very clear when she first arrived, but things went a little awry. Some extenuating circumstances changed things. And she's determined to finish the school year before we marry. I don't know Jenny well, or where she stands on what she wants. I just met her myself a few days ago. But she is Olivia's dearest friend, so I feel responsible for her." He slapped Ren on the back.

Ren didn't budge.

"And now I can trust you to look out for her as well. Does that sound like a plan?"

Was Luke looking to partner with Ren on watching out for

Jenny? Did that mean he was the one to protect her and able to escort her around? He cleared his throat.

Luke pointed his thumb over his shoulder. "These men can be relentless. Don't let them discourage you. And if Miss Millard tells you to back away or stop following her, you don't stop. Just keep a little more distance."

"I'm not sure I understand."

Luke chuckled. "If she is anything like Olivia, she will not like having a man trying to protect her. Womenfolk can be mighty independent in their actions and thinking. But they still need someone to care for them and stand up for them. Miss Millard may not always welcome your good intentions. And I do expect them to be good, Ren. You come across as someone I can depend on."

Ren's heart lifted. It was a gift to have someone say it directly to him.

Luke thrust out his right hand. "Give me your word you'll do right by her, and I'll support you with whatever you want to do in the future." His smirk told him Ren hadn't fooled Luke about his interest in Jenny.

Having someone on his side might be helpful. Ren glanced at Luke's hand. They had shaken several times now, and Luke still never hesitated to reach out to him. Gideon was right in stating that Luke would make a good friend. An unfamiliar warmth filled the empty spots in his soul as he placed his hand in Luke's. Ren would show all his scars to the entire town of Sacramento if it meant being able to watch over Jenny and protect her. As they shook, Ren's senses felt every part of the connection, as if the nerve endings were coming alive.

Maybe they were. There were parts of Ren he never thought would feel the way he did. Upon releasing their handshake, Ren asked, "Do I tell her what I'm doing? How do I go about this?" He hated to ask but needed some guidance.

Luke shook his head. "I wouldn't. Just keep an eye out so she can go about her business. That's the best thing you could do." He glanced over his shoulder. "I need to get the girls home. I'll talk with you later, Ren."

"Later, Luke." Ren stood there and let the last few minutes wash over him.

He had been asked to watch over Jenny. He had a reason to talk with her and be seen with her. It was as if he had a blessing to be around her, which was exactly what he wanted.

His spirits lifted in anticipation.

Fifteen

As I write this letter to you, God, I'm still not sure how I'm supposed to do this. My heart yearns for something I can't name.

—From the journal of Jenny Millard

Luke Taylor came by the forge Tuesday morning after driving his sisters to town. He asked Gideon to send Ren out to speak with him.

"What's up, Luke?" Ren pulled off his gloves. Did he forget a project Luke wanted him to work on? He glanced at Luke's expression and froze.

"Remember yesterday I mentioned I'm trusting you to look out for Miss Millard?"

Ren leaned forward, braced for the bad news. "Yes."

"Olivia shared with me that someone went through their things in their room while they were out."

"When was this?" Ren asked.

"Sometime Sunday, possibly while we were in church, because that's when everyone was away from the Martin residence. The girls didn't notice until they went to bed that night. Olivia told me late yesterday. I wanted to talk with Arthur first before I spoke with you," Luke said.

A fierce protectiveness rooted deep inside Ren. His mind instantly thought of Goose and Dusty, but he had no proof they were up to no good. Just a gut feeling. Ren moved his feet further apart and crossed his arms.

"Their things were rifled through. Olivia's journal is missing. They both say they remember seeing it and now it's not there. Shook them both up, of course."

Ren's heart ached for Jenny, who he knew was looking for peace and contentment here in Washton. "Do you have any idea why? Was it a man who was looking for valuables?"

Luke hesitated. "We can discuss this in more detail later. But Olivia came west because of a situation back home with her family. It's not my place to divulge her secrets, but we both think it might be related to that. Which means she could be in danger. And since Jenny is with her all the time, she could be too. Have you noticed anyone new around lately?"

Ren stiffened. "I'm new." And he had been at the house Sunday.

Luke shook his head. "Other than you. We aren't considering you at all, so don't get your dander up."

Ren blew out a breath. "Because I'm new, I don't know who is from around here and who isn't. But I observe really well. I'll keep my eyes and ears open and let you know if I see or hear anything."

"I'm asking you to look after both of them. I can't be on my ranch and in town at the same time. I appreciate your help. I'm thankful you're here in town." Luke placed his hat back on his head. "You know, Gideon is lucky to have you assisting him. Your work is fantastic."

"Thanks. I appreciate the compliment." Both of them.

They shook hands. The fact he didn't hesitate to place his right hand out told him he was learning to trust. It probably helped that he was being trusted as well.

Luke headed for the door.

He hesitated before deciding to go ahead and ask. "Hey, Luke?"

Luke turned. Raised his eyebrows.

Ren felt funny even asking this but straightened his shoulders anyway. "I'm interested in buying a hat. What type of hat is yours?"

Luke came back toward Ren. "I'm not sure if Jacob Woodward at the Woodward's store across the street can order one like this for you. It's a Stetson hat. It's big, but it provides enough cover when I'm in the saddle all day. There's also a haberdasher shop in Sacramento that can order a custom fit hat for you," Luke said as he took off his hat to show it to Ren. "I have to tell you, though. Some hats cost you a couple months' wages. But they are well worth it."

Ren didn't flinch at the cost and studied the head cover. He knew hats could be expensive. He just hadn't wanted to spend the money on one before.

"What type do you recommend?" Ren noticed several other customers wore hats as well. Because he worked mostly inside every day, he'd never had a need for one. But he also observed that those who wore hats were more involved in town than those who didn't. It was a funny observation, but that's how Ren's mind worked. He noticed things. And since he was interested in fitting in more, for the first time, he wanted a hat.

"Since you don't work on a ranch, maybe one that Jacob has would work for you. Make sure it fits well, stays on your head when riding, and protects the parts you want protecting."

"Thanks, Luke. I appreciate the tip. I'll talk with Jacob."

Placing his hat back on his head, Luke pulled on the brim.

Exactly the way Ren wished to salute those he met on the street.

If Ren had been asked a few weeks ago whether he would be sitting in a pew at church, eating food at a social gathering with others, and greeting customers in the front of the shop, he would've never believed it. God had a way of pushing him out of his comfort zone, molding and shaping each and every day, till his original plan had changed slightly. Hardly noticeable until afterward, when the new shape was formed. Much like his work with metal.

* * *

THE NEXT MORNING Jenny rose at the same time Livvy did for another school day. Today was Wednesday, and they would be back in the schoolhouse. Excited for what lay ahead, she hurried to get ready.

When they arrived at the one-room building, both Teddy and Emily Woodward were there helping load wood in the stove and setting up the slates on the desks. It was obvious they had done all this before.

Livvy showed Jenny where she kept things, and the routine she'd set when she first arrived. Soon, it was time to ring the bell hanging on the porch.

Bert screeched as they reached the doorway.

Screech.

"Right on time, Bert," Livvy called out as she rang the bell.

Screech.

He jumped off his tree stump and ran toward some of the children. Jenny's eyes widened, and she went to veer him off, but Livvy touched her arm. "He won't hurt them."

"Are you sure?" Too many memories of mean rooster pecks flooded her mind. She didn't want the children hurt.

Livvy showed no concern. "I'm sure. Just watch."

Sure enough, Bert circled around them, one wing extended.

Screech.

The kids squealed in delight and ran toward the porch. Almost as if they wanted Bert to chase them.

Which Bert did for a while before he broke off and hurried toward a few other children. Time and again he pushed them all along till they were lined up on the porch, ready for the start of school. Jenny had never seen such an outrageous thing before.

Bert traveled over to his stump and gave one last screech, shook his wings and head, and then jumped onto it.

Why did they need a bell when they had a bird? She shook her head and followed the students into the classroom.

The children all seemed to know what to do. Boys sat on one side, and the girls on the other. Younger kids were in the front. Everything was orderly.

As the day progressed, Jenny's mind strayed from Livvy's instruction. She fidgeted with the slate in front of her. Not wanting to dwell on any negative thinking, Jenny went to offer support to the nearest student, but one of the older students was already helping her. She turned to the next one, but they didn't need her help either. No one did.

She sat in the back of the classroom, feeling a little useless. She was used to keeping busy. Always having something to do. But if no one needed her, why was she here? She didn't want to be ungrateful, but also didn't want to be a 'bump on a log' as her ma would sometimes tell her. Is this how it would be every day from now till the end of the school year?

Livvy moved on to the next lesson, and Jenny waited to see if anyone asked for her help. No one did.

She focused her energy on watching Livvy as she commanded the room. Would the students be eager to learn from her instead of Livvy? What if they didn't, and they rebelled? Being compared to a beloved teacher all the time would not help Jenny's confidence.

Screech. Screech.

"Class, please put your things away and clean up your desk before you grab your pail and head home," Livvy called out over the din. "We will see you all tomorrow morning. Great job, today." She straightened up her desk as Jenny banked the fire in the stove and set the books in a pile by the slates.

At least she could help with that.

Luke was waiting for them with Caroline and Rose when they headed out the door.

Livvy picked up the pace as she hurried toward them.

Jenny followed a bit more sedately.

Bert stood nearby, clucking and pecking the ground. When he saw them approach, he raised his head and spread out his wings.

"Thought I'd give you ladies a ride today back to the Martins'." Luke pushed up his hat.

Livvy must've talked with Luke yesterday about what happened.

Jenny ground her teeth knowing someone had been in their room, touching their things. Her ears burned knowing Luke was aware. But maybe that was for the best. Her newfound security was a little broken again, and she was thankful to not have to be dealing with it alone this time. She knew Livvy was upset, although she did a good job in hiding it today.

Livvy smiled at her beau. "That's very thoughtful of you." She approached him and touched his arm.

He lifted her up onto the wagon seat. Then he faced Jenny. "You're next." He held out his hand for Jenny to use for support as she climbed in after Livvy.

The wagon rocked and bumped as they traveled the dirt road back to Main Street. The walk was not long at all, and Jenny enjoyed the exercise, but for now, she'd ride and feel protected and watched over.

She gazed around town, taking in the storefronts and the people along the boardwalk. It was a different sight from the middle of the street. Jenny's heart galloped at the sight of a man who was built like Ren. But then she noticed he was wearing a hat and dismissed him.

"Whoa." Luke slowed the wagon. "I see you found one," he called out.

Jenny looked at Luke, then followed his gaze to the man she had just rejected as Ren. But it *was* him, and he was wearing a hat. He smiled and stepped into the street closer to the wagon.

"You were right in suggesting I ask Jacob. He had one at his store that fit my head." Ren grabbed the brim and pulled it down a bit. It covered his eyes for a moment, then he pushed it back.

Jenny covered her mouth to hide her smile. He looked dashing in his new hat. Although he was already charming in her mind. He didn't need a hat. But it didn't hurt, and he fit in just a little more. Her heart lifted that he was becoming more comfortable with himself here in Washton. Much like she was.

Ren's dark eyes found hers, and he nodded.

She smiled. She shouldn't encourage him, but she couldn't help it.

"Glad you found one. It suits you. Well, I'm off to drop these ladies at home. Talk later, Ren," Luke said.

"Sounds good. Have a good rest of your day. Ladies," Ren said as he pulled on his hat brim again and headed in the opposite direction.

Luke flicked the reins, and the wagon jerked into motion again.

Within a matter of minutes, Luke helped hand each of them to the ground. Jenny went inside right away to give Luke and Livvy a few minutes alone. Well, as much alone as they could, standing in the middle of Main Street with Caroline and Rose with them.

At that moment, Jenny was thankful not to be the one who had everyone's notice. Maybe being the assistant had its merits after all.

Sixteen

I'm sorry for being impatient and indecisive, but I don't know how to plan or imagine the future. I must wait on other's decisions first. Waiting is so hard.

—From the journal of Jenny Millard

Ren banked the fire for the day. He'd finished pounding out the latest piece of iron and set it in the water to cool. He brushed his forehead with his sleeve.

Gideon stopped a bit earlier, and Ren said he would clean up. His boss was looking a bit more haggard and needing more naps lately. Ren was a little worried.

He didn't want to, but he left the smithy more than once this afternoon. First to procure a hat from Woodward's store. And second was to visit the livery. Since he suspected Goose and had a reason to be at the livery, he figured showing up at different times would possibly shed some light on what he was up to.

So far, he hadn't found anything out of the ordinary.

Ren secured his apron on the hook.

"Hello, Ren?" Luke's voice traveled from the front.

Ren hurried out to meet him. "Did something happen?"

"No. Praise God. I'm getting ready to meet with Arthur in his office, and thought you'd like to join us," said Luke.

"I sure would. Give me one more minute, and I'll be back out."

"I'll wait for you."

Ren ran to the back and finished the nightly ritual of closing off the heat, wiping the anvil, and storing the tools. It was important for safety and to be able to start work right away in the morning to finish all the steps. Once done, he grabbed his new hat and jogged to the front. "Ready."

The two men exited the smithy, crossed the street, and entered the city building.

Arthur waited for them in the front. "Glad you are both here. Let's go to my office."

Ren followed Luke's lead and entered last. The room was simple, with basic furniture. Clean.

"Have a seat." Arthur gestured to the two chairs in front of his desk. He shook his head. "I keep wanting to ask Olivia if they might've imagined the whole thing. The idea of someone in my home, going through their things, angers me. We haven't needed to lock our door before, but now we are all a bit jumpy. Sheriff Jackson won't be back for another week. Until then, any thoughts of what we can do?"

Luke shook his head. "I don't know." He turned to Ren. "To fill you in a bit, Livvy's father had conducted business with the wrong people, and that came to light after he and his wife, Livvy's mother, died in a carriage accident. Livvy came home one day and found all her belongings being seized, along with her house. She had nowhere to go. And no funds. We both think someone is after money that doesn't exist."

Ren listened, taking in the facts. "So, someone who is desperate or won't take no for an answer, then?"

They all sat there in silence, nodding.

"Has anything happened at the schoolhouse?" Ren asked.

"We've been busy rebuilding after the flood. Today was the first day they were officially back in it, so no, not yet," Arthur said.

Ren searched for ways he could help. "Is there a lock on the door and windows? If not, I can make some."

"Yes. And Olivia has the key. I'll mention tonight she should lock everything up tight each day. I don't want to scare her, but I think she'll understand," Arthur said.

Luke's expression grew darker. "I don't want to be suspicious of everyone, but I will be. We all need to. In my bones, I feel this isn't over."

"I agree, but we need to not tip off anyone that we might be on to them," Ren said.

"Wise words, Ren. I'll mention that to the girls. They can talk to only us three about anything else that happens until we can get to the bottom of this." Arthur stood and reached out his hand to first Ren, then Luke.

"I almost lost Olivia once. I won't allow anything to happen to her or Miss Millard," Luke said through clenched teeth.

Ren nodded. He was in complete agreement. Time to make another surprise visit to the livery tonight.

* * *

Ren strolled down the boardwalk, even though what he wanted to do was run. He crossed the street and entered the livery. Instead of calling out for Goose, he decided to assess things first. So far, nothing looked amiss.

Coal stood in his stall, munching on hay.

"Hey, boy, how are you doing tonight?" Ren reached out a hand and patted his neck.

His horse lifted his head around, his large dark eyes searching Ren's hands.

Ren laughed. "I don't have any treats right now. I'll bring some tomorrow."

"Ren, is that you?" Goose called out.

Ren closed his eyes, willing his heart to stop thundering. He had to be careful not to give away anything. "Hey, Goose. How's everything? I missed my boy, and thought I'd come over to say goodnight."

Goose walked up on Ren's right side and placed his arms on the stall gate, never fully looking at Ren. "Things have been quiet. Gets a little boring around here, honestly. Not sure how Stevie manages. Hard for me to stay here all the time."

Ren nodded, hoping Goose would continue talking. So far, he hadn't said anything helpful, but he was sharing something, so that was a start. "Where would you go, if you weren't here?"

"Oh, that's easy. I'd go find me a saloon and a pretty gal." Goose grinned.

Ren cringed. But kept up the conversation. "There aren't any saloons in Washton."

"For now." Goose laughed. "I go to Sacramento. They have a lot there. More people to play cards with as well."

Was that how Goose met Dusty? At a saloon in Sacramento? Ren was grasping at straws.

"I'd love to open one here, though. But you have to have money for that. And I won't make enough in this job. So, I got to figure something out," Goose continued.

Ren remembered Luke's words from earlier. *Have to be suspicious of everyone.* Goose could have gotten wind of the situation if word traveled west, and he wanted to find the funds for himself. The idea of Goose touching Jenny's things had his muscles quivering. He closed his hands into fists to prevent himself from acting on his emotions.

"But I'm not sure yet what I'm going to do. I made a commitment to Stevie, and I have to stay here until he's back. But then, maybe I'll move on for a bit and come back after I make some money." Goose's gaze searched the rafters as he spoke.

Ren didn't read any malice in his voice or hidden meaning. Just a guy with a dream. Maybe not the best dream, but a dream nonetheless. He couldn't begrudge him that. He patted Coal one more time and pushed away from the stall. "I'll check back on all the horses tomorrow."

Goose waved to Ren. "Come all you want, Ren. It gets lonely here. And the one person I thought was going to be around has disappeared, and I don't know when he's coming back."

Ren would be back. And he hoped that Goose's friend would be too. He'd like to have a little chat with him to see what he could find out.

* * *

DUSTY WATCHED both schoolteachers exit the building and lock the door. He had been waiting and watching all week to figure out how best to search the schoolhouse. He didn't think there were enough children for two teachers, but what did he know. Unless one wasn't going to be teaching any more. Was Miss Carmichael going to run? All the more reason to finish this job.

He waited until the crazy rooster followed them. He

couldn't understand this town. This rooster clucked all over the place like he was a pet and had every right to walk amongst them. He squawked and flapped his wings at everyone, and they all talked back to him as if they understood him.

Dusty stayed clear of the beast. He had learned that day at the train station. It's like he picked up on the fact Dusty was up to no good. Which he was.

When the two ladies and the bird passed the church, Dusty pulled out of his hiding place behind the trees. The porch creaked as he stepped onto it. He had seen them lock the door, so he tiptoed to a window on the east side of the building and maneuvered the latch. These locks were easy compared to the ones he had to break through in Cincinnati. He sat on the window sill and rotated his legs and body through the window, and gently placed his feet on the floor.

The last of the afternoon light shone in from the west, allowing him time to survey the room. Where would she hide money in here? Or a clue about the money?

"I'll hurry." A female voice came from outside.

Dusty's heart skipped a beat. He pulled down the window and ran to the desk, the only thing large enough to hide his body. He squatted into a small ball and squeezed himself into the space between the chair and desk.

Sure enough, the door opened, and small footsteps echoed across the room.

Dusty held his breath.

The steps stopped and shuffled in place nearby. "Now, where was it? Oh, there it is. Can't leave this lying around."

Dusty wished he could see. But if he lifted his head, the tip of his hat would show and give away his position.

The steps retreated out the door. The distinct sound of door closing along with a click in the lock, then dead silence in the room told him she was gone.

He unfolded his legs, sat, and leaned against the desk. This was one female he was tired of following. She didn't do anything interesting. Just led a boring life here in the west. California wasn't too bad. Different from Cincinnati in many ways. If he didn't have to return with the wanted money and look after his sister, maybe he would've stayed. But he wouldn't come back. It was a long train ride out here.

Hoping enough time passed that no one else would come back, he stood.

The afternoon light faded. Soon, it would be hard to see details without a lantern, and he'd have to come back. Lifting the papers, he searched the entire top of the desk. Books, an apple, chalk, and pencils were all he found. He opened each book in case something was hidden inside. When he picked up the Bible, a paper fell out to the floor. He bent and picked it up, a note of some type with the words, *I can do all things through Christ which strengtheneth me.'* Like other phrases in the woman's journal. He shoved it back into the book and restacked them the best he could. Then he opened the drawers, pulling everything out. Nothing stared back at him that reeked of any type of money—green, or gold. He threw the contents back in and slammed it shut.

Nothing in the desk.

By now the light had faded.

Where else to look? Maybe there was a floorboard loose. He stomped across the floor, along the wall, listening for a hollow sound. Continued another pass, and then another. Suddenly, something sounded different, or was that his own brain wishing he heard a different tone? He knelt on the floor and knocked on the wood to double-check. No sign of any hiding spot.

He punched the floor. Then wished he hadn't. Holding his fist, he rose and surveyed the rest of the schoolhouse. He didn't think he'd find anything amongst the children's slates, but he looked anyway, unstacking every single one and then restacking them in haste.

Nothing.

Entire waste of time.

He went back to the window, glanced outside to make sure it was clear, then opened it and exited the way he came. He would search inside the schoolhouse one more time this weekend when the light was better, just in case he missed something. However, with no sign of any money, he'd have to think of what to do next. He didn't like where his thoughts were taking him.

Seventeen

God, I haven't heard anything from you yet. I'm not sure if you are listening, or if you're too busy with everyone else. Maybe I'm not doing this right.

—From the journal of Jenny Millard

Jenny followed Livvy into the livery Saturday morning. They were going to spend the day at the Taylor ranch again. She was looking forward to the outing and hoped to see the Taylors' horse, Fanny.

The livery worker, Goose, was there, but the gig was not ready.

"Hi, Goose, I'd like Arabella harnessed to the buggy so we can go for a drive," Livvy said.

Goose finished putting hay in a stall before he responded. "Hello, there, Miss Carmichael, Miss Millard. Aren't you both looking mighty fine today?"

The way he said Jenny's name made her skin crawl.

Livvy didn't hesitate. "We are a bit late, so if you could hurry, we would appreciate it."

"Where are you off to that you're in such a hurry?" He took his time, slowly pulling the front of the buggy in position and getting Arabella out of her stall.

"Oh, that's for us to know, Goose. Can't be giving away all our secrets, now, can we?" Livvy waved her hand in the air.

"Where's the fun in that? I like secrets. Especially when it's a lady giving them to me." He leered at each of them.

Jenny's hackles rose, but she didn't say anything. The faster they got out of there, the better.

When the buggy was all set up, he lifted out a hand to help Livvy alight. Once she was seated, he turned his attention to Jenny.

She hesitated, and he raised an eyebrow. She would not let him best her, so she placed her hand in his. The feel of his clammy fingers sent unpleasant shivers up her arm. She lifted her foot and pushed on his hand to step into the gig. Something passed over her bottom, and she jumped inside, landing with a jolt.

When she glared at him, he smiled and winked at her.

She pinched her lips, holding her tongue. He was a large man and could overpower them if he wanted to. Better to get out the door as fast as possible.

Livvy snapped the reins as Goose opened the side door. The buggy traveled the dirt road, past the church, then the schoolhouse and out of town.

Jenny closed her eyes and took a deep breath.

"He's a handful, isn't he?" Livvy said. "You okay?"

Jenny nodded and faced her friend. "I will be. How do you do it?"

"Do what?" Livvy's forehead creased.

"Stay so calm."

"Oh, I'm anything but calm. But years of living in polite society back in Cincinnati taught me the art of holding back. It helps mostly. And in a way, by not responding, you don't give Goose the satisfaction. It's what he wants. For you to respond."

Jenny's mind wrestled with Livvy's words. It made sense, but she still didn't like it.

They crossed under the Taylor Ranch sign and Jenny chose to let go of the discomforting sensations and instead focus on the beauty before her. Large cows stood, munching on grass, their horns reaching farther than her arms could spread. Chickens pecked at their feed in the chicken coop, a quiet rooster, less colorful than Bert, kept watch. The house came into view, and Luke and Ren stood on the porch.

Her heart skipped a beat. She forgot Ren would be here.

Both men came down and helped them alight. When she placed her hand in Ren's, the sensations were completely different and very welcome. However, the butterflies in her stomach would need to calm down if she were to eat anything during the picnic.

He held out his right arm, and she slid her left through his.

She glanced at him while he smiled at her. His new hat added a certain air to him, and she liked it.

He led her toward the barn. "Caroline and Rose let it be known that you have a fondness for Fanny, and that I'm supposed to take you to her right away and give her these." He opened his other hand to show two small carrots.

Her heart soared. "Oh, yes. That would be wonderful. Thank you, Ren."

They both lapsed into silence as they strolled along the path. But it wasn't uncomfortable. In fact, it felt most ordinary.

"I wanted to let you know that Luke filled me in concerning what happened the other night." Ren looked straight ahead.

Her face heated. "Oh, it's so embarrassing. Yet scary too. I've been trying to not think about it."

"I'm sorry to bring up something so unpleasant, but I wanted you to know that you and Livvy both can come to me for anything. Between the three of us—Arthur, Luke, and myself—we want to keep you safe and ensure no harm comes your way. We don't fully understand what is going on. But we don't want to let others become aware, either. Which is why I wanted to tell you I knew. So I could be there to help you if you need it."

"Thank you, Ren. That is thoughtful of you. I'm glad you're willing to put yourself in danger's path, if necessary. Mr. Martin told us the same thing. Scary to think about. I was hoping it would all go away, but you all are taking it quite seriously, aren't you?"

"We are. Your safety and security are the most important things to me, Jenny. *You* are important to me."

Jenny fidgeted with her bonnet strings.

"Is something the matter?" he said.

"Well, see ... I'm not sure how to bring this up," she said.

"You can tell me anything, Jenny. Anything." He stopped them before they entered the barn, her arm still through his. "What is bothering you? Did I say something wrong?"

"Oh, it's not you. Just this morning, Goose—"

"What did Goose do?" Ren's eyes turned cold.

She hesitated. "See, this is why I was afraid of saying anything. As if I'm reading more into it than necessary."

Ren's nostrils flared. "Please, continue."

"I just have this uncomfortable feeling when I'm around him, which I don't have with you. This morning, he leered at me, if that's a word. And when he offered a hand up into the gig, um ... his hand wandered." She swallowed and looked down. She couldn't meet his eyes.

A moment passed before he spoke. He released her arm, and placed his finger on her chin and lifted her head. The touch sent a shiver through her. "You should trust your instincts. They are sound. I've observed Goose's behavior elsewhere, and I do not trust him. Please, I want you to stay away from him. And let me know the moment anything else happens. And in the meantime, I will speak with him."

She placed her hand on his arm. "Please don't say anything to him. I know you want to protect me, but I don't want to cause additional strife between you two. You have to work together. Today was nothing I couldn't handle. You asked for me to tell you if anything else had happened."

He reached for her hand and held it in his. "I'm glad you did. I meant what I said. You are important to me, Jenny. I care about you. As ... as more than a friend."

Her pulse raced. She licked her lips. Leaned forward. Wait, what was she doing? She frowned.

He stepped back, still holding her hand. "I sound too forward. I apologize if that made you uncomfortable. That was not my intent."

She pulled on his hand to bring him back to where he was. "No, please. Don't apologize. I haven't had someone pay me so much attention before. I ... I like it. Even though I shouldn't."

His brows furrowed. "Why shouldn't you?"

She shook her head. "I ... don't know. It's just that ..."

His eyes searched hers. "Yes?"

"All my life, I've wanted someone to acknowledge me. To really see me. You do. You see me. And I'm not sure what to do with that. Especially if I'm going to teach next year. If I sign a contract with Washton, I can't be seen with you. At all. It's so confusing."

Ren placed her arm back through his. "You deserve to be seen, Jenny. And none of us know what the future holds.

Sometimes, we have to have faith to step into the unknown. That's why there are several Bible verses giving advice for when we worry. For now, let's worry about tomorrow, another day. And enjoy what we've been given today. Shall we go feed Fanny her snack?"

Jenny searched Ren's face. There was no trickery. No false words. Just truth. And a chance to enjoy a beautiful day. He was right. There were so many what-ifs to think about, but they didn't have to be answered right here, right now. Her smile grew, lifting her heart along with it. "Lead the way."

* * *

THANKFUL to not have his time with Jenny ruined, Ren led her into the barn. He would have to deal with Goose, but later. And he would ride back with Jenny. No way would he allow her to be in the livery without him from this day forward.

But for now, Ren had to calm his racing heart.

He breathed in and out. His senses on high alert as he tried to process the multiple messages he received outside the barn.

First, she trusted him. That alone meant so much. But he wanted more. When he shared with her that he cared, she didn't go running. Did that mean she wanted to be more than friends too? Which led into his third observation—did she want him to kiss her?

He sure wanted to, especially when she licked her lips. Now his mind wouldn't sway away from the idea of kissing her. But then she frowned, and he panicked. She didn't reject him outright, but she didn't believe she deserved someone caring about her. But maybe it was more than that. That she was unable to look past his scars and love him more than a friend.

There was much to process, but for now he shoved all of it aside.

Fanny placed her head over the stall, happy to have visitors.

"Hello, girl. Did you miss me?" Jenny approached the horse.

Ren handed her one of the treats.

"We brought something for you." She held out her hand palm up with the carrot in the center.

Fanny's lips curled up as she reached for the treat. Her long tongue lapped it up quickly.

Jenny giggled. Oh, how he'd love to hear that sound all the time.

Coal neighed, and he went over and gave him the other treat. "Good boy." He made sure his horse had enough water and then went back to stand next to Jenny.

Together they stood, quiet, letting the animals have their say, petting the mare, sharing in the peace that surrounded them on this beautiful ranch. He loved what Luke had out here.

When Ren had arrived earlier that morning, Luke showed him all around. Cows, chickens, horses, and land as far as the eye could see. Jimmy, the foreman, joined them, and together they talked about the long-term plans for the property, including their idea for a new metal gate and latch system. Ren was intrigued and liked the collaboration.

But right now, he couldn't take his eyes off Jenny. He was easily falling in love with her, if he hadn't already. She was beautiful, smart, and had a quiet inner resilience he admired. Her acceptance of his scars and his temperamental self touched him deeply.

He had never pursued a woman before and had no idea what he was doing. He still wanted a kiss. Or two. How did he initiate what they started outside?

As if he said that out loud, she glanced him and tilted her

head. His face heated. If she only knew where his thoughts had taken him.

"Thank you, Ren, for bringing me here right away. I was looking forward to seeing Fanny the most. Somehow on my first visit, she and I just connected. I've always wanted a horse." She gazed into his eyes with a dreamy, far-off look.

Without thinking he leaned forward.

She leaned in and closed her eyes.

Something wet and slimy hit Ren in the mouth, just before their lips touched.

"Fanny!" Jenny yelled. Her eyes met Ren's, and she laughed so hard she doubled over.

Ren laughed too. A hard belly laugh that caused his eyes to tear. It seemed either the horse wanted to be a part of their first kiss or didn't want the attention swayed from her. When he finally had enough air, he wondered if the moment was gone now. Or would he have another chance?

Jenny stopped laughing and stood, eyeing Ren warily.

Ren stepped back. "I'm sorry if I overstepped."

Her gaze softened. She bit her lip.

Which drew his attention back to her lips.

"There you two are," Caroline said as she walked into the barn. "I was sent to tell you we are all gathering in the field by the house. It's time for our picnic."

Maybe this was the way it was meant to be. "Great. I'm starved," said Ren. He offered Jenny his arm. "Shall we?"

She hesitated, and his heart sank. But a moment later, she threaded her arm in his and squeezed. "Thank you again," she said.

What was she thanking him for? He studied her, an acute desire to know what she thought.

She stopped, tugged on his arm. "Caroline, I need to do one thing first. We will be there in just a moment."

"Okay. See you outside," Caroline said.

After the young girl ran outside of the barn, Ren looked at Jenny. "What do you need to do?"

"This," she said, a little breathless. She stood on her toes and leaned into him, placing her mouth on his.

Whatever he expected was not that. His nerve endings stirred and tingled as he felt her warm, soft lips on his. A small flowery whiff floated into his senses. It took his brain only a moment before he forgot they were standing in a barn, the smell of horses and hay surrounding them. He wrapped his arms around her and joined in the kiss he had wanted for so long. The one *she* initiated.

Even if she never wanted to kiss again, he'd be a happy man.

She pulled back and slowly opened her eyes. A slow smile grew on her face.

He still held her in his arms. Perfectly.

As the haze in his brain cleared, the obstacles between them popped into his mind. What about her teaching contract? He didn't want to do anything that would cause her to not follow through with her plans.

Although he told her not to worry about tomorrow, for it should take care of itself.

Ren was going to do exactly that for the rest of the day. "Shall we?" He offered her his arm.

Her face glowed as she smiled back at him. "We shall."

He walked out of the barn as if he were walking on air.

Eighteen

He kissed me! Well, maybe I should be honest, I kissed him. Is that proper at all? No, don't answer. I can't wait to see him again, but maybe I shouldn't allow my heart to let this man in.

—From the journal of Jenny Millard

Livvy tapped Jenny's arm. "I'm sorry to break up a lovely day, but it's time we head back."

Jenny's heart sank. She was having the best time today and didn't want it to end.

Ren stood with them. "I'll ride back with you." He followed Luke to the barn to get the horses.

Jenny was sure it had everything to do with what she told him about Goose, and she was grateful. She really didn't want to spend any time in that man's presence. She busied herself, folding the blankets and putting the leftover food into the basket. But it wasn't enough to keep her thoughts at bay.

Had she really kissed Ren? She had, and she didn't regret it. The feel of his arms around her provided the safe haven she had never known. But what did this mean for her and teaching? She'd have to come clean with Livvy and ask her advice. But with Ren riding back with them, that conversation would have to wait till tonight, when they were alone in the room they shared.

Luke led Arabella and the buggy toward them and helped Livvy in.

Just before he reached for Jenny, Ren stepped in and offered his hand. The one with the scars. The gleam in his eyes told her he wasn't paying any attention to his hand, as it should be.

She placed her hand in his, and the current that connected them lit something inside of her. Never had she had such a caring gaze caress her before. He told her she was important to him. He saw her. She mattered to him. And she cared for this man. More than she wanted to admit. It was all moving so fast. Yet, was it? They hadn't discussed anything. Just admitted they liked each other for more than friends.

Jenny had to stop fretting. But all her life, she'd been anxious about something. Worrying was all she knew. Where would the next meal come from? Would there be enough work brought in to cover the expenses? So many things. How could she even think about forming a relationship with someone when she only knew heartache? She didn't want to subject him to that.

Livvy snapped the reins, and they set off for Washton.

Ren rode along on Jenny's side. Coal was a beautiful horse, and together rider and animal worked as one. Ren's hat added to his rugged good looks.

Livvy elbowed her and she turned and faced her friend. Livvy raised her eyebrows. "You haven't taken your eyes off of him the entire time."

"Am I that obvious?"

"Yes, and I think it's wonderful."

"But what about teaching?" she asked, anxious to know her friend's thoughts on the matter.

"What about it? Do you want to teach?" Livvy asked as she handled Arabella around a curve.

She glanced at Ren and lowered her voice. "I do in the sense if that's what I can do to support myself. But—"

"But what if you don't need to support yourself?" Livvy asked.

Jenny's lips parted but no words came out. Could Ren hear their conversation? What if she was getting ahead of herself, and there wasn't going to be anything further than what transpired today?

"Just what I thought." Livvy grinned. "We can talk more tonight." She winked.

They passed the schoolhouse, then the church, turning into the livery from the main square.

Ren followed right after them. Jumped down from Coal and grabbed the bridle on Arabella.

Goose came from the back and headed to help them exit the buggy, but Ren tossed the reins to him. "Here you go, Goose. Jenny, let me help you and Livvy down." He closed the gap in two steps. Instead of holding out his hand, he held her by the waist and swung her down. Her stomach flipped, and the sensation flowed outward to her limbs. She was a little off balance when he placed her on the ground. Her hands were on his strong forearms, and she could feel the muscles flex underneath. They stood there together a moment longer.

"Thank you, Ren." Her lips lifted into a smile she couldn't contain.

Livvy stood in the gig. "My turn, Ren." She held out her arms, and he lifted her by the waist, too, but set her down quickly. "Thank you," she whispered.

His fingers touched the brim of his hat as if he had always

worn one. He held out both elbows. "Ladies, let me escort you home." Then called over his shoulder. "I'll be back, Goose, to check on the horses tonight." Leading them both out the door and onto the street.

"Nicely done, Ren," said Livvy.

"I have no idea what you mean, Miss Carmichael." Ren winked at Jenny.

Jenny narrowed her eyes. "Remember what I said earlier. Please, Ren."

"I know. I promised. And I'll try to keep that promise," he replied.

Livvy leaned over and glanced at both of them. "Do I want to know?"

"No," they said in unison.

In the time it took to converse, they were already at the Martins' porch steps.

"Thank you again, Ren," Livvy headed inside the house.

Jenny turned to face Ren. She'd already told him thank you. What more could she say. She found it ironic that she, not Livvy, was the one now standing in the street with a man for all the world to see.

Yes, she wanted to kiss him again, but was she ready to make such a statement? Was it even proper for them to be standing so close in public? There were so many rules she didn't fully understand, nor did she want to throw herself at him. Did he want to kiss her?

She opened her mouth to apologize for being so forward earlier, but he stepped back, nodded his new hat in her direction, and walked away. Did that mean he wasn't interested anymore?

Later, as Jenny and Livvy readied for bed, Livvy asked, "Did you enjoy your time with Ren, today?"

Jenny nodded, not knowing how to answer her friend.

"Good."

She swiveled around. "Good? I'm not sure what I'm doing."

Livvy grinned. "Then you're doing something right."

"I'm not sure I want to talk about Ren tonight, but I do want to talk about praying in my journal. With church tomorrow, I'd like to learn how to pray better."

"Jenny, there is no right or wrong way to pray to God. He just wants us to talk with Him. So be yourself, and write what is on your heart." She picked up a piece of paper. "Here, we can both write at the same time."

Jenny cringed. "I'm sorry you don't have your journal. Maybe it will still turn up."

Livvy pinched her lips. "I hope whoever has it has learned something about God." She shook her head. "And grown a conscience. For now, I'm okay with writing on paper. Let me know if you want help, but I think you're capable of doing it on your own."

"Am I? I felt woefully inadequate yesterday in the classroom." Oh, why did Jenny say that?

Livvy's eyes widened. "You did?"

"Forget I said anything."

"No, Jenny, let's talk about this. Why did you feel inadequate?"

"Because I didn't have anything to do," she blurted.

"I see." Livvy placed her finger on her cheek.

"What do you see?" Jenny asked.

"You equate your worth based on what you can accomplish."

Jenny threw her arms wide. "Of course, I do. Doesn't everyone? That's how we show value to those around us."

"But not to God, Jenny. You matter to Him no matter what you do. You don't have to accomplish anything to receive His love." She opened her Bible. "I wrote this verse down one day to help me understand it better. Romans five verse eight says, *'But God commendeth his love toward us, in that, while we were yet sinners, Christ died for us.'* Nowhere does it say we have to do specific things. He just loves us."

"That's so hard to fathom. If He loves me, why do I feel so worthless?"

"That's because you've been told lies by people who should've loved you all your life. It took me a while to let this sink in as well. Give yourself time. Open your heart. Write a prayer to God, asking Him to show you."

Jenny sighed wistfully. "Ren told me today that I mattered to him. I've never had anyone say that to me before."

"Yes." Livvy raised her hands in the air, then stood and came over to Jenny. Squeezed her hand. "You matter to me, too, Jenny. I may not have said those words, and I'm sorry about that. But I hope you know you matter to me."

Jenny nodded. A loose tear slid down her cheek.

Her friend put her arms around Jenny and hugged her. "Lord, please fill Jenny's heart with Your love. Let her know how worthy she is to You so she may see Your truth. Amen."

"Thank you," she whispered.

"No, thank *you*. I need the reminder too. Come, let's sit down and spend time writing a letter to God." Livvy led Jenny to the bed, where they both sat and wrote.

Jenny wasn't sure what Livvy was writing, but she put down whatever was in her heart.

She hoped the Lord would answer her tomorrow at church. But first, she would try not to worry about tomorrow and instead focus all her thoughts on this moment, right now.

* * *

On Sunday morning, Gideon and Ren sat in the pew behind Jenny and the Martins again. As much as he wanted to sit next to her, he was thankful he could at least be near enough to hear her beautiful voice. Ren found sitting in church with others added to the connection he had felt with God. He didn't know how to explain it, but he could feel it.

The seats were full, and though a few heads nodded, many sat listening intently to what Pastor Will had to say. "You may find you have choices every day, and you don't know which one you should choose. Could God bless you with one of them? Absolutely. Could He bless you with the other one? Absolutely.

"Walking alongside God is not an easy thing to do. Not when we second guess ourselves and have trouble making decisions. Don't let fear get in the way of your faith. You have to pray and believe that He will answer your prayers."

Did Ren do that? Let fear get in the way of his faith? Had the fear of people seeing his burned hand stopped him from believing he could be accepted as he was? Jesus wasn't accepted everywhere He went, but that didn't mean Ren believed less. Back home, he knew how everyone looked at him, but he wasn't fearful anymore. He accepted it and kept to himself. But here, the chance to belong, to fit in, was present, and Ren had been fearful of something going wrong. Such as when he kept his hands covered the first time he attended church. Or refused to help customers and staying in the back of the shop.

When he did those things, who did he hurt? Who was the one he held back?

Himself.

And what about being open for God to use him?

He'd missed all of that because of fear!

Ren never considered himself a fearful person. He would stand up to any man if he had to. Would hunt four-legged beasts when needed. He wasn't afraid of a fight. But he *was* afraid of fitting in. If he could move beyond that fear, beyond the limitations he put on himself, what would his life be like? As he thought about the past few weeks, he could see how God had been helping him face his fear. And he had taken more steps in his faith.

As the pastor asked for everyone to bow their heads to pray, Ren bowed his head. *Dear God. Thank you for all You have provided and done in my life. I never realized I was living in this type of fear. Help me to overcome it. Help me to change, God. I am only able to by Your grace. Amen.*

As he raised his head, he wiped his eye.

Gideon patted him on the back. He didn't think Gideon would believe him if he said he had something in his eye. He looked at Gideon and smiled. This man had done so much for him by opening his eyes so he could see the world a different way. If he hadn't, he wouldn't have had the opportunity to build this new friendship with Jenny.

She looked over her shoulder as they stood to sing a closing hymn and smiled shyly.

He looked forward to spending the afternoon with her again at the Martins' for the Sunday meal.

* * *

WHEN JENNY ARRIVED at church with the Martins and Livvy on Sunday morning, her mind couldn't focus. She replayed the kiss in the barn over and over. And the sensations that came with the warm gaze in Ren's eyes as they sat and ate during the picnic.

What did it all mean? What about her contract? And her future? If she allowed a courtship with Ren, she wouldn't need the contract, would she? She didn't know her Bible verses well but the words Ren shared yesterday were the same words Livvy had said to her before. *Do not worry about tomorrow.* And that was what she was trying to do.

Although today was tomorrow now. So, did that mean she worried about it today, or waited till tomorrow?

She settled in the pew next to Livvy as the service began. After Pastor Will's message about not letting fear get in the way of your faith, Pastor Will asked everyone to stand and sing. "Please turn your hymnbooks to page ten as we sing *Amazing Grace*."

Everyone stood. Chrissy handed their hymnbook to Livvy, and Jenny glanced over her shoulder before she looked at the book. Her heart sped up as her and Ren's eyes met. She quickly turned back around and studied the words in the small family hymnal.

As the pianist pressed the keys, people all around her sang out, the words slowly penetrating her heart.

> *Amazing grace. How sweet the sound,*
> *that saved a wretch like me,*
> *I once was lost, but now I am found,*
> *Was blind but now I see.*
> *Twas grace that taught my heart to fear,*
> *and grace my fears relieved;*
> *How precious did that grace appear,*
> *the hours I first believed.*
> *When we've been there ten thousand years,*
> *bright shining as the sun,*
> *We've no less days to sing God's praise,*
> *than when we'd first begun.*

When the melody became familiar enough she opened her mouth and released the music within—singing the words that echoed in her heart. The congregation repeated the first verse, and tears ran down her face as each word sank in further. Her heart was so full, it wanted to burst. Her voice wobbled, but she continued singing.

When the song ended, everyone sat, and Pastor Will began the community announcements. But the last line in the first verse kept playing over in her mind. She was lost, but now found. She was blind. But now saw. She had found Jesus, and He loved her. She was blind to that love, but now she could see that He did love her and wanted the best for her. Did that mean she mattered to him?

How could something she couldn't see now be seen?

She gasped. Did that mean He'd answered her prayer from last night?

"I'd like to leave you all with one more verse before we end. Psalm twenty-eight verse seven says, "*The Lord is my strength and my shield; my heart trusted in Him, and I am helped. Therefore my heart greatly, rejoiceth, and with my song will I praise Him.'* May you all go in peace and sing and praise the Lord this week."

His words landed in her heart, adding layers to which the lyrics of the song had started. Somehow, she felt whole. Complete. As if a piece of her had been missing. She didn't fully understand it all, so she knew she had more to learn. Questions too. But there was time. And she had her journal. She was still trying to figure out how to talk to God. But with each day, it would get easier.

Announcements completed, the service officially ended, and everyone stood and greeted those around them. Jenny turned to face Ren and Gideon.

Gideon smiled and nodded, then faced Arthur, and they engaged in a deeper conversation.

Ren looked wary. Probably as unsure as her about the kiss

they'd shared yesterday. But she didn't want him to doubt himself, so she reached out her hand with the same boldness she showed in the barn. "Good day," she said.

He held her hand in his, lifting it to his lips. "Good day."

"We should head over to our home and continue our conversations there." Chrissy's words penetrated Jenny's hazy brain as she kept her eyes on Ren.

"That sounds wonderful." Ren released her hand and motioned his arm for her to step before him. His entire focus was on her.

Her heart full, Jenny praised God for the friendships she had made in Washton. She hummed the notes to the song they'd sung as she headed toward the door and outside into the shining sun.

Ren held out his arm, and she gladly placed hers in his. He began to hum the same tune, and she joined him. Together, they blended their voices as they strolled to the Martins' home.

This would be a good day. In fact, her heart felt things were right. She really couldn't find the words. Maybe this is what she had been missing the entire time. If she'd had God in her life, maybe all the bad things in her past wouldn't have happened. Well, at least now she knew. Which meant from this point on, her life would become easier. Without the hardships she'd had to endure before.

Nineteen

Thank you, God, for showing me I matter. Now tell me whether I
should be a teacher or not.

—From the journal of Jenny Millard

Livvy and Jenny headed to the schoolhouse Monday morning, Bert clucking behind them. The sun shone with only a few clouds in the sky. Jenny's spirits were high after a wonderful weekend spent connecting with God and friends.

Yesterday afternoon was filled with laughter and shared stories. She learned more about Livvy and Luke, as well as the Martins and when they first came to Washton. She and Ren were able to share more with each other about their families and the events that pushed them to leave their childhood homes.

It was a very enlightening day.

As they passed the church, Jenny was reminded of the songs sung during the service. She hummed the tune, now fully ingrained in her heart. Soon, the words flowed from her mouth. *How precious did that grace appear, the hour I first believed.*

"It's a beautiful song, isn't it?" Livvy asked.

Jenny continued, nodding at Livvy.

"You have a lovely voice. You should volunteer to lead us in singing."

Jenny stopped singing. "I don't know all the music."

Livvy shrugged. "You learn so quickly. I'm sure Chrissy would help you. Or Pastor Will."

Jenny thought about the idea further as they strode into the schoolyard. "I won't say no. I do love to sing. I've never sung in front of people before."

Livvy touched Jenny's arm. "Maybe you could get Ren to sing with you. The two of you together sound amazing."

Jenny smiled. It would be nice to share an interest together. "I'll think about it. And I can ask him the next time we see each other." Which she hoped would be soon.

Livvy held out the key to the schoolhouse and unlocked the door.

Jenny followed her friend inside. She hung her coat on the hook, and went to the stove to light it while Livvy went to her desk to pick up her teaching lesson for the day.

"Jenny, can you come here, please?" Livvy asked.

Jenny hurried over to the desk. "What is it?"

"Do things look messy to you? Is this how we left things Friday?" Livvy's voice shook as she stared at her desk.

Jenny studied where Livvy pointed. The few books were not in a neat stack. Both Jenny and Livvy liked to stack books largest to smallest on top of each other. She glanced around. One drawer was not fully closed. She opened it. The contents inside looked as if they were dumped out and thrown back in.

Before she could say something, Livvy held a small

parchment paper. "This is a verse I kept *inside* my Bible. Why was it in a different section of my Bible and sticking out the side? I never leave it that way."

Jenny placed a hand on Livvy's arm. "Let's not panic yet. We can go through the room and make a list of everything that's out of place."

Livvy nodded. "Good idea." She picked up a pencil and a new piece of parchment.

"Let's start with the books in a different order, the paper outside of the Bible, and the drawer contents mixed around." Jenny opened the other drawers. "Make that *all* of the drawers are mixed together." She closed them. "I'll help you set them right while you are teaching today."

"Thank you." Livvy's smile was tight.

Jenny moved over to the student's slates. "Is this how the children normally stack these?"

Livvy joined her. "No."

"Write that down as well. What about these books?"

Livvy shook her head. Her face crumbled, and she sat at the nearest bench. "Why?"

Jenny tried not to let her own fear show. "We don't know anything. But we do need to tell Ren and Luke. Once the students arrive, I'll go to the smithy and let Ren know."

Screech.

Bert's cry came from the porch near a window on the side of the building.

Both Jenny and Livvy jumped.

"What on earth are you doing there, Bert?" Livvy and Jenny approached the window cautiously.

"He hasn't done that before?" Jenny asked.

"No. Never. I've never even seen him on the porch before." She reached for the window and raised it.

Screech.

Bert opened his wings, then pecked at the ground.

Jenny saw fresh paint chips where he pecked. She leaned out the window. "Look at what Bert found."

Livvy joined Jenny in the window. "This must've been how they got in. You'll need to tell Ren that as well." She shivered. "Thank you, Bert."

Screech.

He folded his wings and hustled around the building.

Screech.

Children's shouts could be heard from outside.

"We need to get everything ready. Let's not mention this to the children." Livvy rushed to the chalkboard and wrote the morning lesson.

Jenny agreed. She picked up a pile of slates and set them on each desk.

Screech.

"Time to let them in. Ready?" Livvy walked to the front door to ring the bell.

Jenny wiped her brow as she hurried to finish her task. "Ready." She followed Livvy outside. Livvy handed her the list they had made, and then Jenny waited by the railing. Once Livvy took the children inside, she ran down the steps and out of the schoolyard.

Screech.

Bert flapped his wings and ran after her.

Ren would be relieved to know she didn't come all by herself.

* * *

REN HELD the hot iron with the tongs and placed it on the anvil. Using the technique he had taught himself, he held the metal in place with his right hand, and with his left, he lifted the six-pound setting hammer and began to pound. Each metal and tool hit with a different sound, the tone allowing Ren to know how his hits landed.

He listened till the sound changed, then put the metal back into the forge for the next step.

A commotion at the front had him lifting his head. Soon, Jenny appeared in the doorway. She stopped.

"Jenny?" Her face was all red, and wisps of her hair had fallen out of the bun she usually wore. "What's wrong?" Ren headed toward her, hands extended until he realized he had on his leather apron, gloves, and headpiece to protect his eyes. "Hold on." He quickly removed everything, turned to make sure the metal and fire were safe for a moment, then faced her again. He reached for her hands. "Let's go into the front."

She nodded.

He led her into the customer area of the shop and had her sit on one of the benches. "What happened?" Still holding her hands, he sat next to her.

"Someone was in the schoolhouse." She blurted out.

Ren's heart stopped. He stood. "Now?"

She tugged on his hands, and he sat back down. "No. We don't know when, just that the desk had been sifted through as if searched. Things were left a lot like the bedroom was. As soon as the students were there with Livvy, I came to find you."

"You came here alone?" He frowned.

A sheepish look came across her face. "Well, Bert came with me." She pointed out the door.

Sure enough, Bert stood as if waiting for her. He nodded his head at Ren.

"Thanks, Bert," he called out. Somehow, Bert seemed to understand the significance of what was going on. It wasn't enough in Ren's mind, but he had seen the bird in action and decided any help was better than none. He focused on Jenny.

"Do you want me to come out to the schoolhouse and look around?"

"Will it interrupt your work too much?" she asked.

"Work can wait. As I've said before, your safety is more important. Wait here. I'll let Gideon know and then walk back with you." He squeezed her hand, then left her there while he went to the back to talk to Gideon.

Thankfully, Gideon was of the same mind as Ren in that the safety of Livvy, Jenny, and the students took precedence.

He grabbed his hat before joining Jenny again. "I'm ready. Let's go." He waited for Jenny to exit, then followed her outside.

Squawk.

Jenny and Ren crossed the street, Bert waddling behind them. Neither of them said another word. Jenny was in as much of a hurry as Ren. As much as Ren wanted to stroll with Jenny on his arm, they set a fast pace up the hill.

They came upon the schoolhouse and climbed the steps.

"Let me show you outside first." Jenny led him around the porch along the eastern wall. "We think this is how he got in." She pointed to the window. "Bert actually found the chipped paint and alerted us."

Ren knelt on his knee and sifted his fingers through the fresh paint chips. Then he touched the latch on the window. Fiddled with it a little and saw where the intruder would've broken it loose. Guess he would be making new window locks tonight. "It looks like he broke through the latch here. This is a pretty good lock, but whoever it was, knows his locks. I'll make something stronger to put on all the windows." As he glanced in the glass, young faces with wide eyes stared at him through the window. He waved and smiled, hoping that would help.

"You might want to come in and be officially introduced once you are complete with your work outside, Mr. Lyman,"

Livvy spoke to him through the window in a stern teacher voice.

"Yes, ma'am." He stood and brushed paint chips off his pants.

Jenny giggled. "This way." And she led him to the front door. "We weren't imagining things?"

He shook his head. "No. You were correct in coming to get me."

"Thank you, Ren," Jenny whispered the words before leading him into the schoolhouse.

Scaring the children first with Boaz last week, and appearing in their window today was not what he wanted on his accomplishment list. He hoped he could bring a calming presence instead.

Jenny led him to the front of the classroom. Memories engulfed him, and he swallowed. He was not going to be made to wear the dunce cap in the corner, although the fear of experiencing just that rose to the surface.

"Class, I'd like you to meet Mr. Ren Lyman. He is new in town and working with Gideon at the blacksmith shop. He's here to help fix a latch on the window. Everyone, please say, 'Hi, Mr. Lyman.'"

The children repeated the greeting. Caroline and Rose were heard above the others, their smiles settling his nerves.

Rose snuck in a small wave.

He grinned at her, then turned to face the entire class with the left side of his body. "Hello, class. Don't mind me." Jenny had given him the perfect reason to look on the inside. "I just need to inspect all the windows first, and then, I will be on my way." But he wouldn't head back to the smithy quite yet. He planned to visit the livery again. Something in his gut said this Dusty fellow was the one, but he hadn't seen him except that one time.

When he was finished, he grabbed his hat brim and nodded to the ladies, then stepped out of the schoolhouse to a waiting rooster.

Bert greeted Ren with his clucking, then raised his wings and floated down the stairs.

Ren followed. "Yes, Bert, you are correct. That same someone is after something, and Miss Carmichael and Miss Millard may not be safe."

Screech.

"You've done a great job watching out for them. It's important for you to protect them. Understood?"

Screech.

"Good boy. Stay here. Keep watch. I'll be back later today." He trotted down the hill. Bert's squawking grew fainter as Ren neared the livery.

He slowed his steps as he entered the building. "Goose?" There wasn't a quick answer, so Ren went to Coal first.

Coal neighed and brushed his hat off his head.

Ren caught it before it fell on the floor. He forgot he had it on. He'd gotten used to wearing it.

"What's up, Ren?" Goose asked as he exited from the back stall. He held a rake and had hay all over him.

If Ren was correct, there wasn't a horse in that stall, so Goose was most likely taking a nap. Ren took a calming breath. "Just didn't see you, wanted to let you know I was here."

Goose frowned. "I can see that. You've come over an awful lot lately. It's as if you don't trust me."

"Well." Ren rubbed the back of his neck. He couldn't say anything without giving away information Arthur and Luke requested they keep private. "For weeks, Coal and I rode cross country together, and now I barely take him out, so I want to make sure he knows I haven't forgotten about him."

"Sure, I can understand that. In the middle of the day, though?"

"I was out and thought I'd stop by now before I went back to work. Which I need to do." Ren patted Coal's neck, then stepped back. He reached out his hand to Goose. "Thanks, Goose."

Goose stared at his scarred hand.

Ren hadn't ever put himself in the position to be rejected before. Why did he do that?

Goose hesitated a moment before placing his hand in Ren's.

Ren hoped he wouldn't regret the overture later. He still felt Goose was hiding something. Ren trusted his own instinct, but in this case, he hoped he was wrong.

Twenty

How do we not be fearful, when there are things beyond our control?

—From the journal of Jenny Millard

Ren stood at the anvil, pounding a small piece of iron into a window latch.

Gideon came in from the front of the shop. "They need our help down at the railroad depot tonight while the trains are not running."

"I can go." It would give him a perfect reason to be out, looking for anything out of the ordinary. Whoever they were, they were still around. Still searching for whatever they believed was here. "Is it the gears again?"

"Yes. It looks like there might be parts we will have to replace on a regular basis," Gideon said.

Ren worked on window locks through the evening. It was more than three hours after nightfall when he headed toward the half-finished train depot south of town. Storefronts were closed, but lights were on upstairs, where most families lived. No one was out lurking around except him.

He stepped onto the platform, set down his tools, and opened the enclosure where the mechanism rested. Placing the lantern nearby to provide the best light, he worked on taking apart the gears to reach the broken piece. He set the pieces next to him in the order they went, then pulled out the replacement parts. So far, he wouldn't need to carry anything back to the forge.

This should be a quick fix, and then Ren could scope out the area. Possibly walk out to where Bert had showed him Dusty's hiding place and see if the man was still in town. If he was, he was laying low, as Ren hadn't seen him again. And Goose hadn't mentioned anything about his friend since that first day.

Ren reached far inside the box to set the new part in place.

A baby's cry sounded in the dark. *Waaa.*

Who would be out this late with a crying baby?

The wailing continued.

Someone must be walking by since it sounded close.

Ren finished securing the new part, then placed the others in the opposite order he took them out.

The baby's cries grew louder.

He found it hard to concentrate, and his hand slipped.

After several more minutes of non-stop wailing, he stopped and looked around. He didn't see any movement around the train station, yet the baby sounded near.

He tried to block out the cries while he set the final cap over the gears in place. Whoever was tending to the child didn't know a thing about babies. Ren didn't either, for that matter. But he knew when a baby cried it usually meant it was hungry, thirsty, wet, or tired. This young'un sounded miserable.

The baby screamed.

"Hello?" Setting his tools back in his box, his knees cracked as he stood up. He tilted his head to stretch out his muscles that had been in the same position for too long. Checking his pocket watch, he found an entire hour had passed. That poor baby had been crying the entire time.

He strode along the front platform. "Hello? Anyone here? Do you need some help?"

Did something happen? His conscience couldn't not offer assistance, so he picked up the lantern and crossed the tracks to the back platform, where the conductor's office was being built. No one was on this side, either, so he went around the back. There were no steps nearby to discourage people from entering and exiting where they shouldn't, so Ren jumped down and landed in the dirt.

He brushed his left hand on his pants.

The baby's cries grew louder here.

Holding his lantern in front of him, he crept away from the station toward the open field in the back. That's odd. The cries were more muted farther away. He turned around and headed back to the platform. Now they were louder again.

Was a family hiding under the boards? However, not once did he hear a "Shh, baby. It's okay, baby," or any other whispers.

He bent to his knees and set the lantern next to him. Not a position he wanted to be caught in if this was some sort of trap. With a known stranger watching Livvy and Jenny, by now they would know he was a friend. He wouldn't put anything past this someone who had been searching first the Martins' home, and then the schoolhouse. But who would use a baby for a trap?

Ren belly-crawled under the platform.

A pile of clothes sat in the far corner next to one of the

posts. He couldn't reach it from where he was, so he crawled on his belly.

The cries grew louder.

Reaching the bundle, he unfolded the top cloth of the pile. A small baby laid inside, his mouth wide open. He howled at the top of his lungs.

"Hello there, little one." Ren's gruff voice startled the little guy.

Wide blue eyes stared back as his face froze in position to scream again.

"Hey there. It's all okay. No need to cry again." Why was there a baby here?

The baby searched Ren's face. Hiccuped and shuddered. He was tuckered out from all that crying.

"Who do you belong to little guy?" He was making an assumption it was a boy since he wasn't going to take time to find out right at that moment. His one thought now was to get it out of the cold air and into safety. "I'm going to cover you back up while I move you out." Ren laughed on the inside. Like the baby could understand what he was saying. Still, it helped Ren to talk with him as he covered the baby and wrapped his arms around the bundle. Ren wiggled himself out one slow inch at a time, dragging the clothes pile, baby and all, with him.

A small whimper escaped the child.

"It's okay. We're almost out."

Soon, he was out enough he could raise himself up on his knees. He scooped up the crying bundle and held it close to his chest. The baby whimpered again, which brought relief to Ren's ears. The rest of Ren was wound up tight, knowing someone either was missing their baby or dumped him here on purpose.

Why would he be so far underneath the platform?

The baby cried out again.

Ren didn't know what to do.

"Shh," he whispered as he stood and bounced the little one. He remembered his mother walking back and forth with his younger siblings. Talking in quite tones. "It's okay little one. Shh. It's okay."

The baby quieted down again.

That was the encouragement Ren needed. He continued to pace along the train track. Five steps one way, then turn and walk five steps back.

Soon, the baby stopped whimpering. Ren assumed he had fallen asleep.

He wasn't about to leave the little guy outside all night. Shifting his arms, Ren kept bouncing. "Shh. It's okay." He bent his knees so he could reach down and pick up the lantern. He awkwardly climbed back onto the platform and crossed the tracks to the other platform where he had been working.

Thankfully, his tools were still there. He placed the lantern inside the box and awkwardly picked it up, all while still bouncing the baby in his left arm. His right hand pinched. He hoped it could handle the weight all the way back to the smithy.

He crossed the street to the back alley and headed straight for the cottage. Ren pushed open the door with his backside as quietly as possible. Setting his tools on the small wooden table, he wrapped both arms around the bundle and lowered it onto the table next to his tools.

Ren smiled at the sleeping child. Babies were more precious when not screaming at the tops of their lungs.

He slowly unwrapped the clothing in little sections to take a better look at the sleeping baby. Ten fingers attached to two arms. Two legs that had a total of ten toes. He was right. A baby boy.

"All right, little guy, I need to call you something other than him or baby." He studied the little one further. "How about Joshua? The verse that comes to mind is the ending of Joshua one verse nine, *'for the Lord thy God is with thee whithersoever thou goest.'* God was definitely with you tonight for me to find you. I wonder where you came from? And what am I supposed to do with you now?"

Ren was afraid to move him again for fear he would wake and start crying. He scooped him up in his left arm, then with his right, he piled clothing into a pile right next to his pallet. He gently laid Joshua inside the pile, then held very still. When Joshua didn't make any sound, Ren raised himself up and went to the washstand to wash up.

Would someone come back to look for him? What was he going to do with Joshua in the meantime?

His conversation with Jenny at the Taylor ranch sprung to his mind. *Tomorrow will take care of itself.* "For now, let's worry about tonight and getting some sleep, okay little one?" he whispered as he crawled into his bed and laid on his back.

Ren was beat. He needed sleep. Tilting his head to the side, he looked down on Joshua sleeping so soundly. He immediately wanted to pray, but didn't want to wake Joshua up, so he prayed inside his head. *God, I'm not sure why You had me find Joshua. I pray we can find his family or a good home for him and that You will keep him safe. Give me the wisdom to know what to do. Thank You for Your provisions. Amen.*

The thought he wasn't alone filled him. God was with him and Joshua. As well as Gideon, Jenny, Livvy, Luke, and the Martins. Maybe one of them would have answers in the morning.

* * *

Ren stood in the kitchen, yawned deeply and closed his eyes for a brief moment. He shook his head clearly and continued searching for something he could feed the baby.

Joshua cried softly.

"It's okay. I know you're hungry. Hold on." Joshua had woken Ren up twice in the middle of the night, and even though he only had to gently rock him back to sleep, the broken sleep made it difficult for Ren to awaken at crack of dawn like he normally did.

Gideon came out of his room. "What is all this racket I'm hearing—" He stopped when he saw the baby. "Is there something you didn't tell me when you first arrived Ren?"

Ren wanted to laugh, but Joshua's little cries grew louder, and he didn't have much longer before they would be screams. "I found this little guy under the conductor's platform last night. Do we have anything to feed him with?"

"Where are his parents?" Gideon crossed his arms.

"He cried straight for at least an hour when I was there. I searched the area. Never saw anyone or heard anybody."

Gideon frowned. Yet his gentle gaze landed on the baby.

"I couldn't leave him there once I found him. I had to crawl underneath on my belly to pull him out. I didn't know what to do but knew I had to bring him here, at least for the night."

"You did the right thing, Ren. We should call Doc over." Gideon paused. "And probably the sheriff and Arthur too. They will know what to do. I'll get the forge fired up and then walk over to them both. I might be able to get some milk from the Martins as well. You try to get some water in him, and I'll be back as soon as I can."

Ren nodded and bounced Joshua in his arms while strolling around the room. At this rate, Ren wouldn't get any work done. He was terrified to put him down. He walked to the kitchen cupboard and picked up a cup. How was he to pump water with a baby in his hands? Glancing around, he saw a pitcher. Two steps, and he was peering inside. Relief swept through him to see it held enough for a little sip. He switched arms, then picked up the pitcher and poured what was left into the cup.

Sitting at the table, he held Joshua with his left arm, then placed the cup up to his mouth pouring just a little toward the baby's lips. Joshua's tongue pushed at the cup, but he couldn't put his lips around the edge like an older child would know how to do.

How old was he? He couldn't do much himself, so he had to be young.

A loud pop came from inside the forge. Ren knew it was the fire, but Joshua didn't. His eyes creased, his face bunched up, and he let out a loud wail.

Ren found himself automatically standing to rock him. But this time Joshua couldn't be consoled. He screamed louder and louder. Hungry and most likely needing to be changed, he wanted something Ren couldn't provide.

Ren shifted Joshua to a different position and wandered around the room again.

Maybe Gideon would bring someone with him. Ren wasn't much help. But he would do everything he possibly could for this little guy. A secure string was already attached to Ren's heart. Which now thumped loudly in Ren's chest. How would Jenny react when she saw Joshua?

Twenty-One

I feel like we're all waiting for something else to be stolen. I can't help constantly checking my things to make sure they haven't been rifled through.

—From the journal of Jenny Millard

Jenny got dressed as excited voices filled the front room. She hurried, tying her hair in a simple knot, then placed her apron over her dress. As she entered the main room, Chrissy and Livvy held their hands to their mouths, and Arthur frowned as they listened to Gideon.

He talked fast and moved his arms all around, stopping a moment to nod at Jenny, then continued sharing his tale.

"As I was saying, Ren found an infant last night and brought him home. We don't know who he belongs to, and we don't have any food or drink that would be appropriate for a baby. He's rocking him now. I wanted to stop here first and see if you could help. Now, I'm headed to Doc's."

"You should probably talk with Pastor Will too." Chrissy suggested.

"Good idea. And I planned to let Sheriff Jackson know, if he's in town," Gideon said over his shoulder as he headed out the door.

A baby! Left with no one to care for it? A helpless little baby. Her heart ached for the wee one, and a surge of energy engulfed her. "Do you think I could take care of the child? I have experience from minding my siblings."

Livvy's face brightened. "That's a great idea, Jenny. Grab your things, and I'll help Chrissy gather a basket for you to take over to the cottage."

"I have milk and an old baby cup somewhere in my cupboards." Chrissy went to her kitchen, opening each cupboard door searching for the item.

This baby needed someone, and Jenny was exactly the person for this job. Her heart pounded as she ran to the room and gathered her things. When she came out, she grabbed her coat off the peg, put her arms in, and cinched herself up as Chrissy strolled into the room.

"Here's a basket with a cup with milk and some cloths to use as a diaper. While you watch over the little one, I'll work on pulling together more items." Chrissy held out the hamper.

Jenny reached for the container. "It's a boy, right?"

"Yes, that's what I heard Gideon say. He said something about calling him Joshua."

"Joshua," said Jenny. Strong name. She smiled. "I'm off to take care of him."

Livvy stood at the door, ready for the day. "I'll walk with you on my way to the schoolhouse."

Bert paced outside the Martin home as if he understood the urgency of what was happening this morning. He clucked over to both Livvy and Jenny.

"Good morning, Bert." Livvy greeted the fowl.

Jenny was too preoccupied to talk to him.

Neither said a word as they crossed the street and stepped onto the wood planks, Bert trailing behind them.

Jenny's mind was far away. Could a little baby tell if no one wanted them? At what age did someone sense they didn't matter to another person? She had no idea when she sensed that herself. Just that, at some point, she did. She was determined to make sure little Joshua didn't feel that way as long as he was in her care.

"Penny for your thoughts?" asked Livvy.

Jenny shrugged her tense shoulders. "Oh, I was just thinking about how sad it was for Joshua."

"To be abandoned?" Livvy's words surprised Jenny. She understood more than Jenny thought.

"Yes. Or forgotten. I never felt like I was wanted. I don't want anyone else to feel that way."

"That's why you're the perfect person to take care of him until we find his family or figure out a permanent home."

"Thank you, Livvy. I appreciate your confidence in me."

"It's well deserved, Jenny. You might think you don't matter. But you're wrong. You do matter. To God, to me, and right now to this little baby. I can hear him crying from way over here."

Jenny could hear it too. "Boy, he has a pair of lungs, doesn't he? I better hurry. Have a good day at school." She hurried to the corner, then crossed the street to the livery. She couldn't get to the cottage fast enough. Without thinking she cut into the alley she had seen Ren use. "Bye, Livvy."

"Bye, Jenny. Good luck." Livvy's voice could barely be heard her over the wailing cry.

Screech.

Bert chased after Livvy, doing his job of watching out for her safety.

Jenny bit her lip. Livvy should be all right walking to the schoolhouse with Bert, right?

A large wail traveled from the cottage.

All thoughts of Livvy fled as Jenny approached the entry. Without a thought, she opened the door and walked right into the room.

Ren paced and bounced a screaming infant in his large hands. The man held the baby gently, and cooed soothing words to him, even though they weren't really helping.

Her heart melted at the sight. She set the basket on the table and pulled out the little cup Chrissy had prepared.

Ren turned and halted.

She reached over and plucked Joshua out of his arms.

"Hey, I was—"

"I'm here to take over now." She cooed and rocked Joshua similar to how Ren was doing it a moment ago.

His lips parted, Ren hadn't moved. "Take over!" He yelled.

Joshua cried louder.

Ren grimaced. "I'm sorry Joshua, I didn't mean to scare you."

He turned back to her, a stern look on his face. "I've been watching over him all night. He's familiar with my voice now. You can't just barge in here and pick him up like that."

"I can, and I am," she said. Where was she getting her boldness from? Never had she spoken to anyone like this before. The energy coursing through her gave her courage she didn't know she had. She cuddled the boy close to her chest and gave him time to suckle on the cup she brought.

The room became startlingly quiet.

"Well, thank you, I guess." Ren rubbed the back of his neck

and blew out a breath. "I knew he was hungry, Gideon didn't have anything here for him."

Jenny nodded. "I was at the Martins when Gideon came by to tell them."

"You have experience with babies?" He frowned.

"I'm the oldest sister of six siblings. Yes, I have experience," she said. "I helped my ma take care of them. With each birth, I handled the newborns while she was bedridden."

Little Joshua held his tiny fists on the cup she held. He blinked his eyes a few times, trying to keep them open.

Now that he was calm, her heartbeat slowed back to normal.

She had never resented taking care of her brothers and sisters. She liked caring for them and showing them love. It had been a while since she held a baby of this size, and a yearning deep down inside crept into her heart.

Ren drew close to her shoulder and peered at Joshua. "You're a natural." He chuckled. "Unlike myself."

"It looks like you did just fine," she replied.

Their eyes met over baby Joshua's little head.

She smiled.

He smiled back.

A picture of the three of them as a family entered her mind and lodged there. She knew it was too early to be thinking these thoughts, but could this be their path? To become a family together with Joshua?

Was Ren thinking the same thing?

* * *

REN FOUND himself mesmerized by the woman rocking Joshua. He stood a little too close, but he wanted to make sure Joshua knew he was there. He didn't want the child to think Ren had abandoned him too.

At least, that's what he told himself.

A hint of rosemary and something else he couldn't name drew him closer. But Jenny didn't notice. She was completely focused on the baby boy.

He ran his hand down the front of his face. He needed sleep and a shave. "Um ..." He spoke, just to have something to do, but had no words. He had had his hands full over the last twelve hours, and now they felt empty without holding baby Joshua. How could he have become so attached so quickly?

She looked up at him with a question in her eyes. "Yes?" She whispered.

"I—" His mind went blank. Her smile was beautiful. It went all the way to her eyes. How he would love to gaze into them every day. He reached out a hand to touch her face. Then realized what he was about to do and laughed out loud to cover his actions.

Joshua jumped.

"Sorry, little one." He moved his hand to the boy's fingers and let them wrap around his thumb.

Jenny and Ren stood and watched Joshua for a few more minutes. He didn't want to walk away.

She wrapped her arms around Joshua a little tighter and looked away from Ren.

He hadn't meant to make her uncomfortable. He did have work to focus on in the shop anyway. "If you have everything covered here, I'll go to the smithy now." He stepped back.

"Do you live here?" she asked.

His face heated as she stared at his unmade bed.

When he glanced at her, the entire room shrunk. And even though Ren stood farther away than a few minutes ago, he was drawn to her again. He had to leave. But he didn't want to be rude. Searching for words, he answered her question. "Gideon has been kind enough to let me stay here with him."

"We are both guests of strangers here, aren't we?"

That's right, she was a guest at the Martins' as well. He couldn't help but ask, "Do you plan to stay? In Washton?"

She shifted Joshua onto her shoulder, not even a hitch in her movement as she patted him on the back.

The baby let out a small burp, then relaxed his body.

She sure knew a thing or two about babies.

"I'd like to." Her voice was so soft he had to lean in to hear her. "But I'm not really needed at the schoolhouse with Livvy teaching. And I'm not sure I want to sign a year contract for all of next year."

What was she saying? Did he see hope in her eyes? Was she thinking what he was thinking, that he'd like a future together? He swallowed but didn't say anything.

She looked at the baby. "So, helping with Joshua is perfect. I need something to occupy my time, and this little boy needs me."

Ren didn't miss the idea that Jenny liked to feel needed. "Please, make yourself at home. If you need anything, I'll just be over there." He pointed to the smithy across the yard. "Come get me, and I'll drop everything and come running."

What he really wanted to say was that he wanted to be needed by someone too.

Twenty-Two

I should remember to expect the unexpected. Which has a way of changing, well, everything.

—From the journal of Jenny Millard

The desire to protect and take care of this little one coursed through Jenny's blood. She had no idea where the desire to nurture came from. She loved her siblings, but the responsibility had sometimes been a burden. But right now, she felt anything but that.

Chrissy showed up shortly after Ren left.

When Jenny set Joshua down to change him, she found a man's shirt folded and tucked all around him as a makeshift diaper. "That man is very resourceful," said Chrissy.

Jenny smiled. Her heart still unable to comprehend what a gentle giant Ren was. And how she had come barging in here, yanking Joshua out of his arms. Ren was more than capable of taking care of this little boy.

"He's a keeper, that one." She sent a pointed look at Jenny.

"What about Livvy's contract?" Jenny asked.

Chrissy waved her hand in the air. "We'll figure something out. Watching you two together. Well, it's like it was meant to be. I don't make it a habit of getting in the way of the Lord's plans."

Jenny didn't know what to say to Chrissy's comments, so she busied herself wrapping Joshua into clean clothes Chrissy had brought with her.

"Knock knock." Doc opened the door to the cottage. "I hear we have a little one to take a peek at." He entered and came right to Jenny. "May I?"

Jenny reluctantly handed Joshua over.

After a thorough inspection, Doc proclaimed him healthy. "He must not have been outside too long before Ren found him."

"Praise God!" Chrissy clapped her hands together. "And praise God that Ren worked at the train depot late last night and found him. It was meant to be."

Jenny agreed. It was nice when things worked in a positive way. Baby Joshua was lucky. And Ren was a good man for rescuing him.

"Doc, I'll follow you out. I'm going to check in at the Woodward's store and see if they have heard anything. We don't need to suffocate the boy, and Jenny, you definitely know what you're doing." She winked at Jenny as she followed Doc out the cottage door.

Word in a small town would travel quickly. She hoped that whoever Joshua's parents were, were all right. Did they leave him and get on the train? Or were they coming back, but won't say anything now for fear of being in trouble? Or did they watch from afar, hoping someone would save their baby?

Jenny didn't think she'd ever be able to leave a child behind. She didn't judge, but she felt sad for the parents. That they had no place to go. And no one to turn to. She had a small sense of what that felt like, yet was thankful Livvy and the Martins had taken her in. Keeping those emotions in check, she focused on the baby. He had fallen asleep in her arms, so she set him down on Ren's bed for a spell. Since he didn't wake when she stepped back, she searched for a place to sit in the small front room. She didn't want to look around too much since this was someone else's house, but boredom took over as well as curiosity. She was about to peek under the desk when she heard someone come in the door.

Not wanting whomever it was to wake the baby, she turned around and ran into a solid wall of man.

Ren reached out, his hands surrounding her arms to steady her.

Her body heated from his touch.

"I'm sorry. I didn't mean to startle you," he whispered in a raspy voice. His warm breath tickled her ear, sending goosebumps throughout her body. "I thought I would whisper in your ear rather than shout from across the room."

She was so close to him she couldn't breathe.

"Are you cold?" he asked. "The cool air feels good after working in the forge all morning."

"No," she said. "You just startled me. Why did you come back so soon?"

He shrugged and she felt the movement. "I wanted to check on the little guy. How's he doing?"

Her mouth grew dry. How was it his closeness could cause her body to react in such strange new ways. She swallowed before responding. "He's doing great. Doc says he's healthy. Baby Joshua is fortunate you found him when you did."

He nodded, and his chin brushed her head. "That's good. I worried how long he was out in the cold."

Jenny caught herself before she leaned her whole body into

Ren's. "No one knows who he belongs to. It's like he popped up out of nowhere."

Ren frowned, then dropped his arms and stepped over to watch Joshua sleep.

Jenny immediately noticed his absence.

He studied every detail of the sleeping babe.

Not knowing what else to do, she rushed out her next words. "Who is going to be responsible for him if they don't find his parents?" Her heart kept going in a specific direction, but her mind wanted to pull back a bit. She held her breath, waiting for his answer.

"I really don't know. I care about his well-being, but I'm not suited to take care of him, and neither is Gideon. But I have this protective sense that I don't want him to leave my sight."

Without thinking, Jenny grabbed at Ren's hands and squeezed them with the earnestness and energy of the moment. "I feel the same way. I already love this little boy." She was so into her feelings for Joshua, she almost didn't notice the flinch Ren made when she grabbed his hands. Almost.

Confusion ran through her as he quickly pulled away. Had she hurt him? Or did he not want her to hold his hands?

His voice sounded strained. "I should get back to work. I have iron heating in the fire and it shouldn't be left alone too long."

She watched his retreating back. Did she say something wrong? Was her touch that repulsive? What about the kiss they shared? Why did he react that way?

All the joy she felt a moment ago shattered. The rejection stung. One she had felt many times before. She stuffed her feelings way deep inside. "This little guy needs me, Ren does not." She glanced around. "So here I will stay. With him."

But Jenny couldn't *stay* in this cottage with Joshua. And they hadn't discussed any other alternatives.

What could she do? She would have to take Joshua with her.

* * *

Ren stopped before he reached the forge. Inhaling long, deep breaths, his racing heart finally calmed enough so he could process what happened. He shook his head. What a fool. There was no reason to panic. But he did. And now that he was not in her proximity, he needed to figure out why he reacted the way he did.

He couldn't face her. Not yet. The rote task of putting on his apron and donning his gloves gave him security he didn't feel. Picking up the tongs he moved the hot iron to the anvil.

Pound. Pound. Pound.

What she must think of him? So caught up in the moment, she had grabbed his hands. The unfamiliarity, the weird sensations in his right hand at being touched, and her enthusiasm in her gaze overwhelmed him. So many emotions, and his body just responded.

And she had seen it all. The love in her eyes would be something he'd never forget. But then the hurt. He had ruined the moment. Hurt her.

Pound. Pound. Clang. Clink. Clang.

The ring of the hammer helped him put all his thoughts in order. And there were a lot of thoughts.

Thwack. Thunk. Clunk.

His body hadn't meant to react that way. He didn't want to react that way toward her.

He finished thinning out the five pieces of metal and placed them in the cooling water, then set down his tools on their cloth, and went over to the bench where his Bible lay. It never was too far. "God, please forgive me," he whispered the words as he sat and opened the well-worn book. "The Bible tells us *'Do not be afraid'* so many times and I know this, and yet I still reacted in fear."

That type of fear hadn't surfaced in a long time. Her actions and his reaction were so unplanned. How did he fix this? He had to figure out a way. It was too important not to.

He opened his Bible to one of his favorite Psalms. One of the ones his mother had added to her list. Psalm 55:22: *'Cast thy burden upon the Lord, and he shall sustain thee: he shall never suffer the righteous to be moved.'* "Lord, I messed up. And I don't know what to do. I need to trust You. Help me. Help me to fix this."

His head bowed, he waited for a nudge from God. Anything. In his mind, he handed both Joshua and Jenny to Him because he had to. The entire situation, along with a potential future. There wasn't anything else he could do.

And in that moment, it became clear. Fear made him think the worst, when what he should've done is trust in an outcome after everything transpired, not the what-ifs or the event itself.

An urgency to go back and talk with her filled him. To explain. And to figure out how they would care for Joshua—together. It was obvious they both cared about each other, possibly even loved each other, and the boy too.

He would have to apologize. Hopefully she would listen. If not, it would crush him for her to see him any other way than the hero she thought he was. But he was getting ahead of himself again. Only God would know how she would react, Ren just had to try.

Fully settled, he glanced at the fire and cringed. He had to finish the rake first. It wouldn't do to have to waste time and materials to redo the entire thing because he got sloppy and left half way through.

Besides, it wouldn't take long.

He heated up the last piece that will connect all the other pieces to form the finished shape. Brought it over to the anvil. *Pound. Pound.* The anticipation of the conversation caused his heart to pound in rhythm with the forging.

Once finished, he washed his hands in the bucket. The air was colder as the day turned to late afternoon. He hoped Joshua hadn't cried anymore and felt safe. Ren knew baby Joshua would be showered with love from Jenny.

The cottage was dark when he entered. The fire had died in the fireplace and the stove didn't have anything warming on it. That wasn't usually a cause for alarm, but today wasn't a normal day. There should be a baby and a woman whom he cared about deeply inside. "Jenny?"

No answer.

He grimaced. Maybe she and Joshua were sleeping. He shouldn't yell and wake them up. She wouldn't lay down on his pallet, but maybe she was in Gideon's room. However, that felt a little awkward. Where was she? It didn't take long to walk around the entire home and find it completely empty.

No one was here.

His pulse quickened as a number of scenarios ran through his mind. Was Joshua hurt and she had to take him to the doctor? Did the perpetrator they've been looking for find her and take her and Joshua? White hot fear, different than earlier, filled his body as he searched for a note or some sort of clue. Anything to tell him where to look first.

Then he noticed something. There was nothing here that would've given any hint Joshua was ever at the cottage. A kidnapper wouldn't bother with that, would he? So, that left only one conclusion.

She had left on her own. And she had taken baby Joshua with her.

* * *

JENNY PLACED Joshua on a blanket on the floor while she prepared warm milk on the Martins' stove. She froze. "Oh, no." She placed a hand over her mouth. So upset, she had had to leave as quickly as possible and so she hadn't thought of leaving a note.

Well, she had, but she didn't feel it was necessary to leave one at the time. But now, her outrage had diminished. And Ren would be worried. She didn't want to worry him, but she hadn't felt much charity toward him at the time either.

How could she not take his reaction personally? She'd been pushed away from her parents, from the schools, and parents of her students. People didn't want her around. And Ren had pushed her away as well. Her battered heart couldn't handle it. She thought she had found something different with him. But he wasn't different at all. Was he?

Joshua let out a tiny cry.

"I'm coming, sweetheart." She turned off the stove and took the warm milk over to him.

Ren's action had felt like a slap earlier, which woke her from the dream she'd been having about them. A future she should never have pictured.

She switched her frown to a smile as she gazed at Joshua. For now, she had a sense of purpose with taking care of this little one. Something she desperately needed.

He fussed a little bit. "It's okay, sweet little one. Mama Jenny is here. I'm not going anywhere." She picked him up, and carried him outside, sitting in the rocker Chrissy used on the porch.

Joshua sucked heartily from the cup. The noises he made filled Jenny with joy.

If no one else wanted her, then she would just pour all her love into him. Hopefully, Chrissy won't mind that she brought the baby here. She didn't have any other place to go. No money to make it on her own.

The thought added another layer of sorrow on her heart. She didn't like being dependent on others. She had taken the teaching job to become independent. But that hadn't worked out. It seems things never work out the way they were supposed to.

Like Ren and her.

Why did her thoughts keep circling back to him when it hurt so? Because she cared for him. She *loved* him. And she didn't want things to be over. But what could she do?

Screech.

The quiet noise came from the street a moment before Bert flapped his wings and stepped onto the porch. He must've run over from the schoolhouse.

"Quiet," she whispered.

He lowered his head as if in agreement. Then paced. Was he keeping watch?

Jenny covered her mouth to prevent a laugh from escaping. His actions were odd, yet comforting. But what about Livvy at the school?

Gurgling noises had her shifting her focus from the rooster to the child. Small gray eyes blinked at her.

Babies were so precious. They needed so much tender care, quiet loving words, and arms to hold them. All things she was capable of giving. And wanted to give.

Her heart ached with love for this little one. The song they had sung in church filled her heart. She hummed while the words played in her mind.

Amazing grace. How sweet the sound, that saved a wretch like me, I once was lost, but now I am found, Was blind but now I see.

Bert had stopped pacing, and his beady eyes studied her. His head twitched a little, but his feet stood still.

The sun lowered and shadows emerged on the street, cooling things down. She closed her eyes, continued rocking, while she hummed the melody over and over, letting the words wash over her.

Twenty-Three

I think I know what I'm supposed to do.

—From the journal of Jenny Millard

Ren stormed out of the house, into the alley, and onto Main Street, his mood dark. In some ways he hoped she had left on her own. Either way, the scare he just had caused his body to shake. Did she even know how much he cared for her?

It didn't take long to reach the midpoint to the Martins' home, especially with his long legs and the fast clip he set. He must've had a serious look on his face because people cleared a path for him along the way. At the moment, he cared little about the impression he was leaving with others.

A beautiful sound filled the air, and he almost missed it because of all the steam coming from his ears. But, as the Martin's house came into view, it sunk in. He'd heard the voice and the song before.

Jenny. There, on the porch, she sat holding the baby. She

had her eyes closed, as she rocked and hummed and fed him. The sight filled him with something he couldn't name.

Ren's steam abated. He would get whiplash with his emotions zigzagging back and forth. The beautiful sight reminded him what was important. He had no right to be angry. She was way more equipped to take care of Joshua. Ren didn't even know how to feed a baby. But she did.

A bright mix of color flapped on the porch.

Ren hadn't noticed Bert until he opened his wings. He now marched down the steps, his beady eyes on Ren the entire time. Ren knew if he took a step closer Bert would squawk loudly and ruin the precious moment.

Should he be relieved or worried? Would the rooster keep Ren away from Jenny and the baby? What if he considered Ren a threat? The way Ren behaved earlier would qualify as one.

A fear like no other caused panic in his heart. He didn't want to give up the little guy. He didn't want to give up Jenny. So, he had to talk with her. No matter what the fowl did.

He looked up to the sky. "Don't let me mess this up, God." Then strode to the porch.

Bert halted mid-step, tracking Ren's moves.

Ren cleared his throat to catch Jenny's attention. He didn't want to interrupt, but he had to follow through before he lost his nerve.

The singing stopped, and she opened her eyes. They searched all around before they landed on his. Her face didn't show any emotion. He wished he could read her thoughts.

"Hello." Considering himself intelligent, he felt very dumb with his choices of words right now.

"Ren," she replied cooly. Her eyes narrowed, watching him closely.

He held up his hands in surrender. "I came to apologize. For earlier."

She shifted Joshua over her shoulder and patted his back. A large belch came out, and her face turned a hue of pink.

Ren chuckled.

"You don't need to apologize. I understand. I shouldn't have grabbed you like that. You were startled. The honest truth of your reaction reminded me why it would never work between us. And I should apologize for not leaving a note. But I was hurt and mad, and I didn't feel I could remain at the cottage. And I'll just stay away from you from now on."

He grabbed the railing. What was she rambling on about? "Jenny, I don't want—"

Screech.

Bert's warning caused both of them to turn and see Chrissy arriving home.

"How's that baby of ours doing?" Chrissy asked as she climbed up the porch steps. She swooped in and picked up the baby and faced him to her completely oblivious to the tension in the air. Or maybe she was aware and helping to diffuse it. "Aren't you a cute one? Did you drink all your milk?"

Ren was left with his statement unfinished.

Bert flapped his wings, then flew down to the dirt and scampered off somewhere.

Jenny's attention zeroed in on Chrissy. Ignoring him completely. "Any news?"

"No. Not a single lead." She sat next to Jenny, glanced at Ren, and then Joshua.

At least Chrissy hadn't dismissed him, so he stayed.

"It doesn't make any sense. Where would they have gone? There were no trains running last night, and the doctor doesn't think he was outside for long. It's like he's our little miracle baby." Chrissy looked at Joshua again and rubbed her nose up against his. "Yes, you are!"

Ren glanced at Jenny but still couldn't read her thoughts.

He wanted to counter every word she said, but he preferred to not have an audience. He squared his shoulders, prepared for her rejection. "Jenny, would you take a walk with me?" Ren asked. It was a bold move, but he couldn't walk away. Not now.

Her lips parted, and her eyes darted back and forth between Chrissy, Joshua, and Ren. "I can't leave—"

"Go on. I would like some time with this one before we eat dinner." Chrissy stood and carried Joshua inside, leaving Ren and Jenny alone.

He stood and offered his arm.

She hesitated, but finally stood and placed her arm in his. She held her chin high as if raising a shield around herself. Well, he was very good at doing that, too, so he wasn't going to give up that easily. Instead of traveling down Main Street, he led her down the side street toward Doc's home. It would take them around to the church yard. They could continue on to the school yard if they needed more time to converse.

She turned her body away from him.

He placed his hand over hers and jumped into the conversation. "Jenny. What do you mean it would never work between us? You must know, I care about you deeply. And I won't give up that easily."

She glanced his way and then down at her feet.

"I didn't mean to hurt you. And I'm sorry if I did. I don't know why I reacted the way I did, but I'm ashamed of my behavior. It was not what I wanted to do. My hand ..." He hesitated. "It's not used to being touched at all. More so with handshakes lately, but that's with a lot of foresight on my part. But when your hands touched mine, I was unprepared for all the sensations the skin contact created." He squeezed her hand with his scarred one to let her know he could touch hers and not respond so poorly. "You reaching out to me was exhilarating and scary at the same time. I had no time to mentally prepare, and that was unfair to you. I'd say it won't happen again, but I'll need you to please be patient with me."

She didn't say anything, just kept walking beside him.

He couldn't stand the silence. "Please say something, because I've never said so many words in a row like this before. Tell me you will not walk away from whatever is starting between us. Would you be willing to forgive me?" Ren didn't have any other words he could say. He held his breath, waiting for what felt like hours for her to say something. Anything at all.

Would he be able to court her? Or would he have to let her walk away?

JENNY TRIED HARD NOT to look at Ren, but failed miserably. Why did he have to say such beautiful words? She would not be able to keep the frail walls up around her heart when he shared from his own so openly. A tear dripped down her cheek, and she rubbed it on her shoulder.

"Hey." Ren stopped them and turned her to him. They had made it all the way to the church yard. Thankfully no one else was around. "I've made you cry. I'm such a monster—"

She shook her head. "No. No, you're not—" but he wasn't listening. He had dropped her hand and placed his on his head, walking away. Was he groaning or moaning? "Ren!" She ran after him and reached for his forearm, careful of his hand. Placing her other hand on his cheek. "Please, stop beating yourself up, and listen to me."

He froze.

"I'm sorry too. I shouldn't have expected things a certain way. And I shouldn't have run away. I can see that talking about how we feel is important. That I can't make assumptions. I really thought you might be repulsed by me touching you."

"What? That is the last thing I would ever think. What would make you think that?"

She shrugged. "People have pushed me away. Even my own parents, when I wore out my usefulness. I don't know any other way."

"I'm sorry I reminded you of your past. That is not what I wanted to do. I hope you know that." Ren's eyes were filled with compassion and something else she couldn't name.

"This is all so new to me." Her heart ached to go back before they had this argument. Before she ruined things by not realizing his struggle with his past as well. She had to learn to not take things so personally.

He smiled. "Me too."

She nodded. "And we are messing it up, aren't we? I wish we could start over."

He gazed into her eyes. "I love you."

She blinked to hold back tears. She had never heard those words said to her before. Ever. Did she imagine them?

"I can tell you don't believe me, so I'll say it again. I love you, Jenny Millard. And I want to keep loving you for all our lives. I would like to ask you to marry me, but I feel like it's too soon, and we should work out some things first."

Her vision blurred, and she let out a small laugh. "I would like to work toward courting, if that's what you are asking."

"What about teaching? I want to respect your plans."

"I don't think I want to keep teaching if there is a chance I could become your wife during the next year. But for now, I guess we need to figure out where little Joshua will go, and I can be his nanny."

"Or his *mama*."

Her heart soared. "I would like that very much." She let the idea of becoming a mother sink in. But soon, her smile turned to a frown.

"What?" he asked. "What's the matter?"

"It's just that every time I look forward to something happening, it doesn't happen in the way I planned or hoped for. I don't want to count on that, and then for it not to happen. I know that sounds selfish."

"No. It doesn't. It's actually a faith thing."

She looked at him and frowned.

"Hear me out. In fact, can we step inside the church for a little bit first?" he asked. "It would be good to sit down and invite God into the conversation."

She'd been trying to invite God into a conversation, but so far, He hadn't said much. Maybe with Ren, it would be different. "Okay."

He led her into the main door, and into a pew in the front. He let her sit first, then sat next to her. He picked up her hands. "Lord, we invite you into our hearts and into our lives. Please be a part of our conversation. Know the desires of our hearts. And we ask for your blessings as we move toward them, if it is Your will. Please pave the way for Jenny to be able to watch Joshua. And if his parents can't be found, that she be able to take on the role of mama, if that is what she desires. Thank You for Your love. Thank You for Your grace. Thank You for Your mercy. Be with us in all we do. Amen."

She shuddered, trying to hold back some of the tears pouring out of her.

"Hey." He placed his arm around her and held her while she wept. "It's okay. We're going to be okay. Joshua will be okay."

It took her a few moments before she could say anything. "Thank you, Ren. You don't know how much this all means to me. I ... I ... care about you. A lot. There's just so much to take in. God. Joshua. What I need to do."

"I do understand. And you can take as much time as you need. I'm not going anywhere." He pulled back a little but left his arm around her. The comfort from him was something she hadn't had before and it filled up the holes in her heart.

Ren spoke as Jenny opened her mouth. "If I might make a suggestion, I think you have done a wonderful job in taking care of him today. The cottage is not a place for him. Do you think Chrissy would let you keep him at her house?"

She gave him a small smile. "Thank you for saying that."

"It's the truth."

"We'd need to go back and ask her."

"Let's stay here a while longer and just be still and let God commune with us for a bit before we head back."

"Okay." Jenny hugged herself and leaned her head on Ren's arm. *God, if You can hear me, I need Your help. I'm not sure what I need exactly, but I know I need You. I want You in my life. Helping me not to fear what my future is, but to have faith about my future. A future I hope I can share with Ren and with Joshua. Thank you for listening. Amen.*

Jenny caught Ren watching her when she opened her eyes. "You are beautiful, Miss Millard," he said.

He leaned forward, his eyes in question.

She placed her lips to his and closed her eyes.

After a short while, he pulled away. Cleared his throat.

She wanted to tell him she thought he was handsome, but she couldn't get the words out before he stood and offered his arm again for them to walk back.

When they arrived at the Martins', Chrissy was on the porch, so they sat and joined her. She eyed both of them shrewdly, no doubt catching the blotches on Jenny's face from all the tears. After listening to their ideas, she responded, "Ren,

I think you have a point. The only thing is that she is our guest, and I'm not sure what Mr. Martin will say about having a wee one under our roof again. For now, he can stay tonight. And we can talk about it more tomorrow. Maybe a longer solution will arise if we take some time to pray about the situation."

Ren nodded. "Thank you, Chrissy. We already started praying on our walk."

She beamed at Ren. "I can tell you care a great deal about Jenny and our little boy here."

Jenny watched Ren blush. Her heart seized.

He cleared his throat. "I need to get back to help Gideon anyway. Thank you, Jenny, for your help today. And let's not forget that there is still someone out there who might cause some trouble. We haven't seen anything else for a bit, but I don't want us to let down our guard. Luke and I both want to keep you and Livvy safe." He nodded, then walked away.

Jenny's gaze followed him as he stepped onto the boardwalk and grew smaller as he went farther down the street.

"That's one amazing young man." Chrissy sighed.

Jenny inwardly smiled, then searched her lap, then Chrissy, who was studying her intently.

She grinned at the woman, who had become like a mother to her in such a short time. "Yes. I think so too."

Chrissy smiled back. "Well, he's welcome any time." She glanced down the street and waved.

Jenny turned to see who Chrissy was waving at and saw Livvy being driven home by Luke and his sisters.

Screech.

Bert flapped his wings at the approaching wagon.

"I'm glad Luke could escort Livvy home today." Chrissy faced the rooster. "Bert had to leave Livvy at the schoolhouse today, choosing between the two of you." She glanced over her shoulder at Jenny. "He has his work cut out if you two remain in separate places in the future."

"If we are here with you, we should be safe, right?" Jenny asked.

Chrissy shrugged. "Hard to say. Let's go inside and set up a place for this little one to sleep. I pulled out our old cradle earlier just in case …" Chrissy entered the house, and the rest of her words were cut off.

Jenny stood to follow her, but couldn't help but look down the street at where Ren was moments ago. Where part of her heart was right now. What will the new dawn bring?

Twenty-Four

Early the next morning, Ren sat on a barrel and opened his Bible. Knowing he was spending time with God warmed his soul. The anticipation of reading and learning what God wanted to teach him was a welcome emotion, given everything going on lately.

He took out the paper his ma had given him. On it was the verse 1 Corinthians 2:9. He turned the paper-thin pages till he found first Corinthians, then chapter two. Starting at the beginning of the chapter, he moved his finger over each line till he reached verse nine. *'But as it is written, eye hath not seen, nor ear heard, neither have entered into the heart of man, the things which God hath prepared for them that love him.'*

His mom sure knew what verses to share. God had a plan for him, but waiting was challenging. Throughout the years,

Ren had been a patient man. One needed to be patient for the metal to sit right or for the horseshoes to turn out even so a horse didn't stumble.

He'd also learned if you wait long enough, people, at some point, trip over and make fools of themselves. He'd observed this firsthand on numerous occasions by being the guy sitting off by himself and watching.

But now it was his turn. He made amends last night, but he wanted to learn from this and be better—for Jenny and Joshua.

Some people learned from their experiences and became stronger, while others did not and continued to make poor choices. It was clear in this verse how God's intentions for each person came in ways some never dwelled on or thought about. Whether it was to a town that needed a blacksmith, a country that needed a soldier, or a little boy, who needed someone to find him under the train depot.

Gideon stepped outside and sat down next to him. "Nice to see a young man like yourself spending time in the word."

Ren smiled at his friend.

Gideon placed his hand on Ren's shoulder and squeezed. A fatherly gesture that meant a lot to Ren. In a short time, Gideon had become a second father to Ren. "I've seen a lot in my long years, and you can tell what is really going on in a man by how he spends his time. I see you every day, pull out your Bible, and spend time praying. You are quiet and not very social, but there is a strength in you, Ren. One I haven't seen in too many other young men around here. I'm glad you showed up at my door."

Ren's throat closed, and he blinked a few times. He cleared his throat, but all that came out was, "I'm glad too."

Gideon squeezed again and raised himself, knees creaking as he did. "I'll leave you to your own time. God put the words on my heart, and I needed to say something." He turned and walked back into the smithy.

Later, Gideon and Ren used rounding hammers to pound out a delicate shape. It took much skill to pound, then place it in the fire again to keep it at the same temperature while they continued to mold and shape it into the design they wanted.

Gideon dropped the tongs and clutched his arm and chest with his right hand. He looked pale as if he couldn't breathe.

Ren held onto hot metal, so he placed it in the water before running over to help Gideon into a chair. "Gideon, Gideon … can you hear me?"

Gideon mumbled.

Ren interpreted it as a yes.

"Can I leave you to get Doc?"

The pain must've subsided a little as Gideon was able to nod his head.

"I think we need to get you out of this heat. Let's have you lie down first." Ren helped Gideon stand and, with shuffling feet, moved him outside and over to the porch at the cottage. He pushed the door with his back to prop it open as he maneuvered Gideon inside. Then he laid Gideon on the pallet Ren usually slept on.

"I'll be back in a bit." He ran out the door, into the alley, and across the street. Ren hadn't played outside like other kids, but he could run fast when needed. Before yesterday, he wouldn't have known where Doc's house was, but he and Jenny had passed it on their walk last night, so he knew exactly where to go. He found the little house with a doctor sign in the window and hustled up to the door.

Knocking in fast succession, Ren shifted from foot to foot. What felt like hours took only a moment for the middle-aged doctor to come to the door.

He already had his bag in hand, since a knock on his door usually meant he was needed.

"It's Gideon," was all Ren said. He ran back to the smithy. He didn't like leaving Gideon alone for as long as he had.

Doc was right on his heels. "Tell me his symptoms."

How could Doc speak so evenly while walking that fast? He was in better physical shape than Ren had first thought.

"He lost his grip," he paused. "And then clutched his arm." Longer pause. "Couldn't speak or respond for a few seconds." Ren bit his lip. "Oh, and he looked pale, like he saw a ghost."

"Hmm." They had entered the alley and soon were at the cottage door. Doc placed his hand on Ren's arm. "You've done well, son."

"Will he be okay?" That was the only thing that mattered to Ren.

"Let's pray for the best." Doc's words faded as he went into the cottage ahead of Ren.

Ren followed and leaned over Doc's shoulder, catching Gideon propping himself up on his one arm. Gideon's color looked a little better, but Ren worried for his friend.

"I'm fine, I'm fine. Just a little chest pain. It's all gone now." Gideon swatted at Doc's hands.

"Let me look at you anyway, Gideon." Doc didn't bat an eye at the rudeness of his patient.

Gideon swung his legs over the side of the pallet and wobbled. "I have to get back to work."

"I can work on it," Ren said. "You rest." He nodded to the doctor and then headed back out the way they came. It was better than standing there, feeling so helpless.

Ren knew it had something to do with Gideon's heart. Back home he had heard about old man Tom clutching his arm. It was the last thing Tom ever did, so Ren knew this could be serious.

What would happen to him if Gideon died? Ren knew it was selfish of him to think about those things, but Ren did just that. Over the past few weeks, he loved working with the man. He didn't want anything to change.

What was it he'd told Jenny? *Don't let fear get in the way of your faith.*

That was what he needed to remember. He couldn't expect her to believe if he was casting doubts with his own fears.

Pound. Pound.

He struck the metal evenly as he worked out all the terror and panic running through his body. Lost in his thoughts, he didn't hear the doc approach.

Doc cleared his throat.

"Hold on just a moment," Ren shouted and put the piece he was working on to set. He banked the fire. Wiping his hands on a rag, he walked toward the man who could deliver good or not so good news. "How is he, doc?"

* * *

"Doc said he'd need to take it easy for a few weeks," Ren told Jenny. She had joined him on the cottage porch at the end of the day after hearing something had happened with Gideon's heart. Word had traveled quickly, and she asked Chrissy to watch Joshua so she could check on Ren.

He placed his head in his hands. "I can handle the workload in the smithy. But today, I found myself stopping every hour to come back here and check on him. He was resting each time, but what if he has another episode, and I'm too late?"

Jenny listened. She had no words, but she could offer comfort. The fact that he wanted to share his troubles with her touched her deeply.

"What exactly happened?" she asked.

"One minute we were working, and then another, he grabbed his chest. I helped him here and then ran and got Doc. Doc says it's his heart. There's no way to know if it would happen again or not. Gideon accepted resting today, which tells me he really doesn't feel good. But he's not one to stay idle. I have to remember God is in charge, but sometimes that's difficult to do." He sat up. "Here I am boring you with my troubles. Let's talk of lighter things. How is Joshua today? Why didn't you bring him?

She smiled. "You are not boring me. I'm honored you would like to talk with me about your worries."

He picked up her hand in his and placed it on his knee.

Her stomach flipped over a few times, and she lost her train of thought.

"And Joshua?" he prompted.

"He's doing okay. He's showing some sniffles—

"What?"

Jenny held up her other hand. "He's fine. It's perfectly normal for babies to have them from time to time. Both Chrissy and Livvy are watching over him. They had sent me to find out how Gideon was doing, and ... well, to, um, give us a little time together." She bit her lip and glanced at their connected hands.

"Hey." He lifted her chin with his finger, holding it there for a little while before moving his hand to brush back a loose piece of hair behind her ear.

The gesture sent warm tingles throughout her body.

"Does that mean I have their permission to court you? You don't have a brother or father around, but someone needs to make sure I'm up to snuff before I'm allowed to court you officially. At least that's what I would expect." He grinned.

She grinned back. "Something like that."

"Any word on finding Joshua's parents?" Ren asked.

She shook her head. "Nothing. Chrissy talked with Arthur, and together they agreed that he could stay with all of us for a while. There really isn't anyone else in a position to help. And between Chrissy, myself, and Livvy, we can take turns and still do our chores and work at the schoolhouse.

He nodded.

"I did hear Livvy and Arthur talking about the end of the school term. And possibly finishing early. Since it's obvious someone has been lurking around, he didn't want anything to happen to us or the schoolchildren, although Bert keeps a pretty good eye on us." She giggled and covered her mouth.

"That he does." Ren laughed with her.

"No one has mentioned to me anything about next year or a contract. Nor has Livvy talked further about a wedding with Luke." She paused. "But with Joshua now in the picture, all of it looks different. Who knows what will happen next?"

"There's been no sign of Livvy's journal?" His fingers fidgeted in hers. He was unaware that his agitation was showing, but Jenny thought it highlighted how deeply Ren cared and worried about the situation and hopefully, her.

"No. She keeps thinking maybe she misplaced it, but we both saw it on the table before we left for church that day. And with the state of the room and the schoolhouse, someone must have taken it. Livvy doesn't even care if they read it at this point, she just wants it back."

Ren's gaze landed on the livery next door. He narrowed his eyes.

She wasn't sure what he was thinking, so she sat there quietly until he looked at her again. His dark eyes held hers, a mix of concern and admiration shining in them. She couldn't look away, nor did she want to. She could sit here for the rest of her life if there weren't other responsibilities needing their attention.

"I really need to get back. Will you be okay here watching over Gideon tonight?"

"I'll escort you back to the Martins'. And that way I can say hello to Joshua. You really shouldn't be walking anywhere by yourself these days." He stood and then placed his hand under her elbow and helped her stand. "And yes, Doc is coming by soon to check on our patient again. Besides managing my fear, we will be okay." He led her through the alley and then, once on the street, he offered his arm.

She placed hers in his. "More things to pray about. I'm thankful I have my journal, although I feel guilty writing in mine when Livvy can't write in hers."

"Yes, praying is something we can do and should. The list seems to be growing, doesn't it? So does Livvy just sit watching you write?"

"No, she is using parchment paper in place of her journal, so we still are writing together."

"That's good."

With nothing more to say, they walked in silence the rest of the way.

When they arrived, Joshua's gurgles and smiles had everyone cooing over the latest Washton resident. Ren declared he had his daily dose and headed back to the smithy, not wanting to leave Gideon for too long.

Jenny watched him leave and wondered if and when she wouldn't have to say goodbye to Ren on a daily basis. But with Gideon needing to be watched over and Joshua needing to be taken care of, would there be time for the two of them to marry and set up a place of their own?

Jenny tried not to picture the future in her mind. What were the words? *Do not worry about tomorrow.* Instead, she would keep praying for the Lord to help her take things one day at a time.

Twenty-Five

The heart is an interesting organ. We can't stop it from reacting the way it's going to. Who it chooses to love, when it decides it needs to rest, or when it isn't able to stop someone from hurting someone else.

—From the journal of Jenny Millard

Two weeks had passed, and Dusty had yet to find any money hidden amongst the schoolteacher's things. He'd searched the schoolhouse twice now, including the extra room built on the back of the one-room school building, after going through the mayor's house and not finding anything there. Which meant kidnapping the schoolmarm seemed the only option left.

He cringed. He didn't like the idea of kidnapping, yet if he wanted to stay alive and his sister fed for the next year, he had to deliver something—*or someone*—to the Boss Man.

Other than watching her every day, he hadn't been able to figure out what to do. His boss back in Cincinnati would be fuming for answers by now.

The only thing of importance he found was the lady's journal. As he read through every single entry, the words had begun to worm their way into his twenty-six-year-old heart. How she developed a new relationship with God and the people in this town. How she found a new life.

Something he now desired more than anything. But he had a job to do, and he must see it through, for his sister's sake. But he wasn't sure he had the tenacity to pull it off.

He'd seen the teacher dress down a gentleman one day, keep fifteen children in line, and talk back to a nasty rooster, who clucked in the direction where Dusty had hidden a few times. Thankfully, no one had thought to check. He learned after that first encounter to stay clear of the bird, who had followed him to his first camping spot. Dusty did not want to wrestle with that rooster, because the rooster would surely win.

Waiting again for the cover of darkness, he walked along the train tracks to enter town. He hadn't been here for a week or so, since he had seen the ruckus his searching the schoolhouse had created. Decided to lie low after another almost run-in with the younger blacksmith, who had taken to visiting the livery at odd times during the day and night. Dusty could tell from his one interaction the blacksmith was a smart man, who would notice even the slightest noise or movement.

This forced Dusty to sleep in the fields beyond town on dirt and weeds, a far worse scenario than the hay padding that had been offered to him by Goose in the livery. But once he realized Goose could blow his cover, he had to stay away.

At the train station, he jumped off the platform and headed toward the river. Walking along the shore kept him far away from the streets and any people. The moon was a sliver tonight, and he could barely see his feet in front of him. The gentle slosh of the water against the bank conflicted with the violent plans stirring in his brain. How would he get her to talk? Sure, he was coarse around the edges, but he wasn't the one the boss called on to roughen up people. With his reading and writing skills, Boss Man used him to find information. Yet, without finding any money, Dusty was sure he was expected to proceed by whatever means possible.

Climbing the small hill to the schoolhouse, Dusty approached the shrub where he could hide. Critters scampered away from him as he settled deep into the brush for the night. He didn't know if he should capture her inside or outside. Inside, she might have access to something to keep him from taking her, but outside, she could scream.

As he pondered different options, a twig snapped to his right.

Dusty froze.

No one came out this far at this hour. Who could be making that ruckus?

The click of a gun cocking caused sweat to break out on his brow.

"You gonna come out, or am I gonna have to pull you out?" The rough voice sounded vaguely familiar.

He lifted his hands and scooted out from under the bush. "Slim! What are you doin' here?" If Slim was here, then Boss Man already knew Dusty had failed at finding the bounty.

"Keep your voice down, you nincompoop."

Dusty dropped his arms. "I'm not a ninny."

"That could still be determined. I got a message saying I had to come save your sorry hide. You haven't found the goods yet?"

"I've found nothing. She doesn't have any money to her name. I've checked everywhere. She lives like a pauper. Doesn't spend any money, either. Not at all how her old man had set up his household."

Slim grunted. "Boss Man won't like it."

Dusty shook his head. "Nope."

"What you plan to do, then?"

Dusty hesitated. Kidnapping by himself was one thing, but if Slim got involved, he'd take it to a whole other level. "My plan was to collect her up and question her."

"Hmm. That might work. We could maybe ransom her. She got anyone here with money that's taken a shine to her?" Slim asked.

"The whole town has. That's the problem. Everyone loves her. She's never alone. Goose said that there's a rancher fancy with her, but it's not like I could ask questions anywhere. Everyone knows each other, and I'm a stranger." Dusty brushed the dirt off his hat.

"Okay, then, here's what we are gonna do." Slim searched the schoolhouse yard. "As soon as she arrives in the morning, we'll capture her and take her to Sacramento. I know a hideout there we can take her to, and no one will find us."

On one hand, Dusty was thankful for the help, but on the other, he worried about hurting the young miss. She was a smart, pretty thing, and he didn't want any harm to come to her. He felt as if he knew her now that he had read her journal, which he planned to hand back to her once they were done.

"In fact, I'm going to send you over now. I have a small canoe up the ways you can row over with. You've been here so long, she might recognize you, and that wouldn't do either of us any good. I'll snag her and hide her in the wagon I have and travel on the ferry as soon as I've got her. We'll meet at the field across the train station there." Slim pointed across the wide expanse of water.

He'd have to row over in the dark tonight? Dusty gulped. At least he wasn't the one who was gonna have to deal with the feisty Miss Carmichael.

* * *

"Don't worry about things at the schoolhouse. I have them well in hand, Livvy." Jenny stepped back from her friend as Livvy coughed and sneezed into a handkerchief. "You focus on getting better. Teddy and Emily have been helping me each day, so we have a good routine. The students all miss you, but they're working hard to show you how much they've learned in your absence. Hopefully, tomorrow, you'll be ready to return." And Jenny could go back to caring for Joshua.

This was the third day Livvy was too sick to teach. Jenny was able to step right into the role, so the students didn't miss out on their lessons. Chrissy had taken over the care of Joshua when Jenny was at school. Jenny's heart ached being away from Joshua, even for a few hours. She believed he grew while she was away and found she didn't like missing even that much. But she was also thankful she could help Livvy and the town that had been so welcoming. Being able to lead in the classroom with diligent students was something Jenny enjoyed, but not as much as watching Joshua. In some ways, her prayers had been answered. She now knew she wanted to focus on the little boy, who had captured her heart.

After breakfast, she kissed Joshua on the forehead, gave Chrissy a half-hug, and stepped outside.

Screech.

Bert flapped his wings in an arch and swept over to say hi to Jenny.

He still startled her sometimes, but she was getting used to his ways. "Good morning, Bert."

Screech.

"Yes, Miss Carmichael is still under the weather. She should be back at school tomorrow." She picked up her skirt and hurried across the street till she stepped up onto the boardwalk. After a few strides, she didn't hear any clucking behind her, so she stopped and turned.

Bert stood in the middle of the street, moving his head between her and the Martins' home.

Screech.

His worry for Livvy was palpable. He hadn't seen her in a few days, which according to Livvy, had never happened before. And even though Bert had followed Jenny to the schoolhouse the last two days, he seemed torn as to what to do.

Cluck. Cluck. He headed toward Jenny, then swiveled and went back to the Martins' porch.

Jenny sighed. He was one worried bird. And he was making her late. "Bert, I need to go. If you stay and make enough ruckus, maybe she'll come out to say hi. But she needs her rest. I'll see you at the schoolhouse." She turned and hurried off, a little annoyed that the fowl couldn't make a decision. No matter. She had work to do.

The streets were quiet as usual at this hour. Schoolteachers had to arrive early to set the fire in the room, make sure there was water in the buckets, and prepare lessons for the day. Teddy and Emily Woodward had been so helpful, but she didn't want to count on them doing her work, so she made sure to show up extra early to have enough time to get everything done.

Turning the corner at the end of the street, she climbed the small hill, past the church, and into the schoolyard. She scrambled up the steps and approached the door.

A canvas bag came down over her head, and she sucked in a breath to scream.

"I wouldn't if I were you. Save your breath. No one can hear you anyway." A gruff voice came from behind. One she had never heard before. He grabbed her hands and tied them behind her and then lifted her like a sack of potatoes over his shoulder.

She inhaled a mouthful of whatever was in the sack, causing her to lose her breath. The smell made her eyes water and her throat burn. The man's shoulder pushed on her diaphragm making it challenging to take in a gulp of air.

Where was he taking her and why?

Would anyone notice she was gone?

Where was Bert when she needed him?

* * *

Ren pounded out the metal, shaping it to fit his custom design. Years of honing his skills made this type of project easy to construct. He welcomed simple projects like this as his mind was filled with more things to think about. Jenny. Joshua. Gideon. Who had taken Livvy's journal? The fact that no other nefarious happenings had taken place. All of which made Ren a little jumpy at the slightest unfamiliar noise.

Bert seemed on edge as well, especially with Livvy sick and she and Jenny separated these past few days. Jenny went to the schoolhouse herself and taught all day. Bert walked her in the morning, and Ren walked up the hill to escort her home after she released the children at the end of the day.

Then they, along with Joshua, would sit on the porch until supper, spending time together. No one had come forward yet to declare Joshua was theirs. Both Ren and Jenny were ready to become a family once enough time had passed. The problem was, where they would stay when they did marry?

Pound. Pound.

Ren couldn't leave Gideon alone. And he hadn't found the words to talk to him about the future yet. Didn't want to cause Gideon to collapse into any other health issues.

Gideon had healed and shown no additional signs of heart weakness. He slowly joined Ren back in the forge, working on smaller projects while Ren completed the bigger tasks. It made it harder for him to keep an eye on things outside of the smithy, but there hadn't been any other circumstances that warranted them to take action.

Luke, Arthur, and Ren hoped whomever it was had left, because they hadn't found anything in all their searches. Livvy still didn't have her journal back, but life had sort of gone back to normal.

Pound. Pound. Hiss.

He finished flattening the metal and placed it in the water. Wiped the sweat from his brow.

The two pieces he would meld together reminded him of Jenny and himself and how they made a perfect match. He loved her inner strength. The determination to make a life for herself when everything was stacked against her. That she never gave up. The love she showed Joshua and the willingness to fight for him. But he didn't like that she thought she had to do it all on her own. She was a hard worker like Ren. Fully capable of anything she put her mind to. But she was so much more than all of that to him. He couldn't find the words. He just knew he wanted to be with her.

He blew out a breath, releasing some steam like the water did with the metal. Took a drink of water from the pail. A tightness formed in his gut.

His biggest fear right now was for her safety. He didn't know if Jenny had any idea how dangerous men could be when they were desperate. The fact she had come to him right away a few weeks ago told him she did.

He hoped that was the end of it. But somehow, his gut sensed trouble ahead, which made Ren nervous. He didn't like it when his calm was disturbed. Sure, he read his Bible to stay centered, but that didn't mean his blood wasn't stirred up when he sensed trouble.

Do not worry about tomorrow. The words had become a phrase both he and Jenny recited to each other frequently. A good reminder when one of them had their fears taking over their thoughts more than they should.

Like now. Ren had a hunch the man he had seen with Goose was responsible for the break-ins. That he was the one who had gone through Livvy's things both at the Martins' and the schoolhouse. Ren had realized the first time he laid eyes on the man that he was up to no good.

Ren had known people in desperate straits before. To take the time to follow someone from Cincinnati to California would mean they were desperate. Which meant that if he hadn't found anything by now, he might do something rash.

Ren didn't know what that would be. But he worried it wouldn't be good.

Twenty-Six

It's always when we let down our guard that something happens. As if we open ourselves up to change, and the change comes in a form we don't understand.

—From the journal of Jenny Millard

The man's rough hands dug into Jenny's arms as he lifted her, his breath hot and foul on her neck when he shoved her into the bed of the wagon. He removed the bag but gave her barely enough time to suck in a breath and no time to yell before he pushed a dirty cloth into her mouth and tied it behind her head. The man stayed behind her, so she couldn't see his face. She knew only that his hands were dirty, he smelled as if he hadn't bathed, and he had a rough voice.

When he placed the bag back over her head, she fought the panic swelling inside of her. She couldn't move her arms, nor catch her breath. Was he going to kill her? Why? She wanted to ask a bunch of questions, but the man—if he deserved that title—moved swiftly. Before she knew it, he had her sprawled on the floor of the wagon, covered with thick blankets, and then something hard and heavy to hold her down.

She tried to wiggle her way out, but whatever he set on her made it impossible to move.

The wagon rolled forward, and the bumps caused pain in her side, legs, and head. Whatever lay upon her pushed into those tender spots and hurt with each rock of the vehicle.

Thinking about the pain made it worse, so she went back to trying to figure out why she'd been taken. Jenny had never crossed a single person. Or so she thought. Sure, the other towns weren't happy with the status of the school, but was that because of her?

"Yah! Giddy up." The man yelled to the horses. It didn't seem to bother him to whip them multiple times.

If he was willing to hurt his horses, would he hurt Jenny without a second thought?

She shivered and wanted to curl into a ball. But she couldn't move. And she could barely breathe. She could only manage short pants as she tried to catch air. Tears stung her eyes before they ran down her face. Her nose filled from tearing up, making it impossible to inhale.

Her mind reached for anything to help, and it conjured up Ren. The large, caring man with a sweet disposition who quietly supported her since the first day they met. Frightened by the strong emotions he stirred at the beginning, he had broken down those barriers as they grew closer. Spending time talking and sharing with one another. Slowly chasing away the fear that he, too, would send her away once he grew tired of her, or if she cost too much.

They had been so careful over the past few weeks. Never going anywhere without someone watching. But not this morning. She left Bert with Livvy, Chrissy, and Joshua to manage the schoolroom by herself. An independent streak that had now landed her in rough water. Her unwillingness to ask for help, or impatience to wait, sending her into trouble.

Now, she wished Ren was there with her. His strong presence provided a security she did not feel at the moment. He would come after her, wouldn't he? She hadn't told him she loved him yet. But now, she might never get the chance. And that frightened her even more. What would happen to little Joshua? Ren would probably stay in his life. He loved the little boy as much as she did, and that knowledge provided a little comfort.

She heard water sloshing, horses neighing, and men shouting. Others were around, but no one knew she was there. Was she being taken away from Washton?

Her heart accelerated, and she felt like she might pass out. If she did, she wouldn't know what this man planned to do with her. Or where he was taking her.

But she couldn't think straight because the air was thick, and she couldn't catch her breath.

Ren and Joshua were her last thoughts before she lost consciousness.

* * *

REN PICKED up a new piece of iron and placed it inside the brick furnace. He scooped more coal from the bucket and tossed it into the forge along with the iron. It was imperative to have it hot enough for this next part of the process. The heat seared his face and arms. He blew out a breath. He'd take a break after shaping this last piece.

In order to complete his work, he'd risen earlier every day this week so he could escort Jenny back from school and have time to spend with her and Joshua in the evening. He was tired, but wouldn't change a thing.

He carried the red-hot metal to the anvil and picked up his sledgehammer.

Pound. Pound.

The metal moved in the direction he wanted.

Pound. Pound.

He picked it up with the tongs and inspected every side. Satisfaction filled him. It was fully shaped to connect to the next piece.

Hiss.

He placed it in the cooling bucket, then closed off the chimney. He glanced at the clock. It was early still, but he needed fresh air. He'd head over to the Martins' and spend some time with Joshua. Take him for a walk or something. Give Chrissy a break.

He left the smithy and hurried along the boardwalk to the home that connected him to those he loved.

Screech.

Bert squawked in the street.

Which meant Jenny hadn't left yet.

He reached the Martins' and leaped to the top step. Joshua's cries came from inside. His heartbeat jumped at the chance to help take care of the little one.

He knocked on the door.

Chrissy answered, bouncing a screaming Joshua. "Hello, Ren. How can I help you?"

"My next project is cooling, so I thought I'd spend some time with this little one." He lifted a finger and tickled Joshua's tummy.

Joshua stopped and stared at Ren, tears glistening on his cheeks.

Screech.

"Bert, what are you still doing here? Why didn't you follow Jenny?" Chrissy chastised the bird.

Bert flapped his wings.

Squawk.

Ren's heart seized. "Did Bert not walk her to school?"

Chrissy looked at Ren. "I don't know. She left about twenty minutes ago. Olivia is still sick in bed. Is something wrong?"

The fact that Bert was here and Jenny was not turned Ren's stomach into knots, but Ren didn't want to cause any undue panic. He breathed deeply. "Not that I know. Call it God's nudging, but something compelled me to come here this morning. But I thought it was this guy. And maybe if Jenny was running late, I could walk her to the schoolhouse. No offense, Bert."

Screech.

He eyed the bird. Why had he not followed Jenny today? That behavior was not normal for Bert. The knot in his stomach tightened. "Maybe I should go by and check on her."

Chrissy nodded. "That might be a good idea."

Screech.

"I don't know what has gotten into Bert this morning." Chrissy's brows furrowed.

A loud commotion came from down the street.

Ren turned. Luke Taylor leaned over Admiral, riding fast toward them. Caroline and Rose rode another horse a few paces behind. Dirt from the horses' hooves left a trail of dust in their wake.

Ren's heart caught in his throat. Something was wrong. Terribly, horribly wrong.

Luke pulled up right at the porch.

Ren stepped down and over to Luke in three strides as Luke jumped down from his horse.

Ren grabbed onto Admiral's bridle. "What's—

"Are the girls here, Chrissy?" Luke's tone was short.

Chrissy's lips parted. "Olivia is, but Jenny already went to open the schoolhouse. What's going on, Luke?"

Screech. Squawk.

Bert strutted over, his head swiveling in the direction of the Martins', then toward the schoolhouse.

"Slacking in your job, Bert," Luke growled at the bird.

What did Luke mean by that?

"Jenny wasn't there when we got there. How long ago did she leave?" Luke gave a pointed look to Ren.

Caroline shouted from on top of her horse. "Students were there, but the schoolhouse wasn't open. And no one else was around."

Chrissy placed her hand at her throat. "She's been gone for over thirty minutes now."

That was all Ren needed to know. He took off down the street. Pumped his legs to propel himself as hard as possible. His mind raced as fast as his legs. Where was she? What happened? He knew he might not find anything, but he wanted to see for himself.

Maybe she walked to the shore. Or had to use the outhouse. There could be any number of things, but his mind kept jumping to the conclusion that the situation he worried about had come to fruition.

Someone had taken her. And he had no idea who that was or where they had gone.

But he would find her. Even if it was the last thing he ever did.

Twenty-Seven

There's praying and then there's praying. I now know the difference.

—From the journal of Jenny Millard

Jenny woke as she was jostled onto someone's shoulders.

"Good. You got her." Another voice came from somewhere. "Why is she all gussied up like a pig?"

There were two of them?

"What did you think I was going to do with her? Ask her to sit next to me in the wagon?" The first man snapped.

"Can she breathe in there?" The man sounded concerned about how the other was treating Jenny. Maybe that could work in her favor.

"Who cares?" said the first.

He carried her down some steps. Each bump sent a dull throb through her aching body. The canvas was on her head still. Through the canvas, she could make out when the light faded to darkness and the air changed from warmth of the day to a bone-chilling cold. The dust and dirt stung her eyes, causing them to water. Slung over her captor's shoulder again, her belly and side ached with each step.

The gag was still in place. She couldn't scream or yell.

She kicked her feet, and the man squeezed her legs together. "Decided to wake up, now, did you? Good. Now, you'll be able to give us what we want."

The man's words caused her whole body to tremble. What *did* they want? She knew it would tear her heart out, but if Joshua was that important for someone to go through all of this, she'd give him to his rightful parents. Although if they were willing to kidnap Jenny to get their child back, maybe they weren't the best of parents, and he'd be better off staying with her. Was there a way she could negotiate keeping the boy?

She saw black spots. Maybe it was better if she had pretended to still be asleep. *God, if You can hear me in my mind, I could use some saving today. Help me.*

A door creaked open, and her backside rubbed against a doorframe. They must be entering a building of some sort. Her senses on high alert, she listened for any clues. She had to find a way to get out of here. If she survived. *Lord, help me survive.*

The man grunted as he swung her into a hard chair.

Sharp pain radiated from her back, then down her legs. She couldn't rub anything because her hands were still tied behind her back. Tender spots on her body revealed several bruises forming. Including one on her backside because of how she hit the chair.

He pulled on her arms to secure them.

"*Mmphdgh.*" That hurt.

"What she saying?" The second man asked. Had she heard his voice before?

"I have no idea. She's gagged." He didn't seem to care he was hurting her. "I couldn't have her screaming and drawing attention. We wouldn't of gotten away from there if she was making noise." He pulled on the ropes now secured to the chair.

Pain shot up her arms. "*Mghdkm.*"

"Don't hurt her." The second man's voice was closer now.

"You want answers, right?" Her captor went to work tying her feet to the chair legs.

Jenny cringed as the man's hands wrapped around her ankles. She wanted air. And a bath. She closed her eyes. Tried to calm her mind. What could she do?

The repulsive man placed his hand on her shoulder as he stood. "You'll hurt yourself more if you try to move, scream, or get up out of this chair," he whispered in her ear.

The hot air through the canvas bag caused her to gag. She tried to cough, and her stomach convulsed.

"You ready with your questions? I don't want to take the cover off until we have to. But we won't get any answers from her if she passes out again."

"She passed out?" The other man kept asking questions. It sounded as if he wasn't happy with how she was being treated.

That made two of them.

"I've never done no kidnapping before, and Miss Carmichael is a sweet lady. She don't deserve this type of treatment." The second man sounded indignant on her behalf.

Miss Carmichael? Did these men think they had Livvy? So, they'd been correct. This was about Livvy all along, and not Joshua. Jenny's mind raced. What would happen when they realized they had the wrong schoolteacher?

"How do you seem to know her so well if you've never interacted with her?" The first man's words held an edge to them.

"You can learn a lot about someone by just observing." The

second man sounded angry now. "This was not how this assignment was supposed to go."

"Well, Boss Man needs to know some things, and he was tired of waiting on you. That's why he asked for my help."

The other man sighed. Scuffling sounded to her right. The click of a door told her she was shut in whatever room this was.

If they treated her this way, thinking she was Livvy, what would they do to her once they knew she wasn't whom they sought?

"We may as well take off the hood now."

Jenny prepared herself for a shock.

The two men stood on either side of her, their pants brushing her arms.

She held herself rigid and ignored the sensation. *Lord, help me.* Those were the only silent words she could think to pray.

The hood shifted as they lifted it off her head.

Her jaw clenched. She blinked at the light from a lantern shining in her face. Everything was blurry, and she couldn't open her eyes fully. Her heartbeat thrashed in her ears.

"What did you do? *That's* not Miss Carmichael." The second man's voice bounced off the walls throughout the room.

* * *

"WHAT DO YOU MEAN, that's not Miss Carmichael? She's the schoolteacher." Slim pointed at Jenny.

Dusty sighed. "That's not her. She's the *other* schoolteacher." This entire stint had gone wrong from the beginning. He knew deep down that Olivia Carmichael was left with nothing from her no-good father. But Boss Man wouldn't accept it. Now, it was his head on the chopping block if he didn't produce the missing funds. But he didn't stand a chance to do that with the wrong victim.

"You didn't tell me there were two of them." Slim's eyes narrowed.

Dusty didn't care. "You didn't ask. Were the two of them together?"

Slim shook his head. "No. Only this one. Why would Washton have two teachers?"

"I don't know. But this one came later and is a friend of Miss Carmichael's." He looked at their quarry. Big brown eyes widened in fear. Dried dirt streaked all over her face. Her hair was tousled with hay stuck in it. They had done this to her. And for what?

Nothing.

He cleared his throat. "Miss. You don't happen to know if Olivia Carmichael has money hidden somewhere?"

Her eyes widened, and she quickly shook her head.

Slim threw his hands in the air. "She's not going to answer when you ask like that." He stormed right up to the woman and put his nose right to hers. "Where's the money?" he growled.

Her body grew rigid, and she pressed herself back against the chair. Tears pooled in her eyes. Her head swiveled between Dusty and Slim. When her gaze landed on Dusty, the pleading in her eyes was too much for him to bear.

"She can't answer with a gag in her mouth." Dusty walked behind her and untied the bandana.

She spit dirt and hay out, then swallowed. Her head swiveled to Dusty and then Slim. "I ... I ... I don't know anything about any money. Why would Livvy come west if she had money?"

Slim squinted an eye. "Because she wanted to hide it from Boss Man, that's why."

She gulped. "Who's Boss Man?"

Dusty pushed Slim out of the way. "He's someone who doesn't take to being crossed. And he believes Olivia Carmichael double-crossed him—or her father did. She ever mention anything?"

She shook her head. "Y ... You're the one who went through our things."

* * *

JENNY TOOK the pieces she now knew and put them together. This was not about Joshua. This was not about her. They thought she was Livvy. And they thought Livvy had money hidden somewhere, and they wanted it, even if it wasn't theirs to take.

Her eyes narrowed as she inhaled fresh air, which caused her to cough. Her parched throat made it difficult to talk, but she pushed the words out. "You broke into our room. Touched our things. You *stole* Livvy's journal. Broke into the schoolhouse and made a mess of things there too. And now you *kidnapped* me because you thought I was Livvy? How dare you?"

The nicer one shrugged.

She glared at him. The idea of her things being touched by him made her itch all over.

Her dry throat seized, and she coughed again. Then swallowed. "For the record." Where Jenny got her gumption, she had no idea. Never before had she spoken up for herself like this. "I've never heard Miss Carmichael—" it felt weird to use Livvy's formal name "—mention *anything* about money. I've never seen her *have* any money. She mentioned the town didn't even pay her in cash when I asked if I could borrow some."

"There's no money." The nicer bad guy sat down on the floor and put his head in his hands. "Boss Man isn't going to believe me." He looked up at the one he called Slim. "He'll believe you. You'll have to go back and tell him."

Slim raised his hands. "I'm not sharing that bit of bad news. My job was to interrogate and get some answers. I don't think I've done enough interrogating."

Jenny kept her gaze focused on Slim. He had hurt her already and was most likely capable of doing more. Obviously, there was someone worse who wanted money. Watching these two grown men be frightened of what could happen caused her stomach to twist. Somehow, she'd gotten mixed up in a plot to kidnap Livvy and extract money that didn't even exist.

Which begged the question Jenny didn't want to ponder—did Livvy have money stashed somewhere?

She didn't think her friend did. Most of the girls at the school, if not all of them, had been escaping or leaving behind a life they didn't want anymore.

So, if Livvy didn't have any money, what would they do to Jenny? Would they let her go?

"What now?" the nicer one asked.

That's exactly what Jenny wanted to know.

Did anyone even know she was missing? Did she matter enough to anyone for them to come after her?

Could she hold out however long that took?

Twenty-Eight

Faith over fear. Faith over fear. If I write it enough, I hope to start believing it.

—From the journal of Jenny Millard

Ren stopped at the base of the school steps and bent over to catch his breath. Schoolchildren ran in the yard chasing each other while a few stood off talking amongst themselves. There was no sign of any adult around. He cupped his hands by his mouth. "Jenny!" he yelled, searching the schoolyard.

The children stopped and gawked at him.

An older boy hustled over to him. "Miss Millard's not here."

"I'm worried about your teacher. Have you noticed anything different this morning? Out of the ordinary?" Ren asked.

"Just that the schoolhouse is locked. There's no way to get in. I usually do the chores before and after school. I'm Teddy Woodward." He thrust out his hand.

"Ren Lyman. You're Jacob's boy." Ren placed his right hand in Teddy's, and they shook.

"Yes, sir. Is Miss Millard okay?" Teddy asked.

Ren studied the young man and decided he needed help right then. "We don't know. I'm afraid someone who might want to harm her was here. And might've taken her." The last set of words was difficult to say. He swallowed.

Teddy's eyes widened. "Where do we start looking?" Teddy's eagerness to help calmed Ren's heartbeat.

Ren searched the ground. "Let's search the outside perimeter. We are looking for anything that could give us a clue. Anything odd. Foot or horseshoe prints where they don't belong. Anything. I'll start over there. You go that way, and we will meet in the middle." Ren studied the dirt pathway Jenny would've taken, then cut across to a set of bushes off to one side near the path. He scanned the area.

One of the bushes had several broken twigs and a hole in the middle, big enough for a person. He got on his hands and knees to search closer. Did someone lie in wait? He crawled around but didn't see anything else that looked out of place. No boot prints. No recently stirred-up dirt.

"Mr. Lyman, over here." Teddy hollered.

Ren backed out of the bush and ran to Teddy, who stood near the river behind another set of bushes.

Teddy pointed at deep wagon ruts in the mud. "There's wagon tracks here. No one ever parks a wagon over this way because the river tide changes every day." He looked at Ren. "Is this a clue?"

Ren placed a hand on Teddy's shoulder. "I think so. Keep looking. Let's see if there's more tracks that might lead somewhere."

They turned their backs to one another, and each studied the ground from a different angle.

"Look, boot prints." Teddy pointed at the indentations in the ground.

Ren was impressed with the kid's good sense. "I see another set here. And they are distinctly different. That means two men. Why would two men want to take Jenny?" He couldn't understand this at all. "Do you see any footprints that look like a woman's?"

Teddy fell to his knees. "No, but these boot prints sink deeper over here by the wagon tracks as if one weighed more. Would that mean she was carried away? And look here. Is that hay?" He held up a small piece of yellow straw.

Ren gritted his teeth. Granted, most everyone owned a horse and wagon, and hay could blow from anywhere, but Ren's mind churned with multiple scenarios. None of them good. Goose came to mind, and his treatment of women and Jenny in particular.

Ren's hand formed a fist. Why hadn't he done a better job at protecting Jenny?

He wanted to growl as he stooped low beside Teddy and continued to search. There were a few pieces of hay, some dirt on top of dirt, and ... he reached inside the bush nearby, which also was hollowed out, and pulled out a brown leather book.

Ren's heart stopped. Was this the missing diary?

"Is that a book?" Teddy whispered.

Fire ignited in Ren's entire body. Hay came from the livery. The livery was where wagons and horses were stored. He didn't know if it was this Dusty fellow or Goose, but Goose would have to know something, wouldn't he? "Goose," he growled.

Teddy glanced at him. "From the Livery? You think he's involved?"

Ren stood. "Not sure yet. I don't want to throw around accusations, but my gut tells me he's involved somehow. He's been seen with a stranger. Someone my instincts read as trouble. And Goose has access to both hay and a wagon."

"Ren!" A shout came from the schoolyard.

Screech.

Ren's head turned toward the commotion and saw Luke arrive on Admiral, followed by Bert.

"Over here, Luke," Ren yelled.

Luke dismounted and ran over. "Sorry it took me a bit to talk the girls into staying with Chrissy and Livvy. Hi, Teddy. Ren, is she here?"

Ren shook his head. "No." He pointed to what they found. "We found wagon tracks, boot prints, and hay. She could be anywhere." He stopped and looked out at the river.

"Hey." Luke placed a hand on his arm. "We'll find her. What's that in your hand?"

"Oh, this? We found it in the bushes." He handed it to Luke.

"That's Olivia's journal." Luke thumbed through the pages. "Does this mean whoever took her journal might now have Jenny?"

"I don't know. I'll follow these wagon wheel tracks on my way to the livery. That's where we need to go next. To talk with Goose." Ren leaned and slowly stepped over the closest muddied ruts left in the ground.

"I'll go with Mr. Lyman." Ren heard Teddy tell Luke. He stepped on the other side of the ruts and mirrored Ren's steps.

"I'll get Admiral and ride back over the path and meet you there." Luke trotted back the way he came. "Bert, you stay here and watch the children."

Screech.

Neither Ren nor Teddy said a word as they followed the impressions left in the dirt.

A few times, Ren's boots sunk in the mud, but not enough

to stop him from searching. The wagon wheel imprints had traveled along the entire river bank all the way to the barge. Off to the side. Where no one would see through the trees and shrubs that lined this side of the path.

Ren stopped when they came to the steamer that crossed the river every day. "Whoever did this was sneaky. Do you think they left town? Went to Sacramento?"

Teddy came up alongside Ren. "I don't know, Mr. Lyman. But it looks mighty suspicious. If you look closely, it's as if the wagon disappeared into the water."

Goose had mentioned Sacramento. Made friends there. Could he pull off something of this magnitude?

Ren glanced across the river. "Where are you, Jenny?" He whispered. He'd never forgive himself if she was hurt.

He turned to the livery. It was time to find out what Goose knew, if he could find Goose at all.

Luke stood near the livery door when they approached. "Ready?"

Ren nodded. Clenched his hands. He'd beat answers out of Goose if he had to.

Teddy nodded.

Ren reached for the handle and swung open the door. "Goose!" he yelled as they entered the building.

Goose stood in the center of the livery, frozen. Next to him was another thin man who had his arm around Goose's chest. Not Dusty. "Where's your friend, Goose? The Dusty fellow that's been hiding out here amongst the horses." Ren stormed up to Goose.

"That's exactly what she's been asking me." Goose snarled.

Ren came up short.

"She?" Luke came up on the other side of Goose and the stranger.

Teddy stood behind Ren's shoulder.

"Gentlemen, can we please not resort to violence." A female voice answered. She tilted her head and narrowed her eyes at Luke, Ren, then Teddy. Her facial features were more delicate than a man's, but her loose britches, shirt, and vest allowed her to pass as a young man. She turned toward the man Ren wanted to punch. "I'll explain more later, but first, Goose, answer this one question. Where's Dusty? What are his plans for Miss Carmichael?"

Goose's face went blank.

Ren's did too. Who was this woman, and how did she so quietly enter into this melee? Ren glanced at Luke, whose stormy gaze told Ren he was barely holding it together as well. "It's not Miss Carmichael who's gone missing, it's Miss Millard." Ren growled out.

The woman startled. "What?"

"Miss Millard is missing." He shifted his gaze to Goose. "Did you have something to do with it, Goose?"

Goose shook his head, his eyes a bit wild. "I don't know anything about no kidnapping. Why would that have happened?"

The woman gripped Goose a little tighter. "Let me ask a different question, then. Is Dusty working with Slim?"

"Who's Slim?" Goose and Ren said at the same time.

"That was all the answer I needed." She pointed to Goose. "You should be a little more careful who you associate with. Otherwise, you could be looking at jail time." She shook her head, mumbled something about hot-headed males, then headed out the door. "He's not involved. But I believe I know who is."

Ren glared at Goose. He still wanted to hit him. Even though he knew violence wasn't the answer or who he was at his core. But the need to pummel something to eradicate the fear inside still thrummed through him. It took all the strength he had to glance at Teddy, then Luke, and follow the strange woman out the door.

Ren had to find out what she knew. New information was better than nothing. Whatever it was, his first priority was to find Jenny. He could deal with Goose later.

* * *

JENNY STRUGGLED AGAINST THE RESTRAINTS. The man, Slim, had tied her to the chair so tightly, there was no way she could loosen the knots on her own. When she pulled, they only grew tighter, cutting into her wrists and ankles, causing shooting pain up and down her limbs. Fighting back tears, she stopped, then hunched her shoulders.

The men had left her alone, and she had hoped she could break free and escape.

She listened to see if they had returned yet. But didn't hear any sign of them approaching. No sounds from the other side of the closed door. She didn't know how long they would be gone, but she knew they would be back.

They were arguing when they left because she was not Livvy, and they didn't know what to do with her yet. That could either work in her favor and buy her time, or not, and it was the uncertainty that pushed her to try to escape.

She wiggled to break free again, but the pain intensified. They had placed the cloth back in her mouth, so she couldn't yell or scream. And she didn't know where she was or if she'd be heard anyway. Somehow, the idea of saving her strength for the right moment entered her brain. She'd have to wait for the correct timing if she were going to save herself.

What else could she do?

Waiting for anyone to find her wasn't an option. She hoped

Ren would be worried and would try, but how would he know where to look?

Somehow, she knew he would look for her anyway.

She closed her eyes. Memories of his intense gaze played in her mind. Their first kiss. The way he smiled at her when he escorted her around town. How he held Joshua and cared for him.

She loved him. And not just because he made her feel safe. He was kind and caring. A strong faith and family was important to him. And he understood her like no one ever had. She felt seen and heard. He had said he loved her. And she hadn't said it back.

Regret filled her. What if she never had the chance to say the words to him? What if she never saw him again? A hollow ache opened in her chest.

She couldn't let that happen. She had to get out of here, somehow.

She twisted her hands in a different direction, and the rope sagged a little. Hope blossomed in the open gap in her heart. She kept twisting and turning her wrists. It didn't matter how much it burned. She ignored the pain, moving slowly and meticulously.

The knot tightened again, and she growled deep in her chest. Determined to try again. And again.

After a few more times, she stilled.

She would not let fear get the best of her. Pastor Will's words echoed in her mind. Faith over fear. She repeated the mantra in her head a few more times, willing herself to believe. Hope filled her heart. *God, if You're there, thank You, I'm still alive. Help me find a way out of here. Or send help soon. Amen.*

She waited. For the door to open and the men to return. For Ren to rescue her. For God to save her. To see what happened next. All the while repeating the words, faith over fear, faith over fear.

The desire to hum the notes to the hymn Amazing Grace filled her. Her sounds were soft, but the action proved powerful in helping her fight back the panic.

She would not let fear win.

Twenty-Nine

When we are faced with hardship, that's when we really learn about ourselves and learn to trust God.

—From the journal of Jenny Millard

When Ren stepped outside, he found the woman pacing. Could she help him find Jenny? She had taken off the man's cowboy hat, and her hair was pulled back into a low knot, flowing down her back. Ren could see how he first thought she was a thin man, but that's where the similarities ended.

He walked right up to her. "Who are you? And how do you know where to find Jenny?"

She stopped. "Look, I know you don't know me, nor believe me, but I'm a friend of Jenny and Livvy, and I can help."

Luke had followed Ren and walked up to the woman. "How do you know Olivia?"

"I don't have time to explain it all. We need to go."

"I'm listening." Ren crossed his arms.

Luke and Teddy mirrored Ren's movements.

She threw her arms wide. "Argh. I don't have time for this. But since my cover is blown at this point, or will be once Jenny sees me, here are the facts. I was at the teachers' school with Livvy and Jenny."

She did not look like a teacher at all.

"Are you Lydia, Emilia, or Violet?" Luke asked.

Surprise crossed her face.

"She told me all about all of you."

Her lips parted. She glanced at each of them. "I'm Lydia."

"And you're a schoolteacher?" Ren glanced at what she was wearing.

She narrowed her eyes at Ren. "I am. But it was also my cover."

"For what?" Luke asked.

"Being able to track down information on wanted criminals." She cringed. "I'd like to explain it all to you when Jenny is back safe and sound."

"And this guy who has Jenny?"

"Is someone I've been tracking for a while. He's dangerous, and we need to get moving if we're going to find Jenny in time."

Ren uncrossed his arms. "In time for what? What's this all about?"

She pushed through the wall the men had formed around her, shoving Ren out of the way. She tucked her hair into her hat while moving toward the ferry. "I'll explain on the way." She sized him up with a quick look. "With your build and brute strength, I could use your help."

Luke held back. "How about I find the sheriff and bring him up to speed? He's already looking for Joshua's parents. I don't know which town he's in right now, but Arthur will."

She stopped. Turned to face them all and sighed. "As much as I don't want to bring awareness to my presence, it might be helpful. You're Luke, right?"

He nodded.

"Livvy mentioned you in her last letter. If she's here, it might be best for you to stay close to her."

"Okay. I'll go fill in Olivia and the Martins about everything and get a message to Sheriff Jackson. Good luck." He reached out his hand to Ren.

Ren shook his hand as the ferry whistle blew.

She glanced at the barge. "We need to be on that ferry. Let's go."

Ren ran to catch up.

Teddy ran up beside Ren.

There was no way Ren wanted to take the young man into a situation he had no inkling about. Anything could unfold, and he didn't want the kid getting hurt. "I'd feel better if you stayed back and kept an eye on Goose for me." Of course, he didn't want this woman by his side to get hurt either, although she looked like she could handle herself—and then some.

Teddy nodded, accepting the dismissal without any complaint. He strode beside Ren until they reached the shore. "I'll be praying you find Miss Millard, and she's not hurt."

The words touched Ren's heart. He reached out his hand for a second time that day. "I appreciate your support more than you know."

Teddy's boots swiveled in the dirt as he ran back to the main part of town.

Ren tapped his boot while Lydia secured tickets, then followed her on board. She found a bench on the backside of the boat and sat.

He hovered over her, and then he sat as well. "Spill. What are we up against?"

She shook her head. "First, you answer my questions. Who are you, and why is Jenny so important to you?"

Ren was not expecting that. He studied the ground. "She's a bright light in my life. I met her the first day she arrived. She needed someone." He shrugged. "I liked being there for her." He stood up. "I can't believe I just told you that." He paced a few steps, as far as the boat would allow.

She smiled, nodded. "That's good."

He stopped pacing and stared at her. "What's good?"

She shrugged. "You care about her." She glanced at the water. "She needs someone to care about her."

This time he sat right next to her. So close he'd know if she was lying or not. "What aren't you telling me?"

She hesitated. Pinched her lips. "I'm a Pinkerton agent," she whispered.

He frowned. "I thought they were only men."

She smiled. "Not all. We women can be an asset at times. I was asked in Cincinnati to join them. Some crime bosses who run things in Ohio are extending their reach. Staging accidents, claiming things that don't belong to them, that sort of thing. I was asked to come out here to keep an eye on a few people. The man I've been following, Slim, came to Washton last night. He's wanted for several crimes. I think he's involved in Jenny's disappearance."

He leaned forward. "So, you teach during the day and follow criminals at night?"

She shrugged. "Something like that." Her gaze constantly searched their surroundings. Haggard, with dark circles under her eyes, she acted as if she had drunk several cups of coffee. Tension radiated off her body. She fidgeted with her hands before placing them on her gun belt. "I don't think Jenny was their target. She got caught in the middle. Who they really wanted was Livvy." The fear in her voice sent a shiver down Ren's spine.

He swallowed. "So, why did they take Jenny?"

She slapped her hands on her thighs. "I don't know. That was something I didn't expect." She looked at him. "Desperation? Mistaken identity? Ransom? It could be any or all of those things." It was clear she cared and was worried.

The knot in his chest tightened. "Where are they now?"

Her teeth bit her upper lip for just a moment. Glanced around. Then whispered, "Slim has a hideout in Sacramento. That much, I know. It rests underneath the city and he has come and gone from there for months. That's where I'm hoping we will find them." She furrowed her brow.

"There's something you aren't telling me. What is it?"

She stood. "I'm not sure what they will do when they find out she's not Livvy, or worse—that there's no money."

"The money from Livvy's father?" Ren stood and faced her.

The startled look came and went. "You know about that then. Good. We're here. No time to explain more. Stay right next to me. We might need to look like we're a couple. Can you do that?" She tilted her head.

"Dressed like that?" That would make them stand out even more.

She looked down. "Oh, fiddlesticks. Well, never mind, then. Off we go. Two men walking through the streets." She joined the end of the line to step onto the dock.

Ren followed, his stomach doing somersaults. His worry for Jenny escalated. Psalm 55:22 entered his mind. *'Cast thy burden upon the Lord, and He shall sustain thee.'*

He closed his eyes as the words sunk in. No matter how big the problem was, or small, the Lord would sustain him. Ren was not alone. The Lord would not let him fall.

The words calmed him so he could better focus on the task at hand. He needed the Lord with Him. And Jenny did too. *Lord, I cast all my worries out to You. Please carry us through this. And be with Jenny. Protect her. Give us both Your peace. Your strength. Sustain us. Amen.*

He opened his eyes and moved off the barge with the rest of the passengers. He followed Lydia onto the train platform and across the street. Two men ambling along with no one the wiser. Except for them.

It was time to go get his Jenny back.

Jenny opened her eyes as soon as she heard voices from outside.

"We need to let her go," Dusty stated as he walked in the door.

"No. She's gotta be worth something. We need to get cash for our trouble." Slim's uncaring attitude is what Jenny feared most. He did not see her as a person at all. Only someone who could get him something.

"Who are we gonna ask? Everyone in the town of Washton is strapped. You know there was a flood this past year. They are all rebuilding and trying to survive. There's no big spender in town. Who's going to pay?" Dusty stopped listing reasons they wouldn't get money and looked at her. "No offense, Miss."

Jenny wanted to let him off easy but didn't say a word.

"She stays." Slim picked up another bandana and approached Jenny. "And we keep her tied up till we get something for her."

She shook her head. There was no way she wanted that filthy bandana on her person. She ducked her head, not knowing where he planned to put it. She still had something in her mouth.

"Hold still." He slapped her on the back of the head. Hard.

Jenny's brain bounced around inside her skull. Her momentary confusion gave Slim time to secure the bandana around her eyes. She gritted her teeth against the gag in her mouth. Her throat was so dry. Tears dripped down her cheeks. After the day she had had, she couldn't stop them. She was tired, hungry, and needed an outhouse.

The last gave her an idea. She turned her head in the direction Dusty last stood.

She heard him approach. How could she communicate this without her words. "Mmmh."

"What's she saying?" Dusty asked.

"Who cares?" Slim replied. The creak of a spring in the corner echoed in the room, then the sound of scraping on wood. Was he whittling?

Dusty leaned closer and whispered, "Do you need something?"

She nodded.

"You're probably hungry."

She shook her head.

"You're not?" His voice showed his surprise.

She nodded.

"I don't understand," he said quietly. "Is this eye-covering necessary?" he yelled across the room.

"Yep. Don't touch it." The threat in Slim's command was evident.

She huffed. Then squeezed her knees together to communicate the necessary.

"What's she do—oh, uh. You need an outhouse?"

Jenny nodded quickly.

"Uh, Slim?" Dusty called out.

She waited for the other man to respond. The whittling

stopped, and the creaks on the bed sounded as if he had laid down. A moment lapsed. "What?"

"Uh. She's gotta go," Dusty said.

"What?" Slim must not have seen her movement.

"She's gotta gooooo," Dusty said the words a little thicker. "Like relieve herself. Where do we take her?"

"We don't *take* her anywhere." The bed creaked. Slim had laid back down.

Jenny frowned. What did he normally use when he was here?

"She can go in the chamber pot over there." Slim's response answered her question.

So much for trying to escape while using an outhouse. She would hold it for another day before she'd go in a corner with them in the room. If she remembered correctly, there was no privacy screen or curtain for her to shelter herself.

She shivered. There would be no chance of escape. Her eyes pooled again, droplets spilling out from under the bandana on her face.

Dusty must've seen her tears. "Sorry," he whispered.

He tried to help her, but he was the one who got her into this mess in the first place. The fact he'd been in Washton all this time bothered her most. She trusted everyone in town. It seemed everyone did. Well, not everyone. Ren didn't trust Goose, and he had mentioned seeing Dusty with Goose early on and how he was suspicious. But he didn't have proof. Ren wouldn't accuse someone without it.

But Ren was right. Now, she was paying the price for walking to the schoolhouse alone this morning.

More tears dripped down her face.

Did they find any clues? Was Ren on his way right now? Did he know where to look?

She was so tired. The chair she was tied to was hard and

unyielding. But she didn't dare move or bring attention to herself. She didn't want to do anything that would give them a reason to be rid of her. She wasn't ready yet to give up on being able to get free.

She had something important to tell Ren, after all.

Thirty

I need to memorize more Bible verses so that if I'm ever kidnapped
again, I can remember them.

—From the journal of Jenny Millard

Ren glanced at the railway station he arrived at only a few months ago. His life was so different now. And he wouldn't go back and change anything, except the kidnapping part.

"Don't glance around so much. Stay close and act like you know exactly where you're going." Lydia spoke out of the side of her mouth in a deep gruff voice.

Ren didn't respond, just followed along as she led them along the boardwalk past several storefronts. He didn't know this city, but it was like any other. People hustled along with their purchases or on their way to make more purchases. Others had arrived on the most recent train and carried their bags to one of several hotels nearby. Several were in the saloons, starting to drown their sorrows even though it was midday.

Children ran through the street between the wagons being pulled by horses obviously used to the clatter. The loud noises were enough to cause Ren to want to head back to Washton. Not without Jenny, though. He wouldn't leave until they found her. In the meantime, he would endure the startled stares of passersby. That was until he pulled his new hat down farther on his face, preventing him from having to make eye contact with those they passed.

They crossed several streets before Lydia turned into an alley. She stopped a moment and examined the area. Then stepped into a hole in the ground.

Ren would've missed it, it was so small.

Lydia disappeared, and he followed her into the gap. Old, battered brick steps caked with dirt led into some sort of underground tunnel. His eyes adjusted to the darkness as they went deeper. Ren covered his mouth at the smell. He could only guess at the mold and mildew formed by years of pooling water from the many storms that came through the area.

Another alley of sorts lay at the bottom of the stairs. She turned down one corridor, then another. They passed doorways with chipped and deteriorated wood. Some entryways were on the verge of collapsing. Ren turned his body to avoid any contact with the timber. All they needed was to have the entire city above to come down on them.

As they navigated their way in the partial darkness, it was clear to Ren he would never find his way out. He had a good sense of direction, but this was challenging.

Were these buildings from the past? Why were they underground? And did anyone visit them, or were they left to rot?

This is where Jenny was taken?

Anger fizzled inside as he thought about how she was being treated. His heart beat double-time as they slowed their progress.

Lydia stopped. Leaned against the closest wall and put her fingers to her lips.

He did the same. She wouldn't have seen him nod. It was too dusty and dark.

She kicked open the door with a loud bang.

They both ran inside. But the dark room held no movement, nor any sign that someone had been there recently.

She trudged back out the door.

Ren followed.

Creeping along the wall they came to another door. She kicked it open.

Nothing.

They followed a pattern all along the corridor, but none of them had Jenny, or signs that someone had been inside.

Ren's frustration grew. He huffed out a breath.

Lydia did too. But she didn't give up.

He had to give her credit. She kept going. Pushing herself to check each location methodically. She had to have had some sort of training. It was obvious she knew what she was doing.

She went around a bend and approached the next door.

Yelling and shouts came from inside.

They both glanced at each other.

Ren's nerves ratcheted up a few more notches. If that were possible. They had his precious Jenny, and he didn't know what to expect nor how to go about things.

Lydia took a stance and pulled out a gun.

Was that necessary? *Lord, help us see this through and get out of this situation safely.*

* * *

SOMETHING SHOOK JENNY'S SHOULDER. She sleepily lifted her head. Where was she?

"Hey, wake up. No sleeping till we get some answers." Slim shook her hard.

Her head rattled with each shake from the hit he gave her earlier. She winced. Tried to look around, but everything was dark. And then it came back to her. The extra bandana on her eyes, being tied to the chair, trying to be untied so she could relieve herself.

"Leave her alone. She doesn't know anything, Slim." Dusty's voice came from across the room. He must've fallen asleep as well because he yawned and stretched noisily.

"I've run out of patience. She needs to tell us something. Now." He yanked on her hair. "Where's the money?"

Jenny whimpered. The only sound she could make with the cloth in her mouth.

"Slim!" Dusty's steps echoed on the floor. "Leave her alone."

The hand pulling on her hair let go. Was Dusty protecting her?

"That was a stupid maneuver. You've gotten soft while here in California, and you just made your own grave, boy."

The sound of a fist hitting a body startled Jenny.

"*Oof*," Dusty called out, then growled before she heard a crash.

The two must be brawling and knocking things over. How she wished she could get this bandana off her face so she could see what was happening. It made it worse, because she couldn't see Slim approach her and there was no telling what he would do next.

Crunching bones echoed in the room. Jenny curled herself inward as best she could. She heard a double punch and wondered who was winning or losing. She ducked to stay out of the way, but couldn't really move. Or see.

Someone went down.

"Don't get up, if you know what's good for you," Slim grumbled.

Her stomach dropped knowing Slim was the one standing. She willed Dusty to get up. He was the only thing between her and Slim. If left alone, there was no telling what Slim might do to her.

Somehow, she knew Dusty was trying to get up. Their individual grunts and groans were enhanced in Jenny's ears, because hearing was the only sense she could use. She heard a roar and then a loud crash. The ceiling above creaked.

White-streaked fear laced Jenny's nerves. Was the roof going to crash down on them?

She looked up even though she couldn't see. Would it hold? Or come down on top of all of them? Now, a new worry entered her mind. What was above them? The unknown scared her more than the danger Slim posed.

The sound of wood splintering continued as if a log or post was ripping apart from the middle. The men weren't paying any attention because she could hear them still rolling around on the ground, punching each other. They were making such a racket, they had no idea the destruction they wrought. Or maybe they did and didn't care.

"*Mmmmhyyy.*" She growled in her throat, the sound barely audible. "*Aaeekk.*" She tried a higher octave. She'd ruin her singing voice, but she wouldn't be able to sing if she wasn't alive, so she tried again. "*Eeeiiii.*"

"Shut up." Slim yelled as he made contact with Dusty again. At least she assumed so by the sounds Dusty made.

The sound of a gun cocked reverberated in Jenny's ears. "Don't even think about it," Slim said. She could only imagine he held a gun at Dusty. "I'll shoot her if you don't stop right now." Somehow, she felt the gun pointed at her, even though she wasn't fully sure.

This was it—how she was going to die. She tucked her head to her chin. Imagined herself squeezed into a ball, and waited. *Please, Lord. Let me get out of here alive.*

A hush filled the air before chaos erupted.

* * *

BOTH REN and Lydia stood still for a few moments, listening to the yells and angry shouts coming from inside. Ren could hear a few *oofs* and growls, which sounded like a brawl. Why were the men fighting? Was Jenny caught in the middle?

Ren's eyes met Lydia's as she held up three fingers and lifted her foot, then stepped aside. Her agitation was evident as she prepared herself to enter, gun at the ready.

He moved into position and prepared to break in the door. Ren's protective nature wanted to be the first inside, but she had the gun, and he couldn't really push, kick, and run at the same time.

An ear-piercing crack came from behind the door.

Ren held still a moment to see what would happen.

A loud rumble, more wood splintering.

He lifted his leg and put all his strength into his push. One, two, three. The door burst open at the same time a gunshot echoed throughout the room.

Ren stepped inside, and then the entire ceiling collapsed.

He didn't know how long he was out, but as Ren lifted his head, he searched his surroundings. Hard to do when lying on the floor. Dust, wood, and debris everywhere. The dim light and the settling dirt made it difficult to see anything. There was no movement. Anywhere. He pushed off the board that had fallen on his back, and it landed with a loud crash. He cringed at the noise, waited for someone to come at him. When no one moved, he eased himself to a standing position.

Muffled noises came from other areas of the room. Was anyone else alive? Where was Jenny?

A boot stuck out from underneath a piece of ceiling. He lifted it and found Lydia flat as a pancake. He leaned over and took her pulse. Blew out a breath. She was breathing but knocked out cold. He'd come back to move her if she didn't wake on her own. For now, he had to make sure there was no threat still in the room.

He picked up a splintered piece of wood to wield if necessary, then slowly scanned the premises, searching each corner as the dust and debris settled. No one else moved, though he didn't know where exactly they were.

He took a risk and called out, his voice dry. "Jenny?"

THE CRASH around her echoed in the walls. Even though the dust settled, her ears rang. Something stuck to her lips, but she couldn't swallow with the gag still in her mouth. Nor could she see anything with the bandana still on. Weight pushed down on her legs and feet. Her right shoulder throbbed. Afraid to lift her head, she held herself hunched over and listened for movement.

A cough boomed in the stillness. Along with a groan. It didn't sound like the two men. And it came from near the door. Was someone else here?

"Jenny?" She'd know Ren's voice anywhere.

"*Mmmfdm.*" She lifted her chin to push the sound farther.

"I'm here, sweetheart. Give me a minute." Jenny heard a loud groan and movement. Wood being tossed to the side.

She turned her head toward the sound. Everything was in shadow, but a shape grew larger as Ren approached. More debris was moved. How much in disarray was the room? She wished she could see.

"Jenny!" His voice was nearer.

She felt the weight on her legs and feet lift and then a loud crash. Then, whatever was on her back was removed as well. She could sit up fully again.

"Oh, Jenny." Gentle hands touched her face, and he rested his forehead on hers.

"*Mmmfdm.*" She wiggled her body, trying to break free. She wanted to throw her arms around him. She wanted to *see* him.

He pulled the bandana from around her eyes.

She blinked away the blurriness as her vision adjusted, and she could see Ren's face. His concerned gaze meant everything to her.

He frowned as he noticed the gag and gently removed that as well.

She blew out a breath. Opened her jaw. Then spit the hay and dirt from her mouth. "Thank you," she croaked.

"Are you okay? Did they hurt you? What did they do? May I touch you?" Rapid-fire words came from his mouth as his hands held her arms. "Let me untie you."

"Please. Everything hurts."

He crouched at the back of the chair and worked on the knots at her wrists. Growling, he covered them with his warm hands. "You're bleeding."

Pins and needles tingled in her hands and arms as he gently swung them into her lap. She cried out.

"Easy. Give it some time. It will hurt at first, then get better. I'm going to work on the ties at your feet now. It's just me touching you there, okay?"

She nodded. He was gentle with her. Tears pooled in her eyes, and the stinging forced her to close them. She sniffled.

"Hey. It's okay. You're okay." His strong presence and gentle steadiness were a balm to her soul. How could she want anything more than this? He was exactly what she needed.

"Are the men still here?" She didn't want to say their names out loud. It would make all that had happened much more real.

"I don't know yet. My first priority was you." He finished untying her legs and slowly moved each foot in front of her.

The same sensation traveled through her feet and legs. Ren was right. Her arms were already feeling a little better, although it would take a while for the rope burns to heal.

"Can you stand?" he asked.

"I'm not sure."

He growled as he rested his palms on her face again. Then hugged her to his chest. Never before had she felt so cherished. That she mattered. She closed her eyes and soaked it in.

Groans came from the other side of the room.

"Ren?" a woman's voice came from the door.

"Over here," he yelled. "I found Jenny."

Jenny looked at Ren. Her mouth opened, but no words came to mind. Why was there another woman with him?

"Why don't you stay here and let me check out the bad guys?" Ren whispered.

He slowly let go of her hands, then limped toward the other groans.

She grimaced. He was hurt because of her.

Thirty-One

—From the journal of Jenny Millard

Dusty woke with a start. His head throbbed as he lifted it off the ground. What had happened? Memories of his fight with Slim filtered into his brain. How determined he was to stop Slim from hurting the lady any further than he already had. But then Slim pulled a gun. And one didn't win a gun fight with fists.

Although he tried.

Where was Slim now? He turned his head to the left. The large wooden beam that Slim had pushed him into now lay splintered beside him, no longer supporting the building. He glanced up. Holes appeared all throughout the ceiling. Not all the way to the next floor above them, but whatever foundation the upstairs floor rested on was severed. More could fall on them at any moment.

Powdered debris floated around, making it difficult to see

too far beyond the post. But he saw Slim lying on the other side of the broken timber, out cold.

Miss Millard!

Dusty's gaze went in her direction, but he couldn't tell if she was okay. He tried to push himself up, but his arm gave way, and his side burned something fierce. He tried again and was able to swing his legs around and under.

She had to be okay. If she was hurt because of Slim and him, he'd never forgive himself. He should've never agreed to kidnap someone in the first place. He knew it was wrong and didn't care at first. But after reading the pages in the journal, his outlook changed.

He had to help make things right. That wasn't who he wanted to be anymore. He didn't know how he would extract himself from Boss Man and protect his sister, but he'd worry about that later. For now, he had to help the teacher.

A male voice came from over her way, and it wasn't Slim's crackling voice. Besides, he was out cold on the other side of the broken beam. Who was in the room with them?

Pushing with his other arm, he sat up on his knees. When he moved his hand from his side, sticky, warm liquid ran down his arm. Slim had shot him.

An urgency to make things right kept him from laying back down and giving up. He searched the darkened room. The dust had settled, and the room looked as if a small layer of snow had descended inside the building.

The man near the teacher was untying her. He should be doing that, but his arm must be broken or something, because it hurt, and he couldn't bear any weight on it.

Pushing to a crouch position, he was relieved his legs still worked. Lifting his body onto his good arm, he shoved himself to a standing position but almost fell over and had to quickly step back and lean against the wall.

His legs wouldn't be carrying him anywhere while he still had a bullet in his side.

* * *

Ren had no words. He placed his forehead on Jenny's again, catching his breath. She was alive. Safe. Injured, but from what he could see, would heal. No matter what, he'd be there for her, whatever she needed.

"I don't want to let you go, but I need to check on the others." He dropped his hands even though leaving her side was not what he wanted to be doing.

"Wait." She gripped his arms. "Is Joshua all right? Livvy?"

"Yes. Everyone is fine. They were all worried about you."

"About me?" she asked. Her brows furrowed as if confused that they would worry. Why was it difficult for her to realize she had people who cared about her? That she mattered to them. Especially to him.

"I'll be right back." He let go of her slowly.

She nodded. "I'm not going anywhere." A hint of a smile appeared. "Thank you for coming for me. I—"

He placed a finger to her lips. "I will *always* come for you. To the ends of the earth, if necessary. But let's have this discussion when we aren't caked in dust, okay?"

Her eyes crinkled, and her freckles shifted as her lips moved upward. "Okay," she whispered.

"That's my girl." He stood, squeezed her hand, then shuffled over to where he saw the men lying on the floor. One had awakened and now stood leaning against the wall, holding his side. Ren recognized him immediately and walked up to him. His hands fisted.

The man held up his good arm. "Please, before you say

anything, I'm sorry. I never meant for her to be hurt. For any of this to happen."

Ren held in his surprise by crossing his arms and placing his body close to the man he met with Goose. He didn't know if this was a ploy or not. "Yet, it did. You're Dusty, correct?"

The man nodded, his eyes not meeting Ren's. "I know. Once Slim was involved, there wasn't much I could do."

"I heard fighting."

The man raised his gaze. " I was trying to protect her. She was the wrong schoolteacher."

"So you would've hurt Miss Carmichael instead?" Ren pushed in closer, his nose almost touching Dusty's. "Explain to me how that is any better."

"It's not." He hung his head. "My boss, back in Cincinnati, believes there's money." He shook his head. "But there's not. There never was."

"But he won't believe you, will he? And he'll just keep sending someone after what he thinks is his?"

"Yes. I don't know how to stop him."

"Well, you're going to have to figure that out." Ren pointed a finger at the man's chest. "Don't move."

"I couldn't if I wanted to. Gunshots hurt." He squeezed his side harder and leaned farther against the wall.

The other man, the one Dusty called Slim, shifted and groaned, and Ren stepped over to him, lifting him up by his shirt as the plaster covering him gave way. "You. What's your name?"

The man pursed his lips. His eyes were a bit glossy from the hit to his head, but he had enough spunk inside to glare at Ren.

"His name is Slim." Lydia crawled over to where Ren stirred. "He's the one I want."

She was injured. How badly, Ren didn't know, but her strength and resilience had earned his respect.

"You got nothin' on me. You hear? It was all Dusty's fault. He talked me into helping him. I didn't do nothin'." He spat out the words, dirt and spittle flying along with them.

"You can explain it all before the judge if you'd like, but don't think it'll do you any good." She looked at Ren. "Help me tie him up?"

"Absolutely." She handed him rope, and he pulled the man's arms behind his back. He wrapped the rope around his wrists multiple times. Tighter than Jenny's had been.

"Hey. That's too tight. I won't be able to sit and ride with it that way." He wiggled around, the rope causing indents in his arms already.

Lydia handed Ren a handkerchief, and he took it and gagged the man.

"I say. This is all a misunderstanding. I—*mmmmdm*."

Slim fought and struggled but Ren pushed him to the ground and placed his boot on his back till he stopped squirming. Then Lydia dragged herself over to Slim's feet and tied up his ankles while Ren held him down. Ren stepped back once Slim was secured. He glanced at the wall to check on Dusty. "Dusty, you still among the living?"

"Still here," Dusty answered.

Lydia looked at Ren, question in her gaze.

"He's shot, and looks like he has a broken arm. He's not going anywhere. Plus, he's claiming he has remorse."

"I do," Dusty called out. "I never wanted any of this to happen."

"There's a difference between wanting and doing. You have to do both, not just one of them," Ren said.

Loud pounding came from above, and more plaster dropped on all of them. The cave-in must've done something on the surface to grab notice. Soon, they would have others in their midst. He wanted to get Jenny out of there, but he had to help Lydia as well. He turned to find out what Lydia's injuries were, but she wasn't where he last saw her. She had dragged herself across the floor straight to Jenny.

He watched as Lydia pulled herself up near his beloved and said something to her. Jenny's eyes widened as she recognized her friend. He joined them as Jenny's face revealed surprise, shock, and then wonder. "Lydia? What are you doing here?"

* * *

Jenny stared at her classmate from the training school. "Why are you here? I don't understand."

Lydia winced. "Hi, Jenny. Are you okay?" She leaned heavily onto her right side. Blood seeped from her left leg.

"You're hurt!" Jenny crawled onto the ground to help her friend, her own aches and pains forgotten until she moved. But she ignored it to hug her friend. "I'm so glad to see you. Although, I'm not sure what to think right now."

Lydia pushed Jenny away. "I'll be okay. It's all part of the job."

"What job?" Jenny wasn't going to be a pushover anymore. She was tired of being in the dark. "Why aren't you teaching at your school right now?"

"I hear voices over here." Someone yelled from the hallway. More people were coming, and her chance to talk with Lydia or Ren in private would be lost.

Lydia laughed. "I could ask you the same thing. Didn't you go to Vallejo, or somewhere nearby? Why are you here in Washton with Livvy?"

Deputies ran into the room. The one leading the others pulled up when he saw them and glanced around. "What's going on here?"

Lydia pushed up on her knees. Ren leaned over and helped

Lydia stand. Somehow, Lydia and Ren worked together as a team to come rescue her. They came for *her*.

Jenny couldn't be more grateful for their efforts. She bit her lip. Lydia was the flirtiest one of the bunch of them, who always had an eye for the men. And she was wearing pants! Would she catch Ren's eye? Or had she already? Doubt swarmed her as she studied both of them as Lydia leaned on Ren. Indecision warred within, but as Lydia took a delicate step forward, with Ren's help, Jenny stepped back, out of the way.

Ren glanced over his shoulder and frowned.

"I'm Lydia Spencer." She looked over her shoulder at Jenny and winced. "I'm a Pinkerton Agent under the direction of Kate Warne, and I give to you this wanted criminal Slim Jenkins."

The men's eyes widened.

Lydia breathed deeply. "I see you've heard of him. I've been tracking him for months. He kidnapped this young woman from Washton and brought her here. We—," she glanced at Ren, "—came to rescue her and take him into custody. The second man is Dusty. He was an accomplice. You can take him into custody now, but the agency will need to bring him back to Cincinnati. Both of them were hired and sent here by a Cincinnati Crime Boss. They have failed, so this might not be the only time someone comes searching. We will need security to keep them safe—"

The deputy held up his hand. "Whoa. Slow down. Let's start with taking these two into custody." He motioned to the others who had entered with him to move, and they secured both Slim and Dusty.

Lydia was matter-of-fact. Jenny had never heard her talk this way before. There was so much revealed in all her words. A Pinkerton agent? What was that? And what did she mean, there could be others sent?

Ren dropped Lydia's arm and strode toward Jenny. "What's wrong?"

Jenny shook her head. "I don't understand any of this."

"I can explain on our way back to Washton. Are you ready?" He put his arm around her and then bent down to lift Jenny under her knees. "Let's go home."

Home. That sounded grand.

"Not so fast. We need you both to provide your accounts of what happened." The deputy moved near the chair where Jenny's nightmare had just ended. He touched the brim of his hat. "Miss, I'm sorry you were put under all this stress. I don't mean to add more, but if you could handle a few moments to tell me what transpired, you won't have to come back to my office tomorrow or the next day—"

A loud crack echoed in the room.

The deputy raised his eyes to the ceiling. "Let's head upstairs first." He raised his eyebrows at Ren.

"I agree. We're right behind you."

The deputy turned and headed out the door.

Ren still held Jenny while he turned to Lydia. "Place your hand on my shoulder, and I'll guide us all out."

Lydia nodded. Winced as she limped closer.

The three of them inched forward, avoiding the fallen bits of wood and plaster. Ren had a hitch in his one leg, and Jenny felt bad for being an additional burden. But she didn't think she could move much. Everything hurt, and she was exhausted.

The hallways were long, and there were several of them. Jenny would've never been able to find her way out of this maze, even if she had been able to break free.

They came to narrow stairs, and Ren had Lydia go first. Then he turned Jenny sideways and carried her up the stairs. He grunted a few times.

"I'm sorry," she said.

"There's nothing to be sorry about. I'm fine." True, he wasn't even breathing hard as they crested the last step and appeared into the late afternoon sun.

The deputy waited for them in a field. The other deputies held Slim and Dusty nearby.

Ren stopped and set Jenny down on her feet but kept his arm around her. His presence gave her the support she needed.

"Let's make this quick so you can go home. Please don't leave out anything. And start from the beginning. With your name."

"My name is Jenny Millard. I was about to open the schoolhouse this morning, when he—S-S-Slim placed a sack over my head, picked me up, threw me in a wagon, and brought me here. He tied me to the chair and demanded I tell him where the money was."

Ren growled.

The deputy frowned. "What money?"

Jenny shrugged. "I have no idea."

"*Mmmmdm.*" Slim struggled against the two men who held each of his arms.

The deputy sighed. "Apparently, he thinks you know."

Lydia cleared her throat. "Sir, if I may. Miss Carmichael is the schoolteacher in Washton—"

The deputy glanced at Jenny. "Who's Miss Carmichael? I thought you said you were Miss Millard, the teacher?"

She exhaled. "I was substituting for Miss Carmichael, who was home with a cold. Slim didn't realize I was not Miss Carmichael until Dusty told him."

"Kidnapping, mistaken identity, stolen money. You've made a mess of things, haven't you?" The sheriff shook his head.

Lydia spoke over him, "If I could continue." Her eyes met

Jenny's. "Miss Carmichael's father had some dealings with this Cincinnati Crime Boss. We believe her parents were killed by him."

Jenny gasped. Ren drew her closer, gripping her side to hold her steady. "Livvy will be so upset to hear that part," she whispered.

"She came west to teach. With a group of ladies from the American Women's Educational Association, which included Miss Millard and myself."

The deputy's eyebrows reached his hairline. "You're a teacher?"

"Well, yes. And also a Pinkerton agent. You can even ask Mr. Pinkerton if you need to. I can provide his information. But to continue with the details of the case, there were rumors Miss Carmichael ran off with a substantial amount of money. I was able to discern quite quickly the rumors were false. But Boss Man didn't. Hence why these men were sent after her." She patted her pants pocket. "If you don't mind, I need to send a telegram to my superior right away."

"His name is Boss Man? So original. Okay. What you tell me lines up with the information I have been given earlier. I recognize Slim's name from one of the wanted slips on my desk, so I appreciate your efforts. I'll escort you to the telegraph office in a moment, but first, I want to hear from him." The sheriff pointed to Ren.

"I'm Ren Lyman. I work as a blacksmith in Washton." He looked at Jenny and smiled. "And I would do anything to protect this woman. So, when I found out she was missing, I wasn't about to be left behind."

Jenny's lips parted, pleased by Ren's words. Her eyes grew misty, and she looked away, her gaze landing on her friend.

Lydia had placed her hand over her mouth, a big grin emerging behind.

Her gaze traveled back to the man whom she loved with all her heart. Yes, she loved him. And he had said he loved her. And his actions today showed he cared. He came after her, didn't he?

Ren faced the deputy. "Can we go home now?"

The deputy chuckled. "I think that will be all right."

Ren swung her up and stepped away.

"Wait," Jenny called out.

Ren froze.

"Lydia. Will I see you again?" Jenny asked.

Lydia glanced at her leg. "I'll need a few days to recover. Maybe I can do that in Washton. But I need to see what my superior says."

"What about your school?" Jenny asked. "Has the year ended already for you?"

Lydia frowned. "My agent work took me away too much, and they had to find a replacement. I don't think I was a very good teacher, although I do miss my students."

"If it helps, I always thought you and teaching didn't mix. But I think you make a pretty good agent." Jenny knew this sounded selfish, but the idea she wasn't the only one of their group who didn't finish the year with her original school made Jenny feel as if it wasn't because of her after all.

"Can I take you home now?" Ren asked.

Home sounded so nice right then. She closed her eyes and leaned against the strength in her life she never knew she needed.

Thirty-Two

Thank you, God, for answering my prayers and giving me more than I ever hoped for.

—From the journal of Jenny Millard

Ren carried Jenny all the way to the dock and on board the first available ferry to Washton, only setting her down once they found a seat. All he wanted to do was get her safely back home to Washton. *Home.* It felt right to call Washton home. A place where he and Jenny belonged together, among people who cared for them and they could call friends.

They must look a sight. Covered in plaster, dust, and dried blood, Jenny's hair was tangled in knots, her wrists cut, red, and swollen. He could only imagine her ankles were too. Her clothes were ruined, torn, and stained in several places. As far as he could remember, she only had a few dresses.

All along the river passage they received strange looks ranging from concern to fear. The other passengers gave them a wide berth, which suited Ren just fine. Thankfully, Jenny kept her eyes closed and didn't see the startled glances.

He held her close, his gaze searching her person for anything he might've missed. A yellow-tinted bruise appeared on her cheek, as well as her arms. Ren gritted his teeth. How anyone could treat a woman this way, he had no idea. He was thankful to have found her when he did, and that the culprits had been apprehended.

As they landed at the Washton dock, she raised her head. Her cheeks held more color, and she'd stopped shaking. She took in her surroundings. "How did we get here so fast?"

Ren kept an arm around her, even though it was not within propriety. "I carried you. It wasn't far. Rest against my shoulder some more until it's time to exit."

"I'm not exactly light."

"You are to me. And I don't mind. Gave me an excuse to hold you." He winked at her.

She blushed and looked away.

He touched her chin, careful not to come in contact with any cuts or bruises nor to be heavy-handed. She allowed him to turn her head. "I meant what I said. I care for you. I love you. And I'll spend the rest of my life proving that to you."

Her lips lifted into a smile while her eyes glistened.

He cradled her face, and she leaned into his palm and closed her eyes. The idea of being able to do this every day with Jenny caused a flip in his stomach. He knew he was worthy in God's eyes, but he never thought he would be worthy of someone else's love. Someone he loved in return.

An older gentleman walked by them, did a double take, then stared at Ren's face for a moment before he hurried to the other side of the boat.

His skin felt raw, so he must have several cuts on his face blending nicely with his past facial scars. A smile emerged as he realized he didn't care one whit that other people saw him. A far cry from when he first arrived in Washton a couple of months ago.

Jenny leaned into him and fell asleep on his shoulder, and he cherished the trust she was offering him. When the ferry was secured, Ren carried Jenny off the boat.

"I can walk. Put me down, Ren." She wiggled and pushed on his chest.

"Let me do this for you. Besides, it will hurt more than you think."

"But you're hurting too."

"I've dealt with worse."

She reached for his face. Touched him gently on the damaged skin under his eye. "When you got burned?"

He swallowed. Then nodded.

"I'm sorry. They don't bother me, you know."

Ren pinched his lips. He hated the scars and what the memories did to him. The years of taunting and teasing. But it had made him who he was, and he could put it behind him now because he wanted to move on more than anything. No more hiding. No more fear of what people thought. It only mattered that they did not bother Jenny.

And she had made it clear they didn't.

"We're almost there."

She slapped his arm. "You distracted me."

He grinned. "And it worked."

She grinned back and then looked at the Martins' home a few feet away.

Several people were gathered on the porch.

Screech.

Bert noticed them first.

Luke looked up and waved. The others glanced at Ren and Jenny, hurried down the steps, and met them in the street.

Arms circled both of them amidst cheers, back slaps, and other exclamations.

Ren was too tired to hear them all, but the relief was palpable.

Screech. Squawk.

Bert circled the group, shaking his tail feathers.

Jenny pushed on his chest, and reluctantly, he set her down. Chrissy and Livvy, who had joined the group, immediately embraced her in a big hug.

Bert stopped screeching and came closer to Jenny. He clucked quietly, while his beady eyes scanned her. As if he was making sure she was okay. Ren didn't blame the bird, but somehow, he sensed Bert felt responsible. He was a good asset to have around.

Arthur held Joshua, who laid his head on his shoulder with a fist in his mouth. Luke and Pastor Will stood next to Arthur, relief on both their faces evident. Gideon stood behind Arthur. It was good to see his friend standing there.

Jenny broke free and went straight for the baby. She hugged the little one close. He squirmed from the confinement, then placed his head on her shoulder while she patted his back.

Ren was happy to see Jenny and Joshua reunited. His heart thumped. Could they become a family soon? Was there any news about finding the baby's parents? He didn't want to be apart from them any more than necessary. He approached the men. "Has there been any word?"

Arthur nodded. "The sheriff sent word this afternoon. He had been searching neighboring cities for Joshua's parents, but hasn't found anything. Will also checked outside of town with some families, and no one knows of any young child missing. Everyone is in agreement that Joshua can stay with Jenny and us until there's additional news."

Relief coursed through Ren, as well as a different urgency. He cleared his throat, gathering everyone's attention.

His heart pounded.

Was he about to do something that would change his life forever? Yes, he was.

The nudging in his soul couldn't be ignored.

He had to do this. Right here. Right now.

* * *

JENNY GLANCED at Ren as he turned to her and Joshua. The intent in his eyes caused her to hold her breath.

"Jenny, as I said earlier, I would do anything for you and little Joshua. Besides the Lord, you matter to me more than anything else in this world. I love you, Jenny Millard, and I want to spend my life showing you how much you matter to me. You are essential to me. I can't imagine my life without you in it. Will you marry me so I can spend the rest of our lives showing you how important you are to me?"

Tears streamed down Jenny's face. Was he declaring himself in front of all these people? She could feel the smile blossoming on her face. Her mouth opened, but no sound emerged. She stood there staring at Ren and then around her at the new family she had gained.

Livvy stood next to Luke, a wide smile forming behind clasped hands. She nodded encouragement.

Chrissy nodded at Jenny as well, her eyes glistening with tears.

Arthur's fatherly eyes glowed with affection, and he nodded as well.

Luke gazed at Livvy with deep love in his eyes.

Bert opened his wings and closed them, then nodded his head in her direction.

Squawk.

Joshua's fist hit her cheek, hitting a bruise. But she'd endure any pain to have a family she could call her own. She hugged him closer, her gaze meeting Ren's again. Ren loved her. His actions today showed he would stand by her, no matter what. And his words? For a man who didn't say much when they first met, he sure just said a mouthful. Telling her she mattered. The one thing she had always wanted to hear. Declaring he wanted to spend the rest of his life with her.

"Well, don't leave him in suspense. Answer the man, Jenny," said Livvy.

Tongue-tied and her mouth dry, she swallowed as she returned Ren's intense stare. She croaked out one word. "Yes."

He picked her up, placing Joshua between them, and swung her around.

Bert belted out a screech.

"Ouch," she cried out.

"Sorry." He placed her down gently. Stared into her eyes. He looked so relieved. "You have made me the happiest man in all the world."

Had she put that smile on his face? *Her.* Jenny Millard, soon to be Lyman. Her heart leaped at the new moniker she would have soon. Someone wanted her in their life. To belong as a family. Not because of what she did or how much work she could produce. Just her.

Ren reached out and circled his arms around her and Joshua, sending a warm sensation straight to her heart. He rested his chin on her head.

She closed her eyes and soaked in the love flowing between her, Ren, and Joshua. Thankful to be safe. Home. She and Ren would start a life together. Things wouldn't always be easy, but they had God, and they had each other to lean on.

Jenny had never felt so much love.

Chrissy tapped her on the shoulder. "As much as this family reunion is nice, you aren't an official family yet." She raised her eyebrows and looked over at Ren, then back to Jenny.

Jenny tucked her head into Joshua's.

Ren let go. "Yes, ma'am. But we will be as soon as possible. Right?" Ren glanced at Jenny.

Jenny smiled, nodded, and then glanced at Chrissy.

Chrissy grinned. "I think we can figure something out in a few days time."

A few days! Jenny's heart leaped.

Screech.

Luke slapped Ren on the back. "Now you've done it. You've captured the heart of our next schoolteacher." He glanced at Livvy. "There might be a slight change in our plans. Again."

Everyone laughed as an idea formed in Jenny's head. They still had another person who could possibly help them out. If she showed up like she said she would.

Livvy approached Jenny. "I'm so glad you're all right. Chrissy and Luke filled me in. I'm so sorry that my past caused you all this pain. This is my—"

Jenny stopped her friend. "This is not your fault. And this could've happened to you. I'm glad it didn't, and I'm thankful Ren found me." She glanced over her shoulder and sent him a smile. She would never be able to express how much it meant to her that he came for her. She faced her friend. "And you will never believe who helped Ren."

Livvy's brow furrowed. "Who?"

Chrissy interrupted the two of them. "You'll have plenty of time later to discuss all that, let's get Jenny inside so we can tend her cuts and bruises."

Livvy nodded. "Yes, let's." She put her arm around Jenny

and led her up the porch steps and to the door. "You need to tell me everything."

Jenny didn't know if she had it in her to relive it a third time after explaining everything to the sheriff back in Sacramento, but she didn't have the heart to say anything right then. The reason she was kidnapped was because of Livvy and the situation with her father. Livvy deserved to know what happened. But first, a bath and a nap sounded wonderful.

She glanced over her shoulder at the man who would become her husband. No longer did she want to be a teacher. To manage her own affairs. She wanted to be a wife, and a mother and never let this child experience or feel the rough emotions of her own childhood.

Jenny couldn't believe how different the direction of her life was headed. Never did she think that losing her teaching position in Vallejo would be what she needed to land her in Washton so she could meet Ren and be there for baby Joshua.

Now she couldn't imagine her life any other way.

Squawk.

Bert agreed.

Epilogue

Jenny stood near the Martins' fireplace, her hands in Ren's, as they faced one another. She couldn't believe this day was finally here. Ren was willing to wait longer, but she was ready to be a family with Ren and Joshua right away. They settled on waiting a week so her body could heal from her ordeal and provide time for Chrissy and Livvy to organize things. She hadn't cared too much about the bruises, but she wanted to stand on her own two feet for her wedding, so she agreed.

"By the power vested in me by the state of California, I now pronounce you Husband and Wife." Pastor Will smiled at Ren. "You may kiss your bride."

The room grew loud with cheers as Ren leaned forward and placed his lips on hers.

In the background, Joshua squealed and clapped his hands.

Ren lifted his head and smiled at Jenny. "I love you."

"I love you too." Her body vibrated with emotion.

Their friends engulfed them in hugs and congratulations within minutes. Though a small gathering, the people who mattered most filled up the room. Livvy, Luke and his sisters, the Martins, Pastor Will, and Gideon. Her new family.

The only one missing was Lydia. Her friend should have been here, celebrating with them. But her injury had forced her into hiding at Luke's ranch, where it was safer. Her wounds would raise questions, so she remained secluded. No one else could know she was a Pinkerton agent, not with danger still lurking. Jenny prayed the threats against Livvy wouldn't continue, but something in her gut told her trouble might still arrive at Washton's doorstep.

Gideon flipped the key toward Ren with a knowing grin. "It's yours for the next few days. I'll be with the doc. He'll fuss over me, but it will keep me out of your hair." He winked.

Ren's face filled with concern.

"I'm fine, truly. We're playing it safe. And providing the two of you space before we adjust to the four of us living together in the cottage. His gaze went to Chrissy, who held Joshua, and his smile softened. "I'm going to enjoy being a grandad to that little one. I'll spoil him rotten." He laughed.

Ren joined in.

Jenny's heart was near bursting. Never did she think she'd find a place to call home. Where she had her own family and people who loved her unconditionally. She glanced around the room, her vision blurred by the tears forming in her eyes.

"Hey" Ren put his hand under her chin and lifted it up so she would look at him. "No tears on our wedding day, okay?"

She smiled. "I'll try, but no promises."

"That's my girl," he said.

She whispered the phrase under her breath. "I like the sound of that."

Still holding onto her chin, he leaned over and kissed her lips.

Cherished. That's how she felt. A peace overcame her as he

pulled away. Her eyes fluttered open, and she looked at him in wonder.

"Yes, *my* girl. Is it all right if I call you that?" He asked.

"As long as I can call you *my* man."

Ren cupped her face, his thumb brushing against her cheek. The warmth of his touch grounded her. "I love you," he murmured, his voice low, rough with emotion.

Jenny's breath hitched. "I love you too." The words settled into her bones, steady and sure. When Ren pulled her close, his arms wrapped around her like a promise, solid and unbreakable.

He leaned in and kissed her again.

Thank you!

Thank you for reading *A Slight Change of Plans*!

I hope you enjoyed Ren and Jenny's story. It would mean so much if you would take a quick minute to leave a review (https://scrivenings.link/aslightchangeofplans)! It doesn't have to be long. Just a sentence or two telling what you liked about the book.

Author's Note

When writing a historical novel, there are specific events that a writer wants to include. For my story to take place when it did, I had to take a bit of liberty with the timeline of some of these events to fit my story.

The main train route from Vallejo to the town of Washington, California, was actually completed on November 11, 1868. For my story, it is 1870. In real life, a train bridge was built in 1870, less than two years after this route opened. This changed the entire course of history for Washington as the train route now bypassed the town to get to Sacramento, directly. Thankfully, my fictional town of Washton will not perish so easily.

I love writing about the research I've uncovered on my blog. Be sure to follow me on my blog, www.denisemcolby.com, and social media, Facebook—denisemcolbywrites and Instagram—denisem.colby to learn more.

Thank *you*, dear reader, for choosing this book and taking the time to read it. I hope you enjoyed Jenny and Ren's story and revisiting the town of Washton. My stories couldn't be written without readers, and I appreciate every single one of you.

To my husband, Ken, who has supported me throughout this entire endeavor. It is not easy being married to a writer. We sometimes tend to spend more time with our made-up characters. Thank you, honey, for all the love, support, and encouragement you have given me. I love you.

To my kids, whom I've dedicated this book to. It's been so fun sharing this journey with you. I love you, and I appreciate all your support and encouragement. It's fun to share this endeavor with you. And a special shoutout to Kyle for drawing Bert, my schoolhouse logo, and creating a great map of my fictional town.

To my dear friend Kaycy, who's thoughtful gift of a jar with Bible verses in it (a homemade devotional) from years ago, provided the idea for the list of Bible verses Ren carried with him. Not all of the actual verses on those cards made the final manuscript, but many did. I just had to convert them from NIV to KJV.

To all my family and friends who have encouraged me by purchasing and reading *When Plans Go Awry*, sending me texts and pictures with the book, and then asking when book two would be released. From the book launch party (which is up there as one of my best days ever), to commenting on my social media, to checking in with me when I was lost in my writing cave—I am blessed.

This story would not have been written without my critique partners Kimberly Keagan, Marie Wells Coutu, and Christina Rich. What a gift you all are to me. I'm so thankful for our small but mighty group.

Thank you also to my Novel Academy Huddle Group—Becky Yauger, Becca Kinzer, CJ Meyerly, Wendy Galinetti, and Lynn Watson.

Also a shoutout to all my other writer friends. I belong to several groups and the friendships I have made are special. I can't list everyone here because the list is long, but I did want to say thank you. I've learned and grown as a writer because of you, and I love that I now get to share promotions and book launches with all of you.

A special shout-out to my publisher Scrivenings Press, and my editors, Ann Harrison and Linda Fulkerson.

Last but certainly not least, I thank God for providing the opportunity to write this story and for it to be published. Writing a novel is not easy. And he has provided the people, the tools, and the story ideas to help me make this a reality. To Him be the glory.

About the Author

Passionate about all types of stories—whether they are from songs, theatre, movies, or novels—Denise M. Colby loves history and constantly finds herself contemplating how it was to live in the 1800s.

An avid journal writer, Denise usually can be found with a pen and notepad whenever she's reading God's word. Each year, Denise chooses a word to focus on. She shares her learnings about that word throughout the year on the two blogs she writes for.

A wife for thirty years and mother to three boys and

daughter-in-love, Denise loves to read, watch movies with her family, sing 80s and musical songs, dance, and spend date nights with her husband.

Writing Historical Christian Romance novels combines her love of learning about history and reading. Visit Denise's website to sign up for her newsletter or connect with her on her social media, www.denisemcolby.com.

A Troubling Suggestion

by Betty Woods

Clarisse Matthews still grieves the tragic loss of her fiancé and doubts she'll ever love anyone again. Particularly if she has to divulge the secret abolitionist ideas she keeps hidden deep inside that only her beloved knew.

After the lady Luke Williams loved spurned him and married another man, he will never risk giving his heart to another woman. Especially not to Clarisse who had to have known about her best friend's ruse and helped the woman to conceal it from Luke. He doesn't need a lady by his side to manage his family's plantation or forge a path to become an attorney.

But when Luke's cousin is deceived by a rogue, who only Luke and Clarisse know the whole truth about, they form a reluctant alliance to protect his cousin. Their feigned attraction grows into genuine love. But will the differences between them become a wall too tall to climb or can they find a way to go around?

Get your copy here:

https://scrivenings.link/atroublingsuggestion

* * *

No Leaves in Autumn

by Terri Wangard

Marie Foubert grew up in an orphanage and struggles with feelings of rejection. As a Red Cross recreation worker, she interacts with the American men based in Iceland during World War II. Her growing attraction to seaplane pilot Stefan Dabrowski excites and concerns her. Won't he disappear from her life like everyone else?

Stefan hears his commanding officer describe him as exciting as last night's bathwater. One of his colleagues constantly berates him because of his Polish heritage and his superior flying skill. Despite being the squadron's most productive pilot, he is threatened with court martial. A showdown approaches to prove who's the better pilot and the better man.

Marie's cousin, passing through Iceland, tries to see her after spotting her photo in *Life* magazine. She declines to meet him, but Stefan encourages her to do so and learn why no one wanted her. She may gain a family after all.

Get your copy here:

https://scrivenings.link/noleavesinautumn

Stay up-to-date on your favorite books and authors with our free e-newsletters.

ScriveningsPress.com

www.ingramcontent.com/pod-product-compliance
Lightning Source LLC
Chambersburg PA
CBHW060622100726

47907CB00006B/1736